Shamrock and Lotus

Cassie Premo Steele

for my grandmothers,
Anna Clair and Eleanor Clare

and for my daughter, Lily

PART I

ONE

Claire was what would have been called in America a stay-at-home mom, except that she hadn't lived in America for over a decade and she never really stayed long enough in one place to have a home to stay in. It was true that she was a mother, and that this was her primary work. She used to write, mostly in her journal, and some small essays and poems published in literary magazines, but that was long ago. And now that Claire's daughter Miriam was seventeen years old and refusing to speak to her much of the time or even eat anything Claire would offer, Claire was starting to wake up. She was waking up, not with thoughts of whether the bedroom window needed new curtains or if Miriam's blue loafers were scruffy, but with the question of what she was going to do with herself.

Claire was having a hard time answering this question because in order to answer it, she had to have a self. Lying under the white down comforter as the low January sun reached the window facing the River Liffey, Claire realized it was not only late in the morning but late in her life. She had turned forty in late November and it was high time she woke up and got going. The breakfast dishes were still on the table from when her husband and daughter had eaten, at dawn, while Claire slept like a stone at the bottom of the river. Miriam would not be back till after nightfall since she had cello lessons after school. Michael would go to the athletic club after work and not be home until Miriam was already in bed. And neither of them would expect a dinner waiting for them—maybe some Indian takeout in the fridge. So, staring at the two coffee mugs and one bowl and spoon on the table in the dark kitchen, Claire had to admit for the second time in the day that she was unnecessary and that she really must do something about it.

She looked at the clock on the microwave, glowing green, and remembered that it was a Wednesday and the maid would come in fifteen minutes. Ellie would turn the lights on in all the rooms and do laundry and vacuum and wash and put away the breakfast dishes, all the while listening to the talk shows on the telly, up loud so she could hear them from every room in the apartment. Claire decided she needed to leave.

Not leave altogether, although for a second her mind laughed at that possibility, *I could leave altogether, ha*, and then it was gone, and she was pulling on black jeans and a red sweater and the new black boots Michael had given her at the holidays and brushing her dark shoulder length hair, thick and straight, and putting on lipstick. No matter how she felt inside, lipstick always made things a little bit better. And then she walked down the newly painted white hall to the elevator where she descended four floors to the street below and finally start going.

She thought about shopping. When they had lived in Paris in the *sixième arrondissement* and Miriam had just started school, Claire used to walk the large boulevards of the shopping districts for hours, meditating on the thin girls on the bus stop posters and the African inspired prints behind the boutique windows in the way some women meditate on the natural world. To her they were a wonder, the way so much of the creativity of a civilization could flow in this one direction, toward marketing and merchandise, toward channeling human desire into a clean river of supply and demand. It made her hot, really, in a perverse way that she'd never admitted to anyone. Sometimes she met Michael at the World Bank for lunch and they made love in his wood paneled office beneath the window with the Eiffel Tower in the distance, and later, they ate Pad Thai out of white cartons while sitting on the carpet, still slightly damp, and she thought of herself then as lucky, a lucky wife, a lucky woman. Just plain lucky. Later in the afternoon, after picking Miriam up from school, still brimming with luckiness, she took her daughter to the carousel and let her ride four or five or six times while she sat on the park bench with other mothers and thought of herself as the luckiest of them all.

Chance, she whispered to herself as she crossed the bridge, *la chance* is what the French called luck. *Avoir la chance*, she repeated to herself. Literally, to have the chance. Claire used to do this when they lived in Paris, translate things literally, and it annoyed Michael, because she knew better, she'd studied French literature in college and she wrote poetry and she knew the metaphoric way that language worked, how nothing was ever quite exactly the same from one tongue to the next.

"You know that," he'd say, and she'd grin. Yes, of course, she knew that, that was why she played with it so, because in playing you could find the hidden meanings to things, you could see the way language molded people into shapes they couldn't see.

She did this in Ireland, too, when they drove in the country on a Sunday; she translated the Irish signs of roads and inns and towns for him. *Lough Dan. Gleann Life. Bealach Mileata*. These were the shapes the people were molded in, she explained to him, this is why they never wholly fit into a British world, a British tongue.

She crossed the bridge where O'Connell Street turned to College Green, as the newly painted Ormond Quay Hotel, upstream, briefly sparkled on the water in a quick flash of sunlight over the river, and then white seagulls bobbed their heads underwater to see where the light had gone. These places, this place, she might explain to Michael if he were there, they have names, and stories underneath their names, just as "to have the chance" lay beneath the word "lucky."

But if Michael were there, he would give her a sullen look, for she knew that he could not very well agree that British influence was a wholly bad thing, since he worked for the World Bank and his living, their shared life, had depended upon believing that a monetary system shared by the world was a useful and noble endeavor. That was why they were there, in Dublin, so that he could act as a liaison between the World Bank and the Bank of Ireland, to help bring Ireland the prosperity it deserved as part of the newly forming European Union. And Michael's clouded face meant that no Way of the Swan or Cow's Crossing would help bring that progress about.

Claire had a chance, now, at the end of the bridge, to make a choice. She could go straight and head to the Bank of Ireland and see if Michael were in his office, for old time's sake, since those early Paris years were on her mind today, or she could go left where she would come upon the gothic spires of Trinity College and catch a lunchtime concert, or she could go right and head to the hip and trendy Temple Bar area for lunch.

Chance. She was taking a chance. She knew that Michael was not the same man as he'd been in Paris, that the Irish offices were not as firmly built as his had been in Paris, that he'd be annoyed at the interruption, and Claire really didn't really want to have sex anyway, so she didn't go straight. And while a concert was tempting—it would give her something to discuss with Miriam in the evening—she was, she realized, very hungry. In her rush to avoid the maid, she hadn't eaten breakfast, and here it was, almost noon, and so she went right.

À la droit, she said to herself. To the right. The opposite of *gauche*. To be right is the opposite of being gauche. Those French, there is style in everything they do, she smiled to herself.

"I am right. I have a right," Claire said out loud, startling the elderly lady on the sidewalk beside her and embarrassing herself, which made her dart into the next restaurant she saw, an Indian buffet she'd never tried before. The sign on the door said their specialty was Northern Indian cuisine, by which, she thought, the owner was taking a chance, since the merest hint of anything from Northern Ireland could keep customers away. "I have a right to take a chance on Northern Indian cuisine," she said to herself, smiling, and walked in.

TWO

The ring awoke Brigid from a dream of green, the bluegreen Irish hills of her childhood and the greygreen sea in the west. Like parents they had been to her, that land and water, more like parents than the parents she'd been given by fate or chance or whatever one called the history of a childhood lived in fear and uncertainty. She picked up the phone, slightly angry about all this, the interruption of the dream and the memory of the past and the end of sleep.

"Hullo," she croaked, the brogue deeper than it usually was, after more than ten years in America, and she waited to hear the voice that was beginning her day in this way.

"Brigid, Brigid," her mother's voice bounced across the ocean, repeating itself as the milky white of a New Mexico dawn was just beginning to glow outside Brigid's window.

"Mum?"

"Yes, dearie, it's me, your old mum."

"What's wrong? Is anything wrong?" As a midwife, Brigid was used to asking this question of her callers, who were usually women with waves of pain cutting across their abdomens, sometimes piercing down their thighs or jabbing their lower backs.

"Wrong? No, dear, nothing's wrong."

"Then why are you calling so early?" Brigid said, waking up fully to the fury of a lifetime of not understanding her mother, not being understood by her, and causing her dream of green to recede completely.

"What do you mean?" asked her mother, also slightly annoyed. "Oh, yes, the time. The time is different there. Here it's noon, dear. It's noon."

Noon in Dublin. The concert at Trinity College would be striking the first chord. Bankers and students heading for lunch on the narrow streets. The low winter sun sitting yellow on the Liffey.

Brigid knew the city well. She and her sister and mother had moved there when she was ten, after their father left, so they could start over.

Fresh, her mother would say. As if life was like laundry one could bleach and get fresh and begin again, clean.

Brigid's life would never be clean. She had chosen a profession where she stuck her hands in mucous and blood. Men asked her, and sometimes women did, too, how she could stand it, all the mess and the danger that came with birthing.

"It's a new chance," she would say. "I don't see the blood. I just see the new chance. To begin again."

They thought she meant the babies, but she didn't. She meant herself. With each birth, she had the chance to add another feather to the balance, to weigh her life just one small bit further away from death.

"Brigid, can you hear me?" Her mother's voice came back to her across the waves.

"Yes, mum, what is it?"

"It's your father."

Your father. Her mother had called him that ever since they'd separated, as a way of distancing herself from him. As if Brigid and her sister were still connected to him while herself she wasn't, as if they were somehow still holding to him while she wasn't.

"What about him?"

"He's coming back."

By "back," Brigid knew her mother meant that he was getting out of jail. The Good Friday agreement, signed in the spring of the previous year, was leading to the release of prisoners suspected of paramilitary activities. Brigid had heard it on the news. It was a show of good faith for the possibility of peace, the radio announcer had said.

"Huh," was all Brigid's throat could say.

Friends shook their heads when they discovered that Brigid was an advocate of the death penalty. A fierce advocate. In fact, she also believed in an eye for an eye. She thought rapists should be castrated, bombers have their limbs cut off, every imaginable punishment was permissible in her mind. Cocktail party chatter stopped when she described how she would deal with sexual abusers of children. Over the years, she learned to keep her solutions to herself.

"He wants to see you," said her mother.

"Huh."

"Brigid, he's sick. He may be dying."

For a second, Brigid misunderstood and thought they were putting him to death. Finally. Fifteen years after his admitted involvement in the bombing during the Conservative Party Conference in Brighton.

"He is?" she asked.

"Yes, dear. And he wants to see you."

"Huh." Her old rage at her mother was beginning to rise with the light across the New Mexico desert outside her window. Why did her mother even speak to him anymore? Why did her mother think she still owed him anything? Why was her mother still passing along this sense of obligation to Brigid?

"Dear, he may not have very long," her mother was saying now, and crying, and as the wind began to pick up outside the window. Brigid's attention turned to the white flakes swirling in the morning light across the brown field. Perhaps the snow was a sign it was time to start over. Fresh.

So Brigid answered clearly, "Yes."

No matter how many springs and summers and falls she lived in this desert, she knew that one day he would return, like winter, like snow, he would blow back into her life.

The snow had caught up with her. She couldn't run any longer. She was thirty-five years old. She couldn't pretend he wasn't her father any more. She would go home. She would face him.

"Yes, mum," she said. "I'll come home."

THREE

Claire was not sure she wanted the tea masala that the kind young waiter declared was so delicious.

"Please, Ma'am," he said. "You have never had anything like this."

She believed him. This restaurant was unlike anything she had ever seen. There were books on each table that had been shelved neatly between carved bookends shaped like elephants, tigers, and snakes. People sat at the tables quietly reading, mostly alone, some in pairs, and when Claire first walked in, no one had been eating.

Claire took a seat underneath a painting of an eight-armed woman and waited. She was hungry. Ravenous. Just when she felt like she couldn't wait any longer, a waiter arrived to deliver menus to each table.

Where is the food, she wondered, and looked to the menu. Indian Treets, the menu said. How could they misspell something so simple, she asked herself. What am I doing here?

She opened the menu and discovered that it was not a menu at all but a newsletter. There were articles on world politics, philosophy, yoga, astrology, even a recipe for vegetable pulau. But what about the food, Claire wondered again, feeling perturbed.

"Welcome to all my guests," said the waiter after he had finished distributing the newsletters. "Welcome, old friends and new," he said, nodding to Claire, and she noticed that his eyes curved downwards in a seductive way. "Welcome to Indian Treets. I hope you enjoy your meal, and if there is anything you desire but do not find, please ask, and I will help you."

How about some food, thought Claire.

He looked right at her and said, "And here now is your meal." Two waiters came from the kitchen bearing platters of food piled high and circled the room, describing each dish and putting some on the customers' plates.

When her plate was full with nav rattan curry, pakora with tamarind chutney, clove-scented rice, and raita, the waiter came over to her.

"My name is Padmaj," he said. "Would you like something to drink?"

"Just water," she said.

He stood there, looking at her. It was disconcerting. He was not being a regular waiter. Clearly this was not a regular restaurant.

"My name is Claire," she said, taking a chance that this is what he was waiting for.

"Are you a poet?" he asked.

"No. Why?"

He looked down at the book she'd chosen. It was a volume from the Irish poet Mary O'Malley. She'd read a favorable review recently in *The Irish Times*.

"'I will tell you the sound the wounded make,'" he said, his consonants thumping.

She smiled, charmed by this waiter who knew contemporary poetry by heart. She'd just read that line before the lunch was served.

"But you are hungry, my poet lady," he smiled back. "Eat now. We will talk later." And with a slight bow, he was gone.

A poet, she thought as she devoured the curry. Its color and sweet taste reminded her of the squash she'd fed Miriam as a baby. Even then Miriam's appetite had been small. Claire ended up finishing the baby food, scraping her index finger along the insides of the jar to get it all.

When she'd finished her plate, the waiters returned to clear away the tables, and Padmaj came back to her side.

"Tea masala, my poet lady?" he offered, a silver tea kettle in his hand.

"Why do you call me a poet?" she asked. Although she had written poetry when she was younger, she had never really considered herself a poet. She had not fully allowed the poetry to become a part of her identity. Then Miriam had been born and she hadn't had the time.

"A poet reads poetry," Padmaj answered. "You go in there to hear the language singing, to start the song in you."

She stared at him. Who talked like this? He sounded like her own, younger self, which she'd thought had been buried long ago, but she was hearing it again, now, through his voice.

"*Commencer la chanson*," he smiled, his downturned eyes curling up.

"You know French, too?" she asked, delighted.

"*Oui, Madame*, and also Hindi, and Urdu, and English, and now, Irish."

Commencer la chanson, she said to herself. *Commencer la chance*.

"This is the best tea you have ever had, my poet lady. You are quite sure you will have none?"

"I believe you," she said honestly. "But I am too full. I cannot eat or drink one more thing right now. And that is unusual for me," she admitted, grinning.

"Very well. I will get a take-away cup. You will drink it later, at home." And he was gone.

She looked around. All of the customers were sipping tea, reading books. Maybe she shouldn't have refused. She felt rude, sitting there waiting for her plastic cup and her check while everyone else was relaxing, settling in, enjoying the hospitality.

She looked down at the slim book of poetry. *Asylum Road*. How long had it been since she'd written poetry herself? Five years? Ten? Miriam had been in elementary school already. They'd been in Paris. Maybe seven years. Claire had finished one of her journals, filled with poems and daily thoughts, translations, notes from her voracious reading, and then she simply hadn't bought another one. It was as simple as that. But is anything simple, she wondered. Maybe not. Maybe I've been trying to convince myself that life can be simple. I called it peace. But maybe I was wrong.

She opened up the sky blue book and read,

...I was born outside the pale

and am outside it still. I do not fit in.

"Here you go, my poet lady. Clear."

"Clear?" Claire looked up at him, the words *strangers may come* still echoing behind her eyes.

"Your name. It means clear in French. Aren't you French?"

"No. I mean, well, a little. I have some Irish ancestry. But I'm American," she said, shaking her head, as if to say, "I'm nothing. I'm a mongrel. I'm from nowhere."

He looked concerned.

"Everyone is from somewhere," he said.

She looked down at the book in her hands, at her hands, at the red weave of her sweater against her pale wrists. She said nothing. Miriam had recently said something like this to Claire. They'd been fighting at the time, and Claire had been furious and not really listening. She was listening now.

Padmaj bent down. He reached his hand toward her. Claire held her breath. His skin was so smooth, she thought.

"Here," he said, picking up the newsletter on the table. "Perhaps you could take a class. Learn about your new home."

She felt embarrassed again.

"Take a chance," he said, softly, handing the paper to her.

"A chance," she mouthed silently. And for the third time, he disappeared.

FOUR

It figures, thought Brigid, that when I'm finally ready to leave New Mexico, I can't go. She had been trying to call the airlines for an hour now, getting frustrated from being put on hold, hanging up, dialing again, and being put on hold again. She was still in bed, and it was still snowing outside, with no sign of letting up.

"Patience, dearie," her mother's voice echoed inside her head.

"Don't lecture me, Mum," she said out loud. "You're the one who put this bee in my bonnet." She smiled at that phrase of her mother's and realized again how easily invaded she was by that past, even here, in the American west, in the dry desert.

"Shit," she said out loud again, hanging up for the final time. "That's enough!"

She pulled on jeans and a black sweater and ran her fingers through her unruly short blonde hair and went to the front door to feel the air. The sound rushed in at her, the tiny patter of snowflakes, the crinkled sound of the wind in freezing air. It made her feel young again, and alone. Homesick.

For ten years she'd lived alone, telling herself that she was sick of home, sick of the ocean and rivers and bogs, everything green and blue and damp. She'd made her home in this summer place, where it was dry and brown and landlocked all around. And now, three days past the new year, she was feeling something new.

Not new, really, she realized as she put on the dusty red coat and scarf and hat and mittens she'd pulled from the back of the closet. Old. What she was feeling was old. An old feeling. Making her feel old.

She left her house unlocked and went out into the new snow, feeling old. She began to walk. The rhythm of her feet and the cold white air would clear her head, she thought. She hoped.

Her neighbor, Mattie, had smoke coming from her tiny adobe bungalow, and in the cold Brigid could smell sage and oil and the sweetness of fry bread cooking, even from the street. A black semi cab was parked out front, which meant Mattie's son was back.

Usually the yellow concrete of the government built houses in the pueblo looked dingy and cheap, but in the snow they almost glowed. Brigid had lived here, in the Laguna Pueblo, for eight years now. Before that, she lived in Albuquerque, where she went to school to learn massage and acupuncture after getting her nursing degree from University College in Dublin. She had been hired as a midwife by the US government as a way of keeping medical costs down for the native women who sometimes went their whole pregnancies without seeing a doctor, which then led to high hospital bills when they came in to deliver. Brigid's reputation had grown and now she was in demand off the reservations, too.

Except for now. One of the reasons she'd agreed to go home was that, for the first time in eight years, she had no clients. None. It spooked her.

And now, this. Her father, getting out of jail. Her childhood mind would say that he'd scared all the babies away. She had to go see him, confront him, so the babies could come back.

Her mind used to work this way. It was a way of making sense of insanity. She was the heroine of the night who fought off devils and witches and made the world safe again for morning. It was why, as an adult, she was not afraid of either death or birth. She'd seen them before. And she'd survived.

Walking along the frontage road that paralleled Interstate 40, Brigid saw that only one vehicle had dared out this morning. The truck tracks went up to the gas station at the nearest exit, and then doubled back. Probably out for a beer run, she thought. She looked at her watch. It was just after eight in the morning.

She turned north after the gas station, down a dirt road that was now completely covered in white. Off in the distance she could see Mount Taylor; usually just the tip was snow-covered, but today it was all white. White road, white mountain, white sky, she said to herself, like an incantation.

Suddenly she was seven years old again, in the middle of a white day in Ireland.

***

They are fighting, her parents, in the kitchen. It is winter, and the sun is low on the horizon over the bay. Brigid and her sister are playing outside in a rare snowfall that has left everything around their house white, but now they are cold.

They bang on the kitchen door. Mum and Da do not even look at them. Then Mum does, briefly, or maybe she is simply looking away from him and the children happen to come into her view.

Her sister hits harder on the glass of the upper part of the door, which she can barely reach. She turned five that fall, and is thin. Her pink ears stick out from mousy hair, her fingers are blue. She hits and hits, her rage rising as Brigid backs away.

There is a strength in her sister beyond her age. When faced with injustice, she rises in righteous anger. Brigid usually retreats.

Suddenly the glass crashes all around. Her sister's hands are red now, to match her ears and her cheeks. Their parents look at them in the blood and silence, and, for a moment, her sister has won.

She has stopped the fight.

***

Brigid noticed tracks in front of her in the snow, and the memory was over, disappeared into the white day as quickly as it had come. What is this? she asked herself. Squirrel? No, too much space between each mark for scampering. Fox? Probably not. Not big enough. Rabbit? Maybe.

She could ask Mattie when she got back. Mattie knew everything. Except how to keep her daughter-in-law alive and how to keep her son away from beer, Brigid thought bitterly. She had equal contempt for children who made their parents' lives miserable as she had for parents who had made their children miserable.

The tracks stayed together, then parted, then came together again. A pair of rabbits dancing, she thought. A good sign, perhaps. She would definitely ask Mattie.

Brigid did not want to cross the tracks, to blemish their dancing with her bootmarks, so she turned around and headed back.

***

Mattie called out to Brigid from the doorway when Brigid reached their street.

"Fry bread for you, early riser?"

"Yes, ma'am," called Brigid. Her voice still had a bit of the sweet lilt in it, after all these years, and it endeared people to her.

"Now, aren't you a vision in red!" Mattie exclaimed as she helped Brigid off with her red coat and hat and scarf and mittens and hung them all on a rack near the fire. "If the boys saw you, they'd have thought Santa was back for a return visit!"

"Where are the boys?" asked Brigid. Mattie had been taking care of her two grandsons, aged eight and six, ever since their mother died, two years ago.

"Out playing with their daddy in the snow," she smiled. "He came back when he heard the weather forecast. Always wants to be part of the good times." She shook her head as she piled the plate high with hot fry bread and placed it on the table with butter, sugar, honey, cinnamon, and homemade cherry jam.

"Coffee?" Mattie asked, and Brigid nodded as she grabbed for the bread and jam.

After serving the sugary black coffee, Mattie sat down. "Heard your phone ring real early this morning," she said. Their houses were close enough, and poorly built enough, that this was possible. "Didn't think there were any babies on the way, though."

"No, it wasn't about a baby," Brigid answered. "'Twas my Mum."

"Oh," Mattie, said, quietly.

"She wants me to come home."

"Oh."

"So I'm going."

"Mmm," Mattie said, sipping the sweet coffee.

"Since there aren't any babies coming, it seems a good time."

"Mmm," she said again, swallowing.

They sat together in silence for a moment.

"Oh, Mattie, I wanted to ask you," said Brigid, glad to have thought of a way to change the subject. "This morning I saw tracks in the snow on the old dirt road heading up toward Mount Taylor. Could they have been rabbit marks? There were two long prints in back, pointing away from each other, like a V, and then two little ones in front, like thumbs."

Mattie smiled. "Could be. How far apart were they?"

"Two feet. Three, even four sometimes."

"Yes, you probably saw some baby rabbits looking for food in the snow."

"Babies? In the winter? Is that possible?"

"Anything's possible, sweetheart."

"But I've never seen baby rabbits in the winter before."

"Everything gets clearer in a snowstorm," said Mattie. "You can see trees in a new way, and nests, and tracks...."

"And the past," said Brigid.

"Yes," Mattie nodded. "The snow makes everything clear."

They sat silently for a minute, and then Mattie noticed Brigid's empty cup. "More?" she asked, nodding to the coffee pot.

"No, thank you. I'm full on your delicious fry bread and jam. I couldn't have another drop."

But Mattie was already up and pouring. "Just take it on over to your house," she said. "It'll give you something to do while you're on the phone with those airlines." She smiled.

"Thank you. You're too good to me," Brigid said, hugging her, careful not to bump the hot coffee pot.

"How long you think you'll be gone?" Mattie asked.

"I'm not sure. There are things I need to get clear."

"That can take a while."

"Mmm," said Brigid, putting on her coat.

"I'll take care of your place while you're gone," Mattie said. "Water the plants and things."

"Mmm," Brigid said again, her mind already on the phone, wondering if she should get an open-ended ticket, half wondering if this was a trip she really needed to make, at the same time as she wondered what clothing she should take, what the weather was like in Dublin.

"Sweetheart," Mattie touched Brigid's shoulder at the door. "Those rabbits."

"What?" Brigid's hazel eyes looked into Mattie's deep brown.

"They're good luck. For what you're about to do."

"You think?"

"I know." Mattie smiled.

"One more thing."

"Yes?" Brigid asked, impatient to go.

"They mean babies are on the way."

Mattie paused, then jumped on in.

"Two." Mattie looked serious.

"Two babies?" asked Brigid.

"Yes," smiled the woman. She looked younger when she smiled. She was only ten years older than Brigid, but she was a grandmother, and her body was stooped and in pain often.

"Don't be bringing more babies for me to take care of," Mattie teased. Brigid knew Mattie would like nothing better.

"Be careful." Mattie said, finally pushing her out the door. "Get clear, and then come on back home."

FIVE

It was almost midnight when Claire finally heard Michael's key in the lock. Miriam had come home hours before, at dusk, and Claire had been excited, wanting to take her to the Indian restaurant for dinner, but Miriam had refused.

"But why? Why won't you eat ever with me anymore?" Claire had asked, allowing her voice to rise.

"I'm just not hungry," Miriam had mumbled and let her long black hair fall over her face like a veil.

"But that's crazy! What did you have for lunch? Did you even eat lunch? Miriam, talk to me!" Claire hammered away as Miriam retreated down the hall to her room, saying she had homework, and then quietly locked her door.

***

It is a choice you make, Claire wrote later, sitting in bed and waiting for Michael in the quiet apartment, after the fight with Miriam. You make a choice—to care or withdraw.

Claire had first felt Miriam start to withdraw from her when they moved to Ireland two years ago, and Claire, calling it adolescence or independence, had simply chosen to do it, too.

No one criticizes such a choice, really. It is cleaner. It avoids private messiness and embarrassing scenes in public. It keeps everything smooth. So it is the choice most people, these days, choose.

But maybe choice is too strong a word. For what option did Claire have? She had no *place* for the feelings. She had stopped keeping a journal, she had kept no close friends, her mother had died, and Michael, working late, coming home exhausted, could not be counted on, either.

So Claire's feelings hid themselves in the only homes she gave them: shopping, sex, and food.

Miriam was simply doing the same thing as her mother. In her case, it was music and school and the control of not eating that gave her feelings a place to hide.

But now that Claire was writing again, now that she had allowed herself that burst of anger toward her daughter, maybe now her feelings could come home to brood.

For it was brooding she was doing, her pen moving quickly across the pages of her journal, as she sat in bed in the clean and quiet room, waiting for Michael to come home. She wanted to tell him everything. She hoped he would be in a good mood.

***

"Michael?" Claire called when she heard his key in the door, resolving not to tell him about the fight with Miriam right away. She wanted to try, first, to recapture the joy she'd felt earlier in the day.

"Yes," he said, taking off his raincoat and hat and shoes in the hallway.

"Come in here. I have a surprise for you."

He came into view, still in his dark blue suit, and looking tired.

"But it can wait," she decided, putting down her journal and getting out of bed to greet him. "How was your day? You look tired."

"I am." He started undressing and told her about the conference call he'd had with the UN in New York. Eastern Europe's role in the new European community was a concern to them, and it was Michael's job to pitch Ireland's economic success as a model for the Eastern bloc.

She was used to this, his coming home late, since much of his work had to do with coordinating projects with New York or Washington, and what was a reasonable dinner time in Europe was the middle of the afternoon on the east coast.

"You look happy," he said to her, after he'd undressed and they settled back on the bed.

"I am," she said.

"Is that your surprise?" he asked, in a tone that might have been taken as critical if she had been in a mind to. Indeed, she'd been unhappy most of the evenings he'd come home since their move to Ireland. She had told him she hated the whiteness of the place—the constant, heavy clouds, the pale people—she missed the color and diversity that she'd come to thrive upon in Paris.

"Well, sort of." She looked away. "Wait here."

As she padded in slippers across the apartment to the kitchen and back, he noticed her new journal and the book of Irish poetry she'd been reading, spread open on the table beside the bed. Before he could reach over to look inside, she came back in carrying two mugs.

"This is the surprise," she said, handing him one mug.

"Tea?"

"Yes. I found a place today, a restaurant, but more than a restaurant, and I'm going to start writing poetry again. Look," she pointed to the journal on the table. "I've begun already. And I've been saving this for you since lunch," she gestured to the steaming cups.

He stared at her. She wasn't making sense. But he liked it. It reminded him of how she was. Before they'd moved to Ireland. Before the fighting with Miriam began. Before.

"Drink this with me," she said to him quietly, "and I'll explain everything later."

He smiled.

They sipped. She slipped back into the bed beside him. Side by side, they looked out toward the dark River Liffey, knowing the water was there, flowing from the west, but unable to see it. It was warm, the tea, and sweet. But also slightly bitter. It made them think back over the years of their marriage, how they'd both yearned to travel when they were young, and then how travel became their life, first from Chicago, where he'd graduated from the school of finance, to the London School of Economics, and then a brief time in Morocco, since they'd both studied French in college, and then back to London, then to Paris, and now Dublin. Their marriage had been a river they flowed upon. Neither had ever made friends who could withstand such movement. All they had, more than anything, was each other.

***

Michael turned to Claire and smiled. It worked, whatever magic there was in this tea, in her change, in her. He kissed her neck. She took the mugs and lay them upon the bedside table, where they tilted and clinked together and left rings on the poetry book. She nuzzled down deeper under the covers, pulling him with her. He glanced back, briefly, to make sure the bedroom door was shut, and then dove all the way under the covers. He pulled on her woolen socks and held the soft underskin of her feet in his hands, which were still warm from the tea. He caressed the tops of her feet, sweetly, and then her calves, as he tugged at her pajama pants and then kissed her thighs. She breathed in, deep, and laughed, quietly, as his tongue moved across her belly and up to her breasts, where he sucked and put his whole weight on top of her and entered her, placing her arms above her head, so that there was nothing holding him up. They were pressed against each other like paper, like water, like the long dark river that ran from the west beneath their window. He kissed her mouth, hard and long, and began to move, and as she shifted her hips, he thought again that this was the reason they were together, not travel or dreams of Africa or the French language or money or even their child. This. This river. This.

***

23

Later she would explain to him the change she felt, what had happened at the restaurant. She'd gone from there to the bookstore near Trinity and bought several books of poetry, a journal and a new fountain pen. She'd balanced the tea in one hand the whole time, wanted to save it for him, to share it with him, to do *this* with him, she laughed. Because he was, she said, the most important person in the world to her.

And after she'd fallen asleep, he lay awake, wondering what kind of potion that tea had been. He'd been so tired when he walked though the door, and now here he was, wide awake, feeling the kind of energy he hadn't felt since he was young. He had felt her desire for him—an urgency, the urgency she'd described when she talked about writing. And he felt it for her, too, for her body, for their bodies together. This was his poetry, what they made together.

Work had never been most important to him, although he pretended to be like other men for whom it was. It was simply a kind of protection, to pretend, for otherwise he would be too vulnerable, for the need he felt was too deep for everyday life, was too deep to admit during the day. Only at night, while Claire lay sleeping and he could touch her soft warm skin under the covers, could he admit to himself, briefly, that she was his center, his home, right before he fell asleep.

SIX

The knock at the door came just as Brigid was about to get into bed.

"Just a minute," she called, and grabbed her pink robe from the closet. As a midwife, she was used to late night visits and phone calls, but this had been a long day, and she was exhausted.

She opened the door and was surprised again to see the white snow glowing under the one street lamp. The cold burst into the room.

"Come in, come in," she said to the short young woman standing there in a puffy gray parka.

"I'm sorry to bother you," said Grace, "but Mattie said it was okay."

"Yes, sure," Brigid said as she went to the stove to put on water for tea, an old inclination. "Take off your coat. Have a seat." Brigid realized she was barking orders, out of fatigue and the leftover annoyance at the way the day had begun, irritated by the ghosts from the past that were, even now, in the room with them.

Grace sat at the little table in the kitchen, which was actually the kitchen and the living room together, as well as Brigid's bedroom, once the couch was pulled out, as it was now. The two existing bedrooms were used for storage of her medical supplies and books, as well as two extra beds, in case clients needed a safe place to be examined or to get a massage or to give birth.

When the water boiled, Brigid prepared two cups of red raspberry leaf tea, which strengthened the uterus, and was a good choice since Grace was already three or four months along, Brigid noticed as she took off her coat.

"I'm pregnant," Grace said as Brigid sat down.

"I can see that."

"I haven't told anyone yet. But I'm starting to show."

"Yes."

"And I was wondering if you would be able to keep me here."

"Here?" Brigid was too tired for this conversation. She should have asked Grace to come back in the morning. She had had pregnant women stay with her before, when money got tight or there was violence in the home.

"I don't want to tell my mom," said Grace, looking into her cup.

Brigid knew Grace's mom. She was a stern Christian woman who lived on the road heading toward the Acoma pueblo. She worked in the little church, sweeping and dusting and taking care of the priest. She'd been a widow for a long time.

"I can understand that, darling," Brigid said, after she'd had some tea. "But I have to tell you, I'm having some trouble with my mum at the moment, too. I'm meant to go home next week."

Grace stared at her.

"Ireland. I'm from Ireland," Brigid explained.

Grace didn't speak. She'd never been outside of New Mexico, and she was only fourteen, and here she was, pregnant, and it was too late for an abortion, not that her mom would want that, either. She looked like a deer in headlights. She couldn't conceive of the idea of Ireland.

"What I'm saying, Grace, is that you can't stay here, because I'll be gone. And I don't know when I'm coming back. I'm sorry. I really am."

They sat in silence for a moment.

"You've talked to Mattie about this?" Brigid asked.

"Yes, ma'am."

"Well, that's good. Mattie knows how to take care of you. She could even deliver the baby, if you wanted her to. She knows at least as much as I do, just not from any school, learned it from her grandmother. She's taught me things they don't teach in school, like this tea," Brigid gestured. "It's made from the leaves of red raspberry plants, and it's good for the uterus."

Grace's eyes tightened, as if she were wincing.

"The uterus is where the baby is, darling. It's where your baby is growing," Brigid explained. "And it's got a lot of work to do. It grows and stretches and becomes a big complex home for the baby. And this tea will help it do its job."

Grace nodded.

"But Mattie can teach you all that. What I think we need to talk about is your mother."

Grace's eyes filled with tears. "I can't tell her," she whispered. "She'll be so sad."

"Do you know who the father is?"

"My father?" Grace asked.

"No, sweetie, the father of the baby."

"Oh, yes, ma'am. He's my boyfriend, Jerry."

"How old is he?"

"Sixteen."

"Is he in school? Or does he have a job?"

"Both. He goes to high school and he works at the Walmart distribution center on 40."

"Good."

"He's a nice, nice boy." Grace smiled.

"Good."

"My mom likes him."

"That helps."

"It's just that...."

"What, honey?"

"Well..."

"You can tell me. I won't tell anyone." If Brigid had learned anything in her life, it was that the silence of a woman could be deadly.

"It's what happened to my mom."

"What?"

"This. Me. She tells everybody she is a widow, but she's not. She went away to California when she was a teenager, and she came back with me when I was three years old, and she told everyone she was widowed, that my daddy had died, but he wasn't dead. He's still in California. He still sends me cards sometimes, too, and sometimes some money. But I haven't seen him since we left California, and I don't really remember him, but he's not dead, and with my mom working at the church and everything, no one can ever know this. She's always telling me, 'Be careful with boys. They'll get you in trouble quicker than a rabbit,' but I never listened. She's always telling me stuff that's right and wrong, and sin all over the place, and Jerry's real nice, and he says he wants to marry me."

Brigid took the last sip of her tea, swallowed hard.

"Look, Grace, first, I won't tell anyone what you've just told me. Okay?"

Grace nodded. This girl was either talking at rapidfire or closed like a clam.

"And I understand your worry over what your mom will say and do."

Grace stared.

"But I think you need to tell her. I think she might understand more than you might guess. When parents have been through something, when they've made a mistake somewhere along the line, they have this instinct to keep their kid from it. You can understand, can't you? They love you and they don't want to see you hurt."

Grace looked into her cup.

"But if something happens," Brigid began, and then realized she was saying this for herself, as well. "If something happens that repeats the life of the mother, well, then, the mother just might have that much more compassion."

Grace seemed to wince again.

"You will understand this more as your pregnancy goes along. But the love a mother holds for her child is very deep. It never goes away."

Brigid's voice started to crack.

"Your mother loves you, Grace," she said. And in her mind, Brigid knew that this was true for her, too. Her mother loved her. All the time she'd spent working with mothers and their babies, she'd told herself that she was looking for proof of the existence of a love she hadn't received. But this knowledge had been there all along, deep within her like a river. Brigid had pushed it down because it would mean that she could finally stop running from its truth.

It would mean she could finally go home.

"Your mother loves you, Grace," Brigid repeated.

And she knew it was time for her to go home.

Finally they were all together in the same room, but not even sitting with each other, and not talking, as the lights dimmed and Miriam's chamber music group struck the first notes of Schubert's *Octet in F Minor*. Two weeks had passed, during which Claire had seen even less of Michael and Miriam than usual. He had been busy at work, she at cello practice, and Claire herself had been preoccupied. She had been writing in her journal every day and attending poetry readings and had even begun taking yoga.

And now, on a late January evening in Dublin, Claire looked up at her difficult teenaged daughter, with her black hair falling against the side of her ruby mouth, and her hands moving across the cello's body like a lover. Claire was once again struck by the girl's beauty, and turned around from where she was sitting up front to look for Michael, standing in the back of the concert hall, having rushed in late from work. They smiled at each other, both acknowledging the beauty they had created together, on stage.

Then Claire settled back into her seat for the somewhat anxious first movement, and she did her usual check to see if Miriam's skirt was pressed, what hose she was wearing, whether her shoes needed replacing, and then it dawned on her that she didn't really care.

The past weeks had changed something within her, she realized, as the tempo slowed a bit. Before the concert, Miriam had refused to eat the snack Claire made for her. Then she wanted to walk to the concert alone. And Michael called at the last minute to say he was running late. All this, in times past, would have pushed Claire into a kind of angry numbness by the time of the concert.

Maybe it was turning forty as she had in November, or maybe it was the return of her writing, or the yoga, or more frequent sex, she smiled to herself, but something was starting to shift. It was as if she was letting go of her role as a mother and rediscovering the person she'd been before Miriam's birth.

No, that wasn't quite right, Claire thought, as the momentum quickened. It wasn't really Miriam's fault that they had both become so numb.

How much she'd loved mothering at first. The soft baby skin, the smell, the constant touch of breastfeeding. She had felt herself growing away from Michael and into a more female world. She'd been glad to have a girl. Someone pretty. Claire had loved the compliments, how people said they looked alike. Before Miriam could talk, when they were still in London, Claire would say thank you, knowing she was living off Miriam's small, dark beauty. Miriam had gotten Claire's thick straight hair but not her pale skin or blue eyes or round face. She was angular, and dark, like Michael, and the still colonial-minded British had had no trouble admiring the little girl's exotic looks.

Later, in Paris, Miriam had been thin enough to be admired, but was too dark to be trusted. She'd been taken for an Arab sometimes, and Claire would protect Michael from it, from the knowledge of mothers who shooed their children away from them at the sandbox, for fear it would awaken his own fears as a Jew, which he'd told himself had been safely buried when his grandparents had settled on Midwestern American soil.

It was not so easy to forget the past in Europe, Claire had learned. When they'd first left the states, it would amaze her even to see the dates chiseled into the sides of buildings. 1350. 1588. 1798.

The music paused and the next movement began, a gentle, slow theme led by the sorrowful clarinet that made Claire miss the newness of America, her homeland. How a mall built twenty years earlier could be considered old. And, as Miriam's cello joined in, her bony shoulder rocking back and forth under the white linen, Claire felt a sudden longing for her own mother, who had died two years before. Her mother had never really gotten to know Miriam. How stubborn Claire had been, to make her parents come to Europe those few times, telling herself it was too much trouble to travel overseas with a young child, that it would be good for them to see London or Paris.

And the week would drag by, as her mother harped that Claire was eating too much, needed to lose ten pounds, just ten, she would say, but the baby, she's too thin, don't you feed her?

I try, mother, I try, Claire said to herself, as the violins winced with her at Miriam's slender calves rising up from her chunky black shoes. Secretly she'd been proud of her daughter's thinness; Claire herself had always been so round, so hungry, never satisfied. But Miriam was more controlled, lived off air, it seemed, air and music.

The nostalgia dissipated as Claire realized her mother would be right. The girl was too thin. Claire sighed with the bassoon as one movement ended and the next began.

Fast, too fast, slow down, thought Claire, as the music rushed along like a child chasing a butterfly. Time flies when you're having children, Michael used to say.

And here they were, at forty and forty-five, with only a year until Miriam was gone.

Pause.

Schubert was twenty-seven when he wrote this, Claire had read on the program while waiting for Michael to arrive. Only a twenty-seven year old would rush things like this, right in the middle. You think you will be rushing forever when you are young. And then you slow down.

"I'm going as fast as I can," Claire's mother had said to her over the phone, just before she died.

Suddenly they stopped. And then it was intermission, people clapping, and Michael by her side.

"Sorry I was late," he whispered.

"It's okay. You made it."

"Are you okay?" he asked.

"Yes," she said, then, "No."

"What is it?"

"I've just been thinking about death."

"Schubert can do that," he smiled, trying to cheer her.

"I'm worried about Miriam."

He glanced at the stage, now empty.

"She's playing well."

"No," Claire shook her head. "It's not that. She's too thin. She won't eat."

"You know she gets nervous before a concert." Claire had told him on the phone about the incident with the snack.

"No, Michael," she said firmly. "She's too thin. She isn't eating. I think she has a problem."

The crowd quieted as the eight musicians came out from behind the curtain. Michael and Claire looked away from each other, toward their daughter. They said nothing more. He took her hand as the lights dimmed and the fourth movement began.

Something cheerful, a diversion, that's what this piece is, thought Claire. The group picked it for that reason, and because they were young, and because it was a challenge. Miriam was the youngest, but the oldest, the first violin, was only twenty-three.

How could Claire still feel this, the warmth of Michael's hand around her own, and the sense of excitement she'd been living with, as if a word, a magical word, might be just hovering in the air as she turned a corner, when her daughter was so thin, so obviously in trouble.

They would speak to Miriam tonight, she decided.

Un mot. A word. A mote. *Un mot* is a mote. What keeps us from each other. What protects our castles. What we must cross to reach each other.

No more motes. Only *mots.*

Claire sat for the rest of the concert, annoyed at its confidence, its charm, seeing only Miriam's sharply pointed elbow moving beneath her white linen blouse. Claire bit her bottom lip, chapped by the winter cold, and wished that this night were already over.

EIGHT

The music irked Brigid with its cheerful simplicity, its tinny quality coming through the airplane speakers, as they sat on the runway, unmoving. What happened to silence in public places, she wondered. When did it happen that we decided we had to fill every space with sound? Cartoons in fast food restaurants, music videos in the car repair shop, even the local high school had televisions in every classroom now, with morning news delivered by satellite and punctuated by ads for candy bars and clothing.

She knew she was being critical because she was nervous. She didn't really like to fly. She'd never flown before she'd come to America. Back then, in her twenties, she'd been so exhilarated at being let out of Ireland that she'd held her breath all the way across the Atlantic.

She hadn't been excited for reasons that most young immigrants get excited — the dream of America, the promise of a new identity, the possibility of romance, the thrill of beginning again.

No, Brigid thought, as the lights dimmed and the plane started to taxi down the runway, she'd simply been grateful that America had agreed to let her, the daughter of a terrorist, into the country.

The Clinton administration was taking a leading role in the peace process, the State Department official had explained over the phone to her mother, and then convinced them that this would be a good opportunity for Brigid to make a fresh start.

So the government had hired Brigid as a nurse midwife for a cluster of New Mexico reservations and had even paid for two years of training in Albuquerque. They'd sent her to massage and acupuncture school, let her serve as an apprentice to a midwife, and gave her a chance to study the history and culture of the Pueblo people.

Brigid delivered her first baby when she was twenty-seven. What she'd been so surprised at was the slowness. The way the minutes dragged between contractions. Brigid hadn't understood, at first, that the rests were part of the process. She'd wanted something to do, and had only felt useful during the parts of pain, the cries for encouragement and help. How young she was, how fast she thought life should proceed. How much she'd learned to slow down, these past eight years.

Life happens in the pauses, she knew now, as the plane left the ground and the lights of earth twinkled like reverse stars in the darkness below.

It had been ten years since she'd been home. Ten years since she'd seen her mother, and fifteen since she'd seen her father.

He had come to her ground floor flat, late one night, while she was still at university. It had been raining, and cold. Dublin could be very cold. Brigid hadn't wanted to let him in but couldn't stand the cold so she'd stepped back, just enough so he could move in and she could close the door.

"They're after me," he'd said.

"I know, Da," she'd said.

"I'm goin' underground. I may not get to see you."

She'd shaken her head, said nothing. She'd seen the pictures from the Grand Hotel bombing on the telly.

"I wondered if I could have a hug from my only girl." His eyes had been red, from crying.

"I don't know, Da," she'd said. She was not his only girl. He had had two girls, plus their mother, but he was like this, lying to try to make a woman feel better, to try to make her feel as if she were the most important one to him. It did not work with Brigid, she told herself.

"Cum on," he'd said, opening his arms.

She allowed herself to be hugged by him. Why did he fecking have to cry, she'd thought as he let out a sob.

"One day, Brig," he'd said as he was leaving, "I hope you'll be able to forgive me."

When she'd heard the news that he'd been captured, she was relieved. He wouldn't be able to visit her unexpectedly anymore. That had been her first thought.

Selfish, she thought now. Young people are so selfish.

In the years she'd spent catching babies and watching them grow, she'd learned how much was out of parents' hands. How much money they had. What language they spoke. If they had an accent. Where they lived. If there were a helpful neighbor nearby. These little things could make the difference between a child well cared for and a child neglected. Or hurt.

Perhaps she was ready, she thought now, to see that this had been true for her own parents, as well.

She'd received only one letter from her father while he was in jail. It was just after she'd been accepted into the graduate nursing program at University College. The letter had come to her mother's Dublin flat. Her mother had sat across from her at the kitchen table, drinking coffee and whiskey, at ten in the morning, while Brigid read the letter that her mother had already opened.

Her father congratulated Brigid on her scholarship, and said he'd always wanted to be a scholar. Growing up, he explained, he saw clearly how the lack of work in County Clare led men to feel despair, or to disappear into drink. He hadn't wanted to do either, so, after receiving high marks throughout his years in the local schools, he'd applied to Oxford. Fecking Oxford, he couldn't believe it now, he'd written, and the blokes in the Real would have his ass if they ever knew, but he'd actually gotten in. A phone call had come to the pub next to their house. They hadn't had a telephone and he'd been too ashamed to admit this in the application, so he'd used the pub's number. And his mother, half drunk, had gotten on the phone and had said, "Is this a Catholic school?" The admissions officer had said no, and his mother had said, "Well, I'm sorry, but my son can't go."

He'd been seventeen. Another woman in the pub, a meaner woman even than his mother, had told him the story shortly after, and, out of loyalty to his mum, he'd never repeated the story until now.

Her father signed the letter, "Be *dána*, my girl."

Dána. Creative. Artistic. The goal of Yeats and his generation. Forming a new nation.

"It's not me, Da," Brigid said to herself, closing the letter and looking at her mother who'd already read the letter and whose face was red from whiskey and tears.

"'Tis beautiful, no?" she said.

"No," Brigid answered firmly. "He doesn't even know who I am," she said, partly as an indictment and partly out of sadness, although she hadn't been able to admit the sadness to herself until now, over a decade later, returning home.

She'd seen the difference a father made in the life of child, in the pueblos over the past eight years. How important an uncle or older brother was, when the father could not be found. How boys and girls alike craved the physical play with a man, his laughter, his strength, his quiet way of listening.

Brigid had dated a divorced man with a daughter briefly, while she was living in Albuquerque. She had gone out to dinner with them once, and it was then that she realized that what she'd seen between them was something she had never had and never would have. Later, alone in her apartment, she'd sobbed, huge wracking noises that scared her cat and made it hide under the bed. She fell asleep still crying. The relationship hadn't lasted long.

Brigid looked at her watch. The pilot announced that they'd just crossed out of the Central Time zone and were now heading north.

Brigid wound her watch ahead. She'd read that this helped with jet lag. Suddenly she lost three hours, and the thought filled her with sadness. She took off her watch and decided she didn't want to know what time it was. And she certainly didn't want to see this stupid movie about Russian spies that was just starting, so she looked out the window toward the sliver of January moon in the western night and then closed her eyes and tried to fall asleep by pretending it was even later than it was.

NINE

Walking between Michael and Miriam in the cold Dublin night from the concert hall to dinner, Claire had to focus on her breathing in order to stop herself from launching into a tirade about Miriam's eating.

After the concert, Michael and Claire had gone backstage to meet Miriam, and Michael had shot Claire a look while hugging the girl's tall, thin frame, which meant "Let me handle this," and so she did.

"You played wonderfully, sweetie," was all Claire said to her, trying to smile as she looked into her daughter's chestnut eyes.

Miriam had looked away quickly and said, "Did you like it, Daddy?"

Michael had taken both of her hands in his and kissed them, saying, "Not the cello, my dear, but *these* are the true instruments of beauty," which made Miriam smile and giggle.

And then Michael had suggested, "How about getting dinner at that Indian place your mom is always talking about?" and Miriam, charmed, had agreed.

Now they were going through the colored beads that separated the outer doorway from the inside of the restaurant, and Padmaj was greeting them, saying, "Poet lady, you've brought your family!" and Michael was telling Padmaj about Miriam's concert and Claire was still saying nothing, so afraid she was to make a mess of the whole thing.

"Well," Michael said, after they'd hung their coats and settled into a booth and ordered Guinness, "That was one fine concert."

He'd said this several times. Claire could tell he was somewhat nervous.

"Your playing has really improved since we've been in Ireland," Claire allowed herself to say to Miriam.

Miriam nodded, and her long black hair fell across her face.

Michael looked at Claire, sitting next to Miriam, and then back to Miriam. No one spoke.

"Here you are," Padmaj said, bringing the three pints. "Are you ready to order?"

"Could you choose, Padmaj?" Claire asked.

"I'm not that hungry," said Miriam, and Claire twitched.

"So I'll bring a little of everything and you can taste-try," Padmaj said to Miriam, "Or not. It's up to you." And he was off.

"Miriam, honey," Michael began. He sipped his dark beer. The foam stuck to his upper lip, and he licked it. Claire wanted to kiss him then, wished they were alone, wished they were not having this conversation.

"You don't eat," Claire blurted, to block the guilt she felt. "We're worried about you."

"Yes," Michael said gently, trying to bring Miriam's attention back to him. "We want to know what's going on."

Miriam sighed. She looked at her hands, her long strong fingers, still red from bowing.

"I'm just not hungry," she said, quietly, not looking up.

Claire and Michael looked at each other, and then scanned the restaurant. It was late, and the restaurant was almost empty. Two men sat reading in the corner.

"Why not, sweetheart?" Michael almost whispered.

"Do you have any idea where we are?" she asked him.

She paused.

"I'm talking about Ireland," Miriam said, looking directly at her father.

Michael sustained her gaze. Claire was looking into her beer.

"Do you know how many people died here?" Miriam asked.

"No. I mean, yes," Michael stammered. "Well, not exactly. What do you mean?"

"The famine. I'm talking about the famine. The population of Ireland today is still less than half what it was before the famine. Do you know why?"

"The potato crop failed," he said, almost a question.

"It wasn't about the potato, Daddy," she said, her chestnut eyes aflame. "It was a project of the British to wipe out the population."

"You're starving yourself because of history?" Claire interrupted.

"It's not just history," Miriam spat back, turning toward her mother. "It's the same thing that Daddy's doing now, with the bank. You call it progress, or globalization, or capitalism, whatever, but the truth is that it kills people. It kills people's culture and it kills them."

Padmaj arrived with the food, steaming plates of aloo palak, samosas filled with potatoes and peas, and channa masala. He said nothing, but he looked into Miriam's eyes as he laid the plates down, and Claire saw him wink gently and then retreat.

Michael was hurt, Claire could see this. Claire tried not to speak, to let him respond, and busied herself by serving up portions on the plates. When she got to the third, she laid the spoon down.

"Take what you want, honey," she said to Miriam, and handed the empty plate to her.

"You don't understand, Mom," she said, laying her hands, palms upward, on the table. Her eyes filled with tears.

"You're right," Michael said, a bit angrily, his fork in the air.

"We're trying to, honey," Claire said as she touched Miriam's arm.

"It just doesn't make sense that you're starving yourself on purpose," Michael said as his fork dove into the aloo palak.

"Please try to explain it to us," said Claire, trying to turn Miriam's attention away from her father. She'd tried to let Michael handle this alone, but she couldn't. Deep down she thought it had something to do with her, as a mother. She thought this was about Miriam's differentiation from her. A teenage thing.

This had surprised them both, this turn toward Michael. Claire could tell he was upended.

In the awkward silence, Claire started to eat. She loved this food. She loved all food, but there was something about this food that she loved more than all other food.

Finally Miriam asked Claire, "When did your mother's grandmother leave Ireland?"

Claire looked up from her plate. "I don't know. My grandmother was born in 1909. Her mother was born sometime in the second half of the nineteenth century. So I guess, 1880s or 90s. I don't know."

"Exactly," said Miriam. "You don't know."

Claire was losing her appetite. She felt slightly sick. For a second she wondered if this was what Miriam felt, why she wasn't eating.

"Do *you* know, Daddy? Do you know when your grandparents came to America?"

Claire and Miriam both looked at Michael. He was pale. He put down his fork.

Of course he knew. It was 1932 when his grandparents had fled Germany, all four of them together, the two men, partners in the banking business, with their wives and children, two of whom would grow up and marry and become Michael's parents.

"Why are you asking us these questions?" Claire said.

"Because Daddy's bank is doing to Third World countries what the Germans were doing to the Jews," Miriam said.

Michael turned red. "Stop it!" he growled through clenched teeth.

The two men at the corner table looked up.

"You have no idea what you're talking about! Where did you *hear* this crap? Is this what you're learning in *school*?"

His long buried suspicion of Catholics resurfaced, their history of hatred of Jews, and Ireland's refusal to join Europe in fighting against Germany in World War II. Just that morning, in fact, Michael had read an interview in the *Herald Tribune* with a scholar who had unearthed evidence that Ireland had even taken measures to aid the Nazis during the war.

Miriam started to speak, but Michael slammed his hand into the table and said, "I'm not listening to any more of this!"

He stood up.

"Don't you dare speak with disrespect of your ancestors, Miriam Irene," he said to her, conjuring the names of her two great-grandmothers who had brought his parents safely to America. "Don't you dare."

And he was gone.

***

Claire and Miriam sat side by side in the booth for a long time, silent. After a while Padmaj came to clear the plates away, silent, too. The two customers in the corner put money on their table and left, quietly.

"Daddy doesn't understand, Mom," said Miriam, finally. "Because he's *in* it."

"Listen," said Claire, carefully, turning to face her daughter fully. "I am trying to understand what you are saying. I care about you. I am worried about you. But I also know that you have a mind of your own. You are almost grown. So I am trying to see what you are saying. But you cannot blame your own father for the history of the Irish. You just can't. It's crazy."

Claire paused when she said that word. Then she said, "I think we need some help sorting all this out."

"What do you mean?" Miriam asked.

"I think we need to see somebody. A doctor."

"Mom…" Again Miriam had tears in her eyes.

"We can't do it alone," Claire admitted. "We need help."

Miriam cried in earnest then, and Claire did, too, as she folded her arms around the girl's bony frame.

***

Claire and Miriam stayed so long at the restaurant that the cook had left and Padmaj sat by himself behind the register in a red chair reading a book.

"Mom," Miriam said to Claire, after their tears had subsided. "Don't you ever wonder about where your people came from?"

It was rare, Claire knew, for Miriam to look at her this way anymore—open and vulnerable—so she measured her response carefully.

"You mean South Carolina?"

Claire knew right away that it was the wrong answer.

"No, mother, I mean Ireland. I mean, don't you wonder why they left? Why no one ever came back? Don't you want to know the story?"

"They were poor, honey. They still are. Daddy's trying...."

Miriam shook her head again, looked away.

Claire looked around the room. When she saw Padmaj reading, an idea struck her. "Wait here," she said, and walked over to another table.

Padmaj glanced up briefly.

She brought back a yellow book of poetry. On its cover was a black and white photograph of a married couple—clean, white, starched—it could have been Claire's parents in the Charleston suburbs in the 1950s, newly married, before she herself had been born.

Claire opened the book to the center and paged through until she found the poem she wanted. "Some people know what it's like," she began to read, in a clear voice. By the time she got to the final lines, her voice was shaking.

to be second-hand
to be second-class
to be no class
to be looked down on
to be walked on
to be pissed on
to be shat on
and other people don't.

Claire looked at Miriam. "This is why our grandparents left Europe for America. And why they never came back," she said. "It's why your daddy works so hard at the bank. He's *helping* people." She looked over at Padmaj behind the cash register, briefly.

"Because, sweetie, it all comes down to food. Your great-grandparents went hungry, Miriam. But we haven't. You haven't. You've never known hunger, my daughter," Claire said. "Hunger that you didn't *choose*."

Miriam tears fell into her hands. "But Mommy," she said. "I do. I do."

And for the second time that night, they embraced, crying.

***

When they finally began to head to the door, Padmaj put down his book to join them.

"It's cold tonight, Poet lady and Poet daughter," he said sweetly. "Do bundle up." He was, as usual, patient, as if it brought him joy to be waiting. He reminded Claire of a rare butterfly she'd seen once when they had lived in Morocco, the way its wings moved in slow motion, taking no moment for granted.

It was in this spirit, and on account of all the restaurant had come to mean to her over the past few weeks – the return of her writing, the renewed passion she felt for Michael, the promise of healing for their daughter – that Claire spontaneously leaned into Padmaj and kissed his smooth cheek just before gliding through the colored beads in the entrance way.

"Mom," Miriam smiled, once they were outside. "Why did you do that?"

"I don't know," Claire admitted. "He looked lonely."

They laughed, knowing this was a secret they would keep from Michael, the way mothers and daughters do, and they walked home hand in hand.

The midnight bells from Trinity Cathedral could be heard in the distance as they crossed the river toward home.

TEN

Brigid didn't feel like sharing a taxi from the airport, but the buses were full to overflowing and the black cabs were the only ones available in the afternoon rush, so she loaded her bag into the trunk and slipped in beside an American family with a toddler son.

"Are you Irish?" the father asked her excitedly after she'd given the driver the address of her mother's flat.

She nodded. She was exhausted. The trip had taken almost twenty-four hours. Albuquerque to New York. A five-hour layover in the middle of the night. Then an early morning flight from New York to Dublin, which, after the time change, got her in at dusk.

"Have you any advice for us?" he asked. "It's our first time here."

She shook her head. "I haven't been here in over a decade," she admitted. "It's changed so much." She couldn't believe the traffic, cars heading home to the suburbs, cars heading into the city for the evening, construction everywhere.

The family was disappointed. They got quiet in the way that foreigners do in a strange place.

The boy sensed the parents' sadness and tried to distract them by exclaiming, "Choo choo!" as a railway car sped alongside the highway.

"Yes, Ian, it's a train," said the mother, patting his head.

"I hear the Famine Museum is worth seeing," offered Brigid, by way of apology.

"Yes, we've heard that," said the father, politely. "County Roscommon, right?"

"Yes," said Brigid.

"Have you been there?"

"No, it opened while I was away."

"Oh."

And for the rest of the ride they were quiet.

***

Brigid gave the taxi driver a big tip and then stood on the sidewalk, holding onto her black bag for a long time after he drove away. People had to walk around her, and some bumped into her, the sidewalk was so crowded. Night had fallen now, and people were hungry, or eager to get to the pub, or coming home late from work. She couldn't believe how modern everything looked. How American.

She'd even passed a McDonald's on the way. She'd never even heard of McDonald's until she moved to America, and here it was.

Here she was. She smelled the beer from the pub at the bottom of her mother's building and wondered how silly it would look to go in with her bag. She always had found it easier to deal with her mother's drinking by drinking herself.

How easily the old ways came back, she thought, and then went to ring the bell in the lobby of the building.

"Brigid Mary!" her mother cried through the speaker. "Come on in!"

***

While the city had gotten newer, her mother had gotten old. Her hair was thinner than it had been, although it was still dyed blonde. Her cheeks were sunken in, the lines around her mouth from smoking were deeper. Her eyes were still the hazel that matched Brigid's, that had made her father call her the spitting image, as both a compliment and an accusation.

"Mum," she said, and hugged her mother's rigid frame.

"You're so thin!" her mother exclaimed. "Don't you eat?"

"I'm healthy, mum. I'm a nurse."

"Hmm," said her mother. "Come eat," she said, and sat Brigid down at the worn kitchen table, the same one where they had read the letter from her father so many years ago.

"I've made a stew," her mother said, picking up a burning cigarette from the ashtray and stirring a large pot on the stove at the same time. "A lamb stew."

Brigid paused. "You know I don't eat meat, Mum," she said, quietly.

"Still?" her mother shrieked. "I would have thought you'd abandoned that foolishness years ago!"

"I'm sorry," Brigid apologized, at the same time as her mother said, "Shit!"

"I can eat the vegetables," she offered.

"Would you rather go out?" her mother said.

Brigid knew her mother was trying awfully hard. She hated to cook, and she equally hated to go out. What she liked to do was to drink and smoke and watch the telly, at home, alone.

"No, really, mum," she said, "It's fine. I'll eat the vegetables. It smells wonderful."

"Okay, then," her mother said, relieved. And then, "Well, take your coat off, for Christ's sake! Don't just stand there!" And while Brigid did, her mother poured herself more scotch.

"I'll have one, too," said Brigid.

"Sure, help yourself," said the mother as she ladled out a bowl of stew.

"Aren't you going to eat?" Brigid asked.

"I had some earlier," her mother lied. "Come on, sit down."

***

They sat in silence while Brigid ate, careful to avoid the chunks of meat. Her mother lit another cigarette.

"You didn't check in first?" her mother said, finally, nodding toward the black bag near the door.

"No. I..." It hadn't occurred to Brigid to make a hotel reservation. She thought she'd stay with her mother. "The traffic was so bad," she said. "It would have taken too long," she lied.

Her mother nodded. "City's changed, hasn't it?"

"Yes."

"You should see Miltown Malbay," her mother said. "A feckin' tourist trap, not the sleepy village we knew," she smiled. "'Tis a center for folk music in the summer. Like, what is that city in America? Nashville? Yes, a wee Irish Nashville."

How did her mother know about Nashville? She thought about the country music the people liked on the reservation. How they'd laugh if she told them she was from the Irish Nashville.

They both laughed.

Then they were quiet again.

Her mother poured herself another drink from the bottle on the floor near her feet. "As a matter of fact, you should probably go see it. Do some touring. You've got time. The appointment isn't until next week."

"What are you talking about?"

"Didn't I tell you? His psychiatrist wants to see you before he'll be set free."

"What?" Brigid couldn't believe this. "I thought *he* wanted to see me."

"No, sweetie. I thought I explained this on the phone." Her mother's voice was rising, as it did when she was lying and she knew Brigid knew she was lying.

45

"The whole reason you're here is because they won't let him go until the psychiatrist meets with you. You must agree to keep an eye on him. It's a condition of the release."

"Mother, you didn't tell me this. If I'd known this, I would never have…"

"Brigid, don't be cold. The man's spent fifteen years in jail and never had a trial. He's sick. The least you can do is…"

"The least *I* can do? The least *I* can do?" Brigid rose in anger.

"Your appointment is next Tuesday. Here's the address," she said quickly, handing her a card from the pocket of her housecoat. She knew she didn't have much time. She knew Brigid would leave quickly.

Brigid crumpled the card in her hand but did not throw it away.

"Oh mum," she said, standing. "You never change, do you?"

Her mother did not stand.

Brigid grabbed her coat and purse and left.

She'd left her black bag behind, she realized, as she stood in the grimy hall by the elevator, looking back at her mother's door. She wanted her mother to come out, to say she was sorry, to ask her to come back. The elevator arrived. Brigid hesitated, holding the door open, remembering how many times she'd wanted this from her mother, a return, an apology, a new beginning.

Finally she got in and went down to the pub on the ground floor, where the music was loud and the lights were dim and she could drink in a corner, by herself, and cry.

ELEVEN

Padmaj was lonely. He'd been in this country for fifteen years, and he had made a success of his business, had many good and loyal customers, and was providing them something more than a restaurant, something more than just food. Still there were foggy nights like this, when he closed up late, after the cook and waiters had left, when he couldn't bear to get into his car and drive out to the little house he called home. The car would be cold; it would barely warm up during the twenty minute drive home. Then his house would echo as he stepped into it, the wooden floors and barren walls reminding him that he was alone.

It was easier, on nights like this, to walk four blocks south and slip into the loud, dim after hours bar and order a beer or two or three. Then, usually, he would walk back to the restaurant instead of driving and sleep on the floor until the morning light fragmented through the colored beads and he would wake with a hangover and stumble into the kitchen to start making the tea masala for the day.

He knew he was lonely because this had been happening more regularly. Twice already this month. This would be the third time. Third time's a charm, he said to himself as he saw the Guinness sign lit in the bar's window. Lucky charms, they're magically delicious, he remembered from his time in America as a college student. He laughed to think of himself as a dark faced leprechaun as he opened the pub door and was greeted by the scent of sour beer and the sight of sad bodies, which faded by the time he was at the bar and ordering, as if, magically, becoming one of the drinkers made him lose the power to perceive them clearly.

The bartender took her time, shaving off the foam on top of the glass with a knife, over and over, to fill the pint to capacity. Padmaj looked around for a seat while he waited. He didn't want to be too close to the band, where one would be expected to join in the singing at some point in the wee hours of the morning. But since he was lonely, he didn't want to sit too close to the door, either, which was where the unavailable married men who told themselves they were on their way out soon, just after this song, sat.

He rubbed his hands together to warm them, still chilly from the walk. His knuckles were dry from wiping down tables and putting his hands in water, but the palms were surprisingly soft. He remembered when the astrologer had held his palm when he was a boy and traced his love line so lightly it tickled. "Two," the old woman had said and looked at his mother. "The boy's love line splits in two!"

The mother laughed to cover her worry. "It means he loves his mother always, even when he goes away. Right, Padmaj?"

His mother had told him he would not stay in Sinsyaru Khala, he would not stay in India for that matter. He would travel to America, to Europe, to as many places as he could.

"This world is big," she would say, though she'd never left the forest where they lived. "And not those who know the most, but those who love the most will be saved and will be able to save it."

As the memory faded, he looked across the room to see a woman he'd never seen before here. He was pretty sure she was Irish—the bar was one of the few that welcomed dark faced foreigners like himself—but she looked unusual.

Perhaps it was because she'd been crying, he realized, as he found himself walking closer to her. He had become a good judge of character since owning the restaurant. He knew the way a sad woman sat at a table as if it were a blanket that could cover her.

Her hazel eyes met his dark pools, and her eyes flashed recognition, just briefly, which made him smile.

"May I sit here?" he gestured toward the table.

"Yes, of course," she said, and slid over on the bench.

He had meant to sit across from her, in a wooden chair, but then he realized that the etiquette of Irish pub life called for everyone to sit facing the musicians. She most definitely was Irish, he decided, as he sat next to her, so close his coat brushed her sweater. They sat together like this, looking at the band, until the set was finished.

By then both their glasses were empty.

"Shall I get us another?" he asked, and she nodded, smiling.

He liked her smile.

***

When he returned, he sat down next to her again, and then took off his coat, which necessitated bumping her arm and leaning his knee against her thigh as he maneuvered in the small space.

Despite her obvious sadness, there was a light from within her body, and as his body lightly touched hers, here and there, he imagined sparks flying out from her skin. He knew he was inventing this. It made him admit that he was lonelier than he thought.

Before the music started again, he offered his name.

"Padmaj?" she repeated, unsure of her pronunciation.

"Yes, correct," he smiled.

"I'm Brigid," she said.
Irish, he thought to himself. Definitely Irish.

TWELVE

Brigid had noticed him from the moment he walked through the door, adorable but slightly skittish, as if he were a rabbit and this were his hole.

"And I am the fox," she thought to herself, bitterly, still stinging from the encounter with her mother. Still angry at herself for even coming to Ireland, still unsure of how long she would stay, not to mention whether she would consent to meet with the psychiatrist on Tuesday.

And then suddenly he was in front of her, asking to sit down. His eyes were so dark, and he looked so young, he reminded her of a baby boy she'd delivered in the Taos Pueblo. His last name had been Riley, and the mother had given him the first name of O'Connell after her, Brigid. This could be the dark O'Connell Riley himself, reincarnated in Ireland, and the thought made her smile and welcome him closer than she would have done only moments before.

She liked his smell. Cumin. Cinnamon. Dark scents, sweet scents. Brigid was very keen on smell. She could smell high blood pressure from a pregnant woman's sweat, a diet deficiency from a baby's pee.

She smelled loneliness in this man.

The music was ending and he was looking into her eyes again, offering to get her another beer, and she was agreeing.

What is it about Ireland, she thought, watching his slim rear as he walked toward the bar, that makes me want to drink and fuck? Good thing I left or I'd be some kind of Dublin whore, she chastised herself. It was something her mother would have said about her.

Her mother. The thought of her upstairs, just above them, drinking, and alone, made Brigid want to flee.

But he was back, and she couldn't leave, not when he was taking off his coat and bumping into her, gently, seductively, revealing broad shoulders covered by a dark green sweater that almost shone in the dark.

"I'm Padmaj," he said, and extended his hand.

She took it. The skin was surprisingly soft. Warm.

"Padmaj?" she repeated, as a way of holding on to him a moment longer. "I'm Brigid," she said, and he nodded, as if he already knew.

***

The musicians had gone home, and there were only a few people left in the place: the bartender, a whore with a tourist at the bar, a married man who'd fallen asleep near the door, and Padmaj and Brigid still side by side against the wall.

"Last call," the bartender said.

"Can I walk you home?" Padmaj asked.

She didn't know what to say. Where would she go?

He interpreted her hesitation as a way of declining.

"I am sorry. I was only…" he stammered. "It's late. I am only wanting to make sure you are safe." He slurred a little from the beer and from fatigue. The "r"s were rough. Sorrhy. Surrhe you arrhe safe.

She took his hand. She was drunk, too.

"No, it's not that," she said firmly. "I'm not saying no. It's that…" she paused. "It's simply that I haven't any place to go."

He had no idea how this could be true, and he might have, at another time, taken this as a warning. Was she homeless? A prostitute? In some kind of trouble? For some reason, though, when she said it, his heart opened to her.

"Come with me, then," he said, his hand still in hers.

"Really?"

"Yes. I have a little house outside the city," he began, and then saw the worry cross her hazel eyes. "Or we could stay here, in my restaurant, if you prefer."

What did she prefer, she wondered. She was suddenly so very tired. She'd come so far. She couldn't make another decision.

He saw all this. He knew this was the face, when he saw it on his customers, that meant, "Serve me. Take care of me. I don't know what I need."

"Leave it to me," he said, suddenly bold. "Wait here. I will gather my car. I will return." And then he was gone.

***

Brigid waited. Soon she was the only one left. She stood up, put on her coat, and paid for their drinks. Just when she thought she would go up to her mother's place, he burst back through the door.

"Pardon me," he blurted. "The damn defroster wasn't working, and I tried to drive, but I couldn't see, and I had to stick my head out the window all the way here!" His hair was blown back and his ears were red, his eyes wet from the wind. They laughed together. She wanted to kiss him.

"Come," he said, and took her mittened hand, and led her outside.

"It's so cold!" she exclaimed. "I'm not used to it!" She was almost shrieking.

He wondered what she could mean. It wasn't really that cold, for Dublin, only incredibly damp, and that was normal.

He opened the passenger door for her and placed her inside.

"I am sorry, the defroster is not working, I am sorry," he was repeating out the right window, as if to the few passersby, as they drove through the almost deserted city streets.

"It's okay," she chattered and laughed.

By the time they reached the highway, the windshield was clear and he could shut the window.

The car was suddenly quiet and warm.

They did not speak again until they reached his house, a tiny bungalow, all by itself, on a small hill.

The perfect setting for a made-for-TV murder mystery, Brigid thought, as they walked to the front door.

Inside, the bare white walls and wooden floors of the living room reflected the overhead light, which was too bright after the pub and the night. Padmaj thought again and turned it off, and groped in the sudden dark for a match. He lit a candle, took Brigid's hand, and led her to the bedroom.

Brigid breathed in, hard, at the doorway, as the flame illuminated an altar within. Brilliantly colored statues waved at them with many arms from a long, high table, and above the table, a huge painting of trees, unlike she had ever seen. They seemed to be gigantic roots, growing from the air toward ground. "Wow," she whispered, and he kissed her.

They both tasted of beer, but he also tasted of the cumin and cinnamon she'd smelled earlier, as well as something hot, a kind of pepper. His kiss was insistent but soft. She wanted to draw him in, closer, closer, but he stayed a bit away, holding her carefully, a bit shy, and it made her want him more.

She tasted of beer and of vegetables and she smelled of airplanes and cigarettes and something else—was it sage? He wanted to know, he wanted to know all her smells, but slowly. He did not want to take advantage of her.

"You've come from a long way," he said, quietly, as he led her to the bed, covered her with a dark saffron blanket, and knelt beside her.

"Yes," she sighed, feeling herself at rest. The candles threw shadows on the trees, the elephant, the tiger, the many-armed woman above, watching them.

"But you are home now," he said.

"Yes."

THIRTEEN

Claire hated hospitals. Even when her mother had been sick, and then dying, she couldn't bring herself to go visit. They were in the middle of the move from Paris to Dublin, she had told herself. But the truth was she hadn't wanted to see her mother in a thin cotton gown, surrounded by uniform white walls, the drafts of other people's food coming down the hallway, the beds that faced televisions bolted high into the wall.

This was the office wing of the hospital, but it was a hospital nonetheless. She could smell the disinfectant, sense the masks on the faces of the receptionists, nurses, doctors, staff—what they needed to wear to face the daily sickness. The daily death. No wonder they'd named the northern Dublin hospital "Mater Misericordiae." Claire had never done that well in Latin class, but she guessed it meant "Mother of All Miseries."

They had brought Miriam to see the doctor the day before. Claire remembered the way her daughter's olive skin paled beneath the doctor's hand as he checked her pulse and then shook his head.

The doctor had told them she must be admitted. It was sudden, he'd said, but it was necessary.

Miriam had retreated under her veil of hair and said nothing, not even when Claire and Michael both hugged her bony frame and said goodbye.

***

Michael was already there, early for once, in the waiting room. He looked tired, but Claire knew it was not his normal fatigue from late night conference calls at work. He was worried about Miriam, and he was not sleeping. She could tell from the empty yogurt containers left on the kitchen counter in the morning, from the newspapers strewn around his chair in the living room.

She kissed him, quickly.

Their daughter was sick, very sick. Claire knew that. That's why they were here. Still, a part of her was writing a poem, scrubbing a pot, doing a yoga pose, far away in her mind, as she sat down next to Michael in the waiting room.

They did this, retreated into themselves, sometimes, over the course of their marriage. It used to worry her. Now she knew it was part of a cycle, part of being attached to a person through good times and bad. It was a kind of comfort, to know you could go away and come back, later.

The nurse was calling them now, and they were walking back toward an empty office, being told to wait.

The office was not the doctor's, it was a generic room with no desk, just several chairs arranged around a circular table. She'd been in a room like this once when, after her mother's death, she'd gone by herself to Charleston, and sat in a chair like this and signed the papers to have her father permanently admitted to a nursing home. He lived there still. In the Alzheimer's wing. Where he talked to his wife, complimenting her on the dinner, and asked his daughter, at eight, to recite a poem during dessert.

Now another doctor was going to ask her to sign another paper to admit that her daughter was sick. All that will be left after our culture is gone, Claire thought, will be our signatures from our most painful days.

"Mr. and Mrs. Levin," the doctor said, as people did who didn't know them, who didn't know that she went by her maiden name, Curtain, but Claire stood anyway, took the doctor's hand as he entered, smiled. "I'm Dr. O'Brien. Thank you for coming."

As if they wouldn't come. But then again, she never did have this conversation with her mother's doctor.

They were seated in the green chairs, and Dr. O'Brien was looking through some papers. Why did they always do that? You would think they could do that before they came in. Was that something they learned in medical school?

"I have to be honest with you," the doctor said, in a heavy brogue, which was not unpleasant. "Miriam is not well. She is very ill. She may be dying."

Claire did not hear this, not really. She was thinking of the mantra she'd chanted that morning at yoga class, "God and me, me and God are one." Was that really true? Was it true now, for Miriam? Had it been true for Michael's grandparents when they'd fled Germany? Could it be true for Michael, who hadn't gone to temple for years, and for Claire herself, an agnostic Protestant who'd spent more time in boutiques than churches?

"Mrs. Levin?" the doctor was asking. "Are you listening?"

"No," she said. "I'm not Mrs. Levin."

The doctor's face reddened. "Pardon me?"

"I'm Mrs. Curtain. I kept my maiden name. My name is Claire Curtain."

"I'm sorry," he said, flipping through the papers again. "There should have been something about that in here. I will make sure..."

"I'm sorry," she said. "It doesn't matter. Please, go ahead."

"I was saying that it's very lucky that you brought Miriam in when you did. And you shouldn't feel bad about taking so long to notice her condition. The parents are often the last ones to notice, usually. So you shouldn't let yourself fret…"

"Will she get better?" Michael interrupted.

"That's up to her. She's on IV now, so she'll begin to put weight back on, whether she wants to or not. You mustn't take it as an improvement. The real test will come when we try to get her to eat solid foods again, which probably won't be for a month or so. We need to give her organs time to recuperate. They were, well," his face reddened again."Eating themselves in order to keep her alive."

"Why?" Michael said. His hair had more gray in it than Claire had seen last, and his face was pale.

"What we think is that anorexia is caused by a mourning of some sort. Sometimes the trigger is a boyfriend who leaves the girl. It could also be changed relations with the significant parent. Or a move. You moved here…." he started sorting through the papers again.

"Two years ago," offered Claire.

"Yes, well," the doctor began. "And before that?"

"My job makes it necessary for us to relocate fairly often," said Michael.

"Well, that could be a precipitate."

They stared at him.

"At puberty, often with girls, there is a deep desire for constancy. And what seems a small change for us as adults—a new school, a change of friends—could trigger a need for control. "

"And so she doesn't eat?" Michael said, angrily.

"Withholding food can give them a sense of control. At least it does, at the beginning. Then, as the disease progresses, it becomes more or less involuntary. That's the hardest part for them. What starts out as a way of being in control grows into a kind of ghost in the head that controls the girl."

"Ghost?" asked Claire.

"Yes, there is almost a kind of possession. Girls often hear voices." Michael put his head in his hands.

The doctor sensed they couldn't take in much more information, and he began to come to closure.

"You won't be able to see her for several weeks. The therapy is intense, and we need to work on establishing the girl as a separate self, separate from the ghost, from her parents, from the past." He pulled out a legal size sheet of paper. "This says that you'll agree not to have contact with her in order for us to move forward with her therapy. Do you think you can do that?"

Claire nodded, took the pen, found herself feeling slightly relieved. It was strange, how she'd been struggling with Miriam about eating for over a year now, and suddenly, she felt disconnected. As if it weren't really her responsibility after all.

Michael did not feel this, Claire knew. She knew that he'd been telling himself everything was fine, just fine, and that now he was eager to make up for his inattention.

"Exactly how long until we can see her?" Michael asked, after he had signed on the line below Claire's signature.

"We can't say, exactly. Give us time. Give her time."

They stared at him, and he stood to leave.

"Take good care of yourselves. I'll be in touch."

After the doctor left, teardrops fell down Michael's cheeks. Claire held his hand. They sat there, without speaking, for a long time. Finally a nurse rapped softly on the door and told them the room was needed. They got up to go.

"I love you," Claire said, unexpectedly, and tried to smile at him.

"I love you, too," he said.

They held hands the whole walk home.

FOURTEEN

Brigid had never seen a couple looking more stricken with grief nor more in love, she thought, as she stepped onto the elevator to leave the hospital.

They were holding hands, and it looked like the man had been crying. His ruddy face was red around the eyes, his black hair was rumpled and unwashed. And yet his hand was so tight around the woman's fingers that there were little white crescent moons at the tip of his fingernails.

The woman's wedding ring had a large diamond, and her skin was as pale as the jewel, almost translucent, like a white silk scarf Brigid had once stolen when she was a teenager.

What could it be? Were their parents dying? They looked like people without parents, people who'd learned to depend on themselves. But they also didn't look Irish, and if one of their parents were dying, it wouldn't be happening in a foreign land. It would be happening at home. But where did they call home?

The elevator bell rung as they reached the ground floor, and Brigid let them step out first, so she could continue to look at them. Is this what married love looks like, she wondered. She'd certainly never seen her parents holding hands in public like this.

The woman was strikingly beautiful, Brigid decided, as she passed closely by her on the way out. Smooth silkwhite skin, almost no wrinkles, deep blue eyes, thick chestnut hair that fell just to her shoulders and shone in the light. Even her plump hips were seductive, like an actress from the forties, like a woman who had gotten used to eating whatever she wanted.

Eating. Brigid had never eaten as much as she had in the last four days, with Padmaj. She'd stayed at his apartment that first night, and since the next day had been a Sunday and the restaurant hadn't opened for lunch, she'd stayed that day, too, and he convinced her to come to the restaurant for dinner and then come home with him again.

"One more night," she'd agreed. "But tomorrow morning I have to go get my clothes from my mother's. I smell like a goat."

He'd laughed. "You don't know what a goat smells like, do you?"

"No," she admitted.

"They're actually quite sweet," he'd teased, and he'd kissed her, in front of the few remaining customers who were buried in their books anyway.

The funny thing was they hadn't slept together. Yet. He'd kissed her, passionately, and often, but not more. And at night, he would give her a thick green robe of his, and tuck her into bed, and kiss her, and then leave with a blanket to go sleep on the wooden floor in the empty living room.

And then Monday morning came, and he woke early, before dawn, made them tea, and brought it in on a tray to the bedroom.

"I'm sorry to wake you," he'd said. "But I go to the market with the cook on Monday mornings, and I did not want to leave without saying goodbye. He'll be here straight away to pick me up. You can use my car to retrieve your belongings from your mother's, and then you are welcome to stay here."

Brigid had shaken her head. "It's not that I don't want to, Padmaj," she'd said, and he'd looked so sad. "I just have some things I need to do in the next couple of days, and I think I need to be alone. I'm not used to all this attention," she'd said as she stared at the tea steaming in her cup. "I'm a solitary creature."

He'd said nothing at first. He understood. He was a solitary creature, too. Despite having been raised in a village of women who never shut doors, who shared the cooking and the childrearing, who didn't believe in being alone, he had spent half of his life alone, first at boarding school in Lucknow, then at college in Massachusetts, and then, for the last fifteen years, here, in Dublin.

Maybe it was this thought, then, that made him put his tea down on the floor beside the bed, and take Brigid's tea from her hands, and put her hands into his.

"Brigid," he said, looking into her freckled face, into her eyes that seemed to twinkle, green-brown, green-brown, into her orange-red lips that always seemed, even when laughing, to frown. "I, too, am a solitary creature. I, too, have traveled far in my lifetime. I, too, have ghosts that haunt me."

She'd looked down. She hadn't told him about her father, about why she was here, but he'd sensed it.

"But I feel…" he'd groped for the word. "Unalone. With you I am unalone." And he'd kissed her. She smelled of morning, and fear, and dreams.

"Me, too, Padmaj," she'd said. "I feel it, too." She'd pulled him onto her, and she hadn't let him go, except once, when the cook honked the horn to the van, and Padmaj, fortunately still partly dressed, had run to the front door for fear the cook would start looking for him, and called in Urdu, "I'm sick. You do the marketing today," and had come back, giggling, and slipped off his pants before crawling under the saffron blanket with her.

He was a tender lover. He'd touched her, everywhere, lightly, in no hurry, lingering over the left hip that stuck out as she arched toward him, over the small indentation at the bottom of her back that he pressed his palm into, over the freckle on her right earlobe, which he kissed, and then sucked, lightly, as he entered her for the first time.

She'd cried, lightly, after, and he did not ask why.

She'd cried, again, when she was finally alone, after she'd gotten her bag from her mother's flat and checked into an inn near Padmaj's restaurant. She'd sat on the bed, and felt the tender places in her body, her breasts, her ears, her thighs, which he'd loved so carefully, and she'd cried.

Maybe it had been a mistake, she thought, to want to be alone. The room was so quiet. The inn was practically empty. No one goes to Dublin in January.

But then, as the hours passed, and as she felt herself become herself again, felt that sense of strength and independence, fueled by need and anger, she knew she'd been right. She needed to be strong for what she had to face the next day.

***

And here it was, the next day, and the appointment with her father's doctor was over, and she was free.

The meeting had been brief, and the doctor simply said that the new medication her father was taking seemed to be working. He was no longer showing paranoia, nor hearing voices. The doctor believed that he was a different man.

"But of course," he'd said to her gently, "I'm not saying that you must see him. It's understandable if you do not."

She'd been surprised at his compassion. The doctor seemed truly to understand how difficult her life had been. Perhaps he even knew more about her childhood than she could bring herself to remember.

"All I'm asking is that if you are in contact with him, and you have any sense that he is not well, that he is planning something again, or that he has any knowledge of plans, that you contact both me and the authorities immediately."

She'd nodded.

"You must do this in order for him to be eligible for release. But you don't have to agree."

She'd stopped nodding. It had never occurred to her that she might one day have this kind of power over her father.

"If you do not agree, he will not be released. It's that simple."

She had paused, but she knew already what she would do. She had not known on the plane, and she certainly hadn't known in her mother's flat, nor in the pub that first night. But she knew now. She knew, when Padmaj made love to her the morning before, that in order to be the kind of woman who could love with her whole heart, she would have to let her father go free.

"Where do I sign?" she'd asked, and the meeting was over.

***

And now she was walking into the restaurant. It had been only a little more than twenty-four hours since she'd seen Padmaj, and when he wasn't in sight, she walked past the dozen or so customers, straight back into the kitchen, past the cook who was equally scandalized and celebratory, right into Padmaj's arms. He wrapped his arms around her, a pitcher of lassi still in one hand, as she kissed him, long, and then she said, "Can I come back, and stay?"

It was the first time in her life she'd ever said those words. Always before, she had been the one to walk away.

Now, as they kissed again, Brigid wanted, for the first time in her life, to be someone who could be counted on to come back. To come back, and to stay.

FIFTEEN

Claire knew. She was beginning to know. As a result of her daughter's illness, she was beginning to learn about hunger and history, immigration and imagination, pain and the process it took—over generations—to heal.

And while she read book after book after book, she also knew that it was more than a little ironic that her only child was having to be strapped into a hospital bed and was being force fed fluids, while Claire herself could not stop eating. She ate huge breakfasts—eggs, potatoes, toast, muffins, marmalade, pots of tea—and then, after her noon yoga class, would stop in at the Indian restaurant for a late lunch. She often lingered there, reading one of the books on the table, or writing in her journal, until it was time for the dinner customers to start coming in. She would walk home slowly, taking a different route each time. Sometimes she would pick up a take-away meal from a restaurant she hadn't tried. Michael would not be home for hours, and this, the newness of the tastes in her mouth, would be all she had to look forward to, in their apartment, alone. She would crawl into bed and watch the cold water running down the Liffey's banks, and eat, and eat, and try not to think of her daughter in a bright hospital room with cold fluids running through her arm.

It was on one of these days, when she was sitting in Indian Treets late in the afternoon, enjoying her tea masala and surveying the books on her table for something to read, when she saw her. Claire felt like she might have seen her before, but she couldn't quite place her. She looked like so many young Irish women with wavy blonde hair and light eyes and thin lines of bones, like a new bird yet without feathers.

She had come in from the unusually sunny day, and when she moved through the colored beads in the entranceway, she threw rainbows around the room. It made Claire slightly dizzy, the colors moving across the walls and floor and ceiling, and she felt the way she had the first time she drank wine, as a teenager. She remembered sitting in the dark of the party, in a house where the parents were not home, and watching the lava lamps and party globes and feeling slightly sick from the sweet wine and the heavy scents of couples making out on couches.

This woman had that, too—the scent of sex on her—which Claire could not exactly smell but could sense from the slightly rumpled hair, the slightly redder cheeks, the slightly looser walk.

Padmaj came out from the kitchen before she'd even taken a seat, and said, "What can I get for you today?" and the woman had slid into a booth and said something, in deep tones, and they'd laughed. Claire found herself feeling, inexplicably, jealous.

Soon he was gone again and the woman was looking around the room. Her eyes met Claire's, and Claire looked down, ashamed at having been caught staring. After a moment, she glanced up again, and the woman was still looking at her.

Claire quickly grabbed one of the books on her table, opened to a page in the middle, and began to read. It was an unusually slim book of poetry, with words printed in two columns. On the left, she read:
a lonely mind unused
to strangers

Yes, there she was. Claire herself. A lonely mind. Among strangers. It was uncanny, the way poetry could open her up like that, reveal her insides with a sharp knife.

And suddenly the woman was there, above her, before Claire had time to let the lines sink in. And she had spoken. And Claire had not heard her.

"Pardon me?" Claire said, with almost a French accent, so used was she to asking the Parisians to slow down, *répétez s'il vous plaît*.

It caught the woman off guard.

"Do you speak English?" she said.

"Yes, why?" Claire asked.

"I...," and the woman looked flustered.

Claire could think of nothing to say, either.

"Let me start again," the woman said, and she literally walked back to her seat, sat down, and stood up again, coming over, as if rehearsing a scene in a play, with a huge grin on her face, and this made Claire burst into laughter.

"That's a funny book to be reading in a restaurant, don't you think?" she said as she approached Claire's table.

Claire looked at the book's title for the first time.

Famine.

It's a book about the famine? she asked herself, and suddenly became very serious.

The woman sensed the change in her.

"I'm sorry. I didn't mean—" It looked like she was going to run away for a moment. She looked that scared.

Claire didn't want her to go.

"Please," Claire said. "Sit down."

And when the woman did not move, Claire reached out and took her hand, tugged at it, clinging as one might do with a child. "Please sit with me."

She did.

"Yes, it is a funny book," Claire agreed, trying to make peace. "Well, not funny, haha, but funny queer. Well, not queer as in gay, but strange." *Etrange*, she said to herself. *Etranger*.

"I think I've seen you before," the woman said. "When was it? Last Tuesday—at the hospital. In the elevator. With your husband. Was it you?"

Claire felt accused. *J'accuse*.

She didn't want to talk about that day.

"No, I don't think…"

And, as if to rescue them from any more of this torturous conversation, Padmaj arrived, with plates of food.

"So, you've met my Poet lady," he said to the woman, as he smiled at them both.

"Well, we haven't exactly met," said the woman. "I was just making a fool of myself in front of her, really." She looked so vulnerable suddenly, in his presence, it made Claire remember that initial impression she'd had—young, sexual, open.

"Well, let me do the honors," Padmaj said politely.

"Brigid," he said, nodding to her, "This is my Poet lady friend, Claire." He then looked at Claire, with tenderness, and said, "Poet lady, this is my…. This is my very good friend, Brigid."

The woman, Brigid, had looked down at her freckled hands when he'd hesitated, and it made Claire feel sympathy for her.

"Would you eat with me?" Claire offered, since Padmaj was still holding the tray of food.

Brigid looked relieved. "Only if you'll eat, too," she said, and smiled.

"I've already eaten," Claire said. "But I can always eat a little more." And she buried the book in the pile and helped Padmaj set the plates down.

SIXTEEN

Brigid had been in Dublin for three weeks now, and she was starting to feel worn out. Her father's release had been officially approved, but an exact date hadn't been set yet, and she didn't know if she wanted to wait anyway. She'd seen her mother a couple of times, but it was always the same, the same sour smell, the same dingy kitchen, the same housecoat. It depressed her.

She knew, she admitted to herself, that she'd accomplished her mission, as far as her mother was concerned, she'd signed the paper, and now her father was going to be released, and her mother didn't really need her anymore.

Brigid needed to be needed. This had been true all her life. First, she'd raised her sister while their parents were too busy fighting; then, after her father's disappearance, she'd taken care of her mother and sister while they were in Dublin. Or tried anyhow. She'd go searching, before bedtime, for her mother, in the neighborhood pubs, trying to get her to come home before it got too late, before she couldn't walk, before there would be a man too willing to help her home.

For a while, in college, Brigid had tried not to help anybody. This was when she herself had started drinking and sleeping with too many people and called it being "independent." The truth was that it made her head hurt and her stomach ache, in the morning, as she lay in bed, hung over, still smelling the stranger's body from the night before.

Then she'd decided to be a nurse. She might as well get paid for helping people if she was going to make a career out of it.

And when she became a nurse, it seemed that the drinking and the sex were suddenly unnecessary. She was satisfied with touching patients and bringing cold sips of water to sick mouths, and later, with birthing babies, at the end of each day, she was tired and wanted simply to fall asleep, alone.

Until now. Returning to Ireland had caused her old desires to flare up again. And old loneliness, too. Now when she thought of her solitary life in the desert, it seemed sad to her.

And yet. Padmaj didn't really need her. Not her help, anyway. He was a dependable, organized, grounded person. He marketed on Mondays. Did laundry on Wednesdays. Paid bills and wrote paychecks every Friday. Meditated every morning at dawn. And took long walks in the countryside on Sunday mornings, since that was the only day he could close the restaurant for lunch. The Irish liked to eat at home after church, have a good midday supper and watch soccer or rugby on television.

So why was she still here? Brigid was wondering that, and feeling like she should leave, but not really wanting to, when she walked into the restaurant late that afternoon.

Right away she noticed, because there were only a few people left in the place, that the woman she'd seen at the hospital was there, alone.

She looked happier, and somehow, heavier, than she had before. She looked like a scholar, maybe. A professor at one of the universities. They often used the restaurant as a place to read and work, away from their offices, away from the anxious graduate students and bored faculty who roamed the halls, looking for someone to help pass the time.

The woman was still, in spite of—or maybe because of—the extra weight, strikingly beautiful. Her cheeks were rounded and rosy. She almost glowed.

And then Padmaj was there, asking Brigid what she wanted to eat.

"You mean," Brigid said, in a low voice, "What would be my pleasure?"

He'd smiled, but she'd sensed that he was slightly uncomfortable. Ever since that day she'd kissed him in the kitchen, he'd made it clear to her that he wanted to focus at work, he didn't want her to hang around and flirt with him, or even help wait tables. He was proud of the success of the restaurant, proud of his independence, she knew, and they'd only known each other for less than three weeks, after all.

"You choose for me, Padmaj," she'd said, in a more serious tone, by way of apology, and then, after he'd receded into the kitchen, she turned to look at the woman again.

Yes, it was definitely the same woman, she decided. Why had she been so sad that day? Why was she alone today? Where was her husband? Was she lonely?

This last question, Brigid knew, was a projection. It was Brigid who was lonely. She'd gotten used to being around people—big, needy pregnant women and their children, and Mattie and her grandsons—while on the reservation, but here she was lonely, waiting all day and most of the night for Padmaj to return home from work when they would make love and talk and make love again. She didn't know how he did it, getting up before dawn each morning, bathing, and then lighting the candle on his altar, while she slept till lunch was almost over, or sometimes even until dinner.

Brigid decided to go introduce herself. On the way over to the woman's table, she noticed she was reading a book called *Famine*. She decided, on an impulse, to make a joke about it.

She often did this, made a bad joke, when she was nervous. It turned people away, usually. She'd even wondered if she would have scared Padmaj away if it hadn't been for the music being so loud the night they met.

And now it was happening again. The woman didn't think her joke was funny. Maybe she was a History professor, had staked her whole life's work on the study of the famine. "Pardon me?" the woman had said. Christ, what a way to start a friendship. Brigid was humiliated.

Because friendship, it dawned on her, was what she wanted from this woman. Nothing less. She wanted to know what was behind those deep blue eyes, that strange accent.

And then Brigid was asking her if she spoke English. The times she'd been asked that, when she'd traveled to Britain, came back to her. Bloody hell. This was off to a bad start.

Brigid decided to start over, in hopes of making the woman laugh. It worked.

Brigid took a chance and repeated the joke again. The laughter stopped. Jesus, I'm going back to America, she thought. There are too many unknowns in Ireland now. Where did all these foreigners come from? The streets were full of new faces, coming to a democracy, wanting to be part of a modern, industrialized nation. This was not the same Ireland. She didn't know it anymore.

And then the woman, the foreigner, the stranger she wanted to befriend, was touching her, holding her hand, insistently, and Brigid felt a kind of tingling go through her arm, as she had the first time Padmaj touched her, and so she said, "I think I've seen you before. When was it? Last Tuesday—at the hospital. In the elevator. With your husband. Was it you?"

And the woman's face turned dark again, clouds entered her blue eyes. Brigid remembered the tears in the husband's eyes, how they'd held hands, and was grateful when Padmaj interrupted them.

"So, you've met my Poet lady," he said to Brigid, and then smiled at Claire. Brigid noticed that he saw it, too. Claire's beauty.

"Well, we haven't exactly met," Brigid said, to draw his attention back to herself. "I was just making a fool of myself in front of her, really." She wondered if it were obvious to him, her coarseness, in front of this woman.

"Well, let me do the honors," he said.

"Brigid," he said, nodding to her, "This is my Poet lady friend, Claire."

Claire. Her name was Claire. Like the county. Like her home.

"Poet lady," he said to Claire. "This is my…. This is my very good friend, Brigid."

What am I doing here, thought Brigid again, and again, the urge to leave swelled in her. The dry arid heat. The intensity of a pregnant woman's needs. These had become her home.

She didn't need this: a man who opened her body and made her feel spikes of jealousy when he looked at another woman.

She didn't need this: a woman whose name reminded her of her childhood, whose blue eyes made her want to look, to keep looking.

"Would you eat with me, here, at my table?" Claire was saying, but Brigid wasn't hungry, the old flight reflex was snapping somewhere deep inside her.

Padmaj, still holding the tray of food, turned his dark pool eyes to her.

The rubber band inside her body loosened.

Brigid didn't want the food, not really, but she wanted them, the two of them. She didn't want to leave, again, alone. "Only if you'll eat, too," she said to Claire, and smiled.

"I've already eaten," said Claire, and for a second Brigid feared she would disappear. "But I can always eat a little more."

Padmaj winked at Brigid as he set the plates down. Did he know how close she'd been to leaving, she wondered. Did she know what had just been decided, within her, just then?

She would tell him tonight. And since tomorrow was Sunday, they would have almost all day tomorrow to celebrate before looking for a job on Monday morning.

Ourselves. Together. No longer alone.

SEVENTEEN

"I met the most interesting woman today," Claire told Michael as he walked through the door that night. It had been a long time since she'd made a new friend—since college, actually; her marriage had meant moving, and moving had meant keeping things contained enough so that they could easily be packed away again at a moment's notice.

Michael was tired, more so because he'd had to work all day on a Saturday, but he could see she was excited, so he feigned interest.

"She's Irish," Claire began, pressing play on the CD remote with one hand, handing him a Dutch beer with the other, and curling her legs under her on the couch. A fire was roaring, and this was the only light in the room except for the stereo lights flashing up and down with the Chieftains' first track. Claire looked beautiful, particularly so in this light and with this music, and Michael told her so by leaning his back against her and stroking her thigh with one hand as he sipped the beer with the other.

"But she's lived in America so long that she feels like home, you know? And she's funny. Quirky. Not afraid to make a fool of herself."

"Hmmm." He wasn't really focusing on what she was saying but on the curve of her thigh as it reached her knee. All this yoga was making her so supple.

"And she's Padmaj's new girlfriend!"

"Really?" He couldn't quite picture the almost effeminate man with a woman.

"Yes. They've only known each other for three weeks, but they're obviously crazy about each other."

"Speaking of that…" he laid the beer on the floor beside the couch and rolled over.

"Come on," she smiled.

It had been nice, having the place to themselves for the past eighteen days. She'd forgotten how it could be. They felt like newlyweds again, undressing in the living room, or making love there. It was as if they'd reclaimed their home from parenthood. And yet, still, the pleasure was rimmed with guilt.

They missed their child so much they didn't even speak of her.

Van Morrison started crooning against the Chieftains' soft harp and flute, and Michael hummed along, "Ease my troubles, that's what you do." Then he pulled up her pajama top and kissed her lightly, all over her belly, which was soft and round. His lips tickled her skin.

Claire sighed, and finally gave in, stopped talking altogether, and decided she would tell him the story later.

"What is this woman's name anyway?" he asked, between kisses, to show that he had been listening.

"Brigid," she said, grinning, as the music's pace quickened and his hips moved up to meet hers.

***

Brigid continued to linger on Claire's mind later, as well, after Michael had fallen asleep on the couch and Claire went to rinse the beer bottles in the kitchen and the Chieftains started to sing about some maid from Malabar.

History, Claire thought. That's what Brigid and Padmaj share. Maybe that's what had made Claire stare at them in the restaurant that day, the way they seemed to share something, something not completely in the present, that Claire could not fully understand.

History. She'd never thought about it before. It had been too concrete to her, as a literature major in college. Too many facts and not enough metaphor.

But now, in Ireland, with her only daughter starving and ranting about history, Claire was having to come to face it. Facts and all.

She had no idea what this meant, really. She knew, of course, that Ireland had been a British colony, just as India had. But these were vague answers on a multiple choice test to her. They carried no feeling for her. No poetry.

After that day's lunch with Brigid, she'd gone to a used bookstore and looked for books about Irish history. Mostly she found huge picture books with glossy green photos and captions that romanticized the past. Or more precisely, romanticised it.

In the end, she'd left the green books on their shelves and bought this Chieftains' CD, at the advice of the shopkeeper, who told her all she needed to know about Irish history could be found in its music.

She'd nodded, agreeing with him as she pulled out her American Express card.

Music carried history just as poetry did, Claire mused, as she began to run a bath. It came from the sounds. Sounds, spellings and accents. These are what hold history.

What was that line Padmaj had said to her when they first met? "The sound the wounded make."

The difference between British and American English, she thought as she added bubbles and saw the words "romanticise" and "romanticize" in bubbles in her head, can be summed up by the difference between an 's' and a 'z.' The British hiss like the snake in the garden, and Americans sleep through it all.

Claire had, certainly, for most of her life. Slept through it all. As Michael was doing now. What would it take, she wondered, for Americans to wake up?

When the tub was full, she turned off the tap and went to get her journal. Sinking into the bubbly water, she lifted her ivory arms up to keep the book dry, and then carefully leaned it against the side of the tub, and began to write.

What came out was a poem about waking.

***

The phone rang early the next morning. It was a Sunday. No one ever called them on a Sunday, especially in Ireland, where Sundays were still reserved for church and family and rugby.

Michael answered the phone.

"Yes," he said, sitting up, surprised.

"What is it?" she whispered.

He held his hand up.

"Really? So suddenly? Today?"

"What? What?"

"Okay. We'll be right in." He hung up.

"What?" she said again.

"It's Miriam."

Claire said nothing. She was afraid of hearing something terrible. She tried to read his face. She kept very still.

"Dr. O'Brien says she's ready to see us," Michael said.

"Today?" Claire smiled.

"Yes."

"Let's go!"

***

On the way to the hospital, she told Michael more about Brigid, about what Brigid had told her about the famine. How the British had, somewhat, planned it, or at least, hadn't worked very hard to stop it once it began, because they wanted the population to be reduced.

When she said the word "reduced," he winced.

The British had wanted to move Ireland from a small agricultural economy to large scale cattle farming. And when the potato blight started, and people started dying, and when people could be induced to start leaving, it was possible to do so. To consolidate the tiny tenant plots into large cattle fields.

She did not say that this must have been what Miriam had been referring to, that night in the Indian restaurant. She didn't have to.

"You know those stone walls we see when we go for drives in the country?" she asked. "Those are from the pre-famine era. A whole family, generations, would have lived within one of those small areas, with maybe one cow or one pig, and some chickens, and rows of potatoes."

Michael did not like thinking about poverty. About how bad things used to be. His own family history had taught him that these stories often covered over other stories of even greater pain. It was wiser to focus on the present. On what could be done to make things better, here and now.

"And Brigid told me something else, too," Claire said. "Something else I never knew. Did you know that even before the famine, the British would give land to people for converting to Protestantism? What was that word she used for it? Oh, I can't remember. I've always been so bad at history."

He kept walking, afraid of what else Claire might tell him that would make him feel more of what he was feeling, a kind of nausea, a kind of shame, as if he'd been caught at something he couldn't quite name.

"Anyway, she said that with my dark hair and blue eyes, chances are that my ancestors were Norman. From France. This would mean they would have been Catholic, would have intermarried with the Irish, and later probably converted to Protestantism in order to get land. Isn't that interesting? I mean, that we've lived, perhaps, in all the places where my ancestors lived. Ireland, France, England, even Morocco, who knows?"

He couldn't quite match the joy she was showing.

The hospital was now in view. Claire got quiet, too. Maybe Miriam was right. Maybe he just couldn't understand.

***

"Mommy? Daddy?" Miriam called to them from her bed, cautiously, as they stood in the doorway of her hospital room.

Her long black hair had been brushed carefully, parted down the middle, and was gleaming. She had a bit of mascara and blush on, too, in preparation for her parents' visit.

Claire suddenly had a vision of Miriam as a little girl, after she and Michael had gone on a vacation by themselves, and left her with a nanny. Claire remembered how Miriam, even then, would tuck away her sadness and her anger. Instead she would dress up, trying to look nice when she met them at the airport. Claire's eyes filled with tears at the memory.

It had only been nineteen days since they'd seen her, but already she'd put on weight, as Dr. O'Brien had said she would, and despite her sadness, it filled Claire with hope.

"Honey," Claire said as she ran to her. "You look wonderful!" They hugged, but Claire was careful not to touch the IV drip, still attached to Miriam's arm.

Miriam noticed her mother's slight hesitancy and felt herself look away, toward her father. Miriam believed he had always been able to give more deeply than her mother.

Michael came in slowly, tears in his eyes, too, and then hugged her.

"Daddy," the girl began to sob. "I'm so sorry for all those things I said."

"It's okay, pumpkin pie," he murmured, and stroked her hair, so thick and straight like her mother's.

"I'm so glad you're both here," Miriam said. "I didn't know if they would let you come. But I've been very good. I've been participating in therapy sessions, and they think I'm making good progress."

"That's great," they said, although they were both holding back, remembering what the doctor had said, how very sick she was, how long this could take.

"They're going to take the IV out today. And I wanted you to be here. So we could celebrate."

Claire looked at Michael. Be strong for me, her eyes pleaded. She was seeing Miriam again as a toddler, trying to walk, but falling, and crying. She was seeing herself as a toddler, too, and her own mother, in frustration, picking her up and carrying her instead of letting her learn, on her own.

"Mommy, aren't you happy for me?" Miriam asked.

Claire sat down on the bed and took Miriam's hand, cold from the IV.

"Yes, I'm very proud of you, of all the hard work you've been doing," she said carefully. "But I'm also sad, sweetie. I…." Claire stopped.

She wanted to say, "I can't do this for you." Or, "I know that you need to do this on your own." Or, "I know how very far you have to go."

But she did not say any of this.

"You're my sweet girl," Claire said. "And I've missed you so. I'm sad because I've missed you." Claire held her daughter tight, felt her own cheeks wet with her daughter's tears, and felt, for the first time since Miriam had gotten sick, that maybe she was going to be well after all.

"I love you, baby," said Claire.

"I love you, too, Mommy," Miriam said.

EIGHTEEN

It was midnight when Padmaj rang that Saturday night to say he was almost ready to close the restaurant. Brigid drove his car into the city, tired from a long day of teaching yoga classes and doing massage. Further, she was unsure about what she was going to say to him. Should she tell him about her decision to stay? Perhaps it would scare him. He hadn't actually asked her to stay. Well, not in words.

He was waiting outside on the curb by the time she arrived, and she stopped the car and opened the door to move to the passenger side.

"Where are you going?" he asked, startled.

"I thought I'd let you drive," she explained.

"Why?"

This was one of the reasons—the many reasons—she loved him. Love? Yes, to herself, she was using that word. He had no preconceptions about what one or the other of them should do—in driving, in cooking, in making love. It was as if he hadn't been raised to be a man. Not in all the usual—and, Brigid admitted, awful—ways she'd come to expect.

She smiled at him as he opened the passenger door, and then she kissed him, and, after starting to drive, she blurted, "I want to stay with you." She was doing a lot of blurting today, she thought, remembering the embarrassing first impression she'd made with Claire.

"Yes, of course," he said.

"I mean," she started to say, and she got scared for a moment. Then she repeated, "I mean," paused, and said, "For good. I'd like to stay here for good."

"For good?" he asked.

Terror filled her. She could taste it, sour, in her mouth. She looked over at him and saw, in his puzzled face lit by the yellow streetlamps, that it was simply a matter of misunderstanding.

"For good," she explained. "It means forever. Or, well, for as far as I can see."

"I see," he said, looking down.

"But if you don't want me to…"

He took her left hand off the wheel, then decided it wasn't enough. He wanted to see her, to see her whole face.

"Please pull to the side of the road," he said.

She did.

Then he took both her hands in his and placed them on his cheeks. He put his hands on her cheeks. "Brigid," he said. "I have only known you for a little while, but, as far as I can see," he said, repeating her phrasing, "my soul feels that we have always known each other. You are my *brahma muhutra*."

Her eyes filled with tears, but she did not blink.

"It means sunrise. You are my sunrise. With you I feel always the day is only beginning."

"Padmaj," she said, as a tear fell down her cheek and onto his hand.

He kissed her, and her tears fell upon his cheeks.

***

Later, with the candle burning low upon the altar in the bedroom, he said to her, "Wait here," and jumped out of bed.

He came back with a bag of dried fruits, mixed with nuts and chocolates.

"This was my favorite sweet as a child. I ordered it through the distributor for you after I met you. It arrived today."

She sat up, grinning. "I feel like a kid again," she said. But it was a strange thing to say, and she knew it. She'd never felt safe like this as a child, nor this joyful.

He placed one of the large chocolate pieces in her mouth. She bit down, and the chocolate crushed to reveal a dried cherry.

"Mmm," she moaned and giggled.

"Tell me why you are here, Brigid," he said, sucking on an almond.

The request took her by surprise.

"I am not talking about here, with me. Tell me why you came back. Here. To your country."

She looked down at her hands as the cherry slid down her throat. "I don't know if I can."

"You can," he encouraged her. "The candy is magical. It will help you be strong."

She looked at him and saw him as a boy of eight who believed this to be true. And she supposed she was ready, somewhere deep inside. She picked a dried mango out of the bag, and took a small bite, and began.

"I grew up in County Clare. It is in the far west of Ireland."

He nodded.

"The reason I am here is that my mother called me one morning." She stopped. "At sunrise," she smiled, then continued. "She told me my father was to be let free from prison as part of the peace negotiations. She said he wanted to see me. So I thought…."

"You would come to make peace," he offered, chewing on a drop of creamy white chocolate.

"Yes, I suppose so."

She chose another chocolate-covered cherry.

"But my mother had lied, as she always does. She tricked me into coming here so I could sign the papers to release him. They wouldn't release him unless I agreed—all the people in his life had to agree—to inform on him if he was planning any…."

She stopped again.

"Yes?"

"Activities. Terrorist activities. He's a suspected terrorist."

"Suspected?"

"There were no trials. People were thrown in jail on suspicion."

He shook his head, dismayed at her pain, what she must carry as his daughter, and also at the failure of the court system. As a new Irish citizen, he wanted to believe in the integrity of the nation's institutions.

"So you don't know. You don't really know if…" he suggested.

"I know," she said.

He tried to look into her eyes, but she was looking away, at the weapons in Durga's many hands on the altar.

"Who is that?" she asked, to take a rest from the telling.

"Durga," he said, letting her. "She holds different weapons in her hands to protect herself. She is a strong woman, like you." He put a chocolate-covered cashew nut in her hand. "Here is your weapon," he joked.

She laughed, sadly. "You are my weapon, Padmaj."

"No," he said, suddenly forceful. "That is not true. You are a strong woman, Brigid, and this is your story you are telling. One day I will tell you mine, and then you will listen as I am listening now. We will help each other in this, but they will still be our own stories. Our childhoods. What we survived. Ourselves. Alone."

She bit down and the peanut was salty.

"I was not alone," she said, in a small voice. "My sister was with me. When I was little, six or seven, and my sister Terri was smaller, four or five, our father began to come into our room after he and my mum had been fighting, and he would…."

She stopped.

"Go on," he said, holding her.

"I can't," she cried.

"I am here."

She cried for a while, pressing her face into his chest. Then she continued.

"He would talk. Crazy talk. Stuff you don't tell a kid, but also, he was insane. Literally. But the diagnosis came later, once he was in prison, after he'd been analyzed. But my sister...."

"Yes?"

She reached for the bag and popped a white chocolate and a dried orange into her mouth at the same time. Could it be true, what he'd said about this candy? She felt it working, she felt it opening her throat, making her say things she'd never said. Not like this. Not all at once. Not to the same person.

"My sister didn't live long enough to learn the diagnosis. She committed suicide. At nineteen."

"Oh, Brigid."

"I was twenty-one. I'd just finished college, was going on for a graduate degree in nursing. My mother called me, in my apartment."

He stroked her hand, lightly.

"Can you believe it? My mother was actually worried *she*'d be arrested! Suicide was a crime in Ireland until 1993, and with my father in jail, my mother was worried the authorities would arrest her for my sister's suicide!"

He shook his head, remembering the way laws had reached into his mother's past, too, in India.

"I couldn't take it. I didn't even go to her funeral. I've never gone to a funeral."

Her tears were falling fast now, as they sat, silently. The candle sputtered and went out, and then they were in the dark.

He moved closer to her, put an arm around her, and she settled in, leaned back against his chest.

Her hand groped in the dark for more candy. She was trying to avoid the nuts. All she wanted were the sweet pieces.

"He would get into bed with us, tell us stories, make us laugh. That was the funny thing, he was actually quite funny and nice. He knew all about literature and mythology." She looked again toward Durga in the dark. "But he also touched us. Under the covers. He would get quiet. His awful tongue would dart between his teeth. He would bite down on his tongue."

For a moment she felt like she couldn't breathe. Padmaj stroked her hair back from her forehead.

"It was after this, one night, was when he told us. He said he'd met some blokes, and that they were planning something big. Something 'revolutionary,' he said. He meant it as an explanation, I guess, of why he would be leaving. Because the next morning, he was gone."

She felt around and found another chocolate cherry, and took tiny bites, afraid it was the last one in the bag.

"That's how I know he was guilty," she said, her voice once again solid.

Padmaj slid further down so that he could wrap his arms around her whole body, and they fell asleep like that, the bag of candy still next to her, and a melted piece of chocolate still in her hand.

***

The phone rang, at dawn. There was chocolate on the sheets, and in the early morning light it frightened her, but he quickly pointed to the bag of candy, reminding her, then went down the hall to the kitchen to answer the phone.

She felt slightly hungover, even though she hadn't had anything to drink, and annoyed, as she always was, from being awakened before she was ready.

"Brigid!" he called.

This bloody better not be my mother, she thought.

It was chilly in the kitchen. He handed her the phone, and then rushed to the closet to get her the green robe.

He was putting it around her as she heard her father's voice. She hadn't heard his voice for fifteen years, but there it was, like a nightmare suddenly remembered in the middle of the day, crystal clear.

"Out, out, damn spot," he said.

"Da?"

"They're letting me out, my lady," he said. He was quoting Macbeth, she knew, and he was trying to be funny because he was nervous, she knew this, too. But the phrase, "My lady," struck her. Hadn't this been something Padmaj said, too? She shivered. She wanted to hang up the phone.

Instead she asked, "When?" and waited.

"Tomorrow and tomorrow and tomorrow," he said.

"What time?" she asked.

"Early. Sunrise. Like Our Lord, resurrected," her father said.

I can't do this, she thought. I can't see him. I can't stay here.

"Will you be there for me, Sunrise?" her father asked.

She felt like she was going to be sick.

She looked at Padmaj, sitting at the kitchen table across from her. His face was calm and still.

"I'll try, Da," she said. "I will try."

NINETEEN

Padmaj woke earlier than usual on Monday morning, to meditate. He knew that Brigid would be up early, too, to meet her father at dawn, and he knew that she might need him to be with her as she got ready to go. He also knew that she needed to go alone.

There are some things, Padmaj had learned, that are best done alone, no matter how painful.

As he lit the candle on the altar in the twinkling darkness, his hair still wet from the bath, his eyes rested on Ganesh, the elephant god who could banish all obstacles.

Open all doors.

Padmaj sat down on his mat, in the lotus position, and closed his eyes gently, and let his mind focus on an inner image of a door.

He had seen many open doors during his lifetime.

The open door of the region's ancient mosque that allowed his mother to attend the funeral of the last living Muslim woman in their village.

The open door of his mother's heart that allowed his father back in after an absence of seventeen years.

The open door of his mother's womb that allowed his father's seed to take root there.

The open door of the hut where he lived with his mother, which his father walked back and forth through, again and again, during the first three years of Padmaj's life.

The open door his father left behind, for the final time, leaving Padmaj and his mother to cling to each other, in sorrow.

The open door the white man walked through, when Padmaj was eight, leaving him with a memory he was still trying to forget.

The open door his mother pushed him through when he was twelve, sending him to Lucknow for school, where he learned French and proper English and excelled especially in the memorization of the poetry of the Celtic Twilight.

The open door of the airplane that took him to America, at eighteen, for college in a city called Boston where, he'd learned in school, the War of American Independence had begun.

The open door of the white envelope that his mother handed to him at twenty-three, which enabled his move to Ireland and the down-payment on the restaurant, which he now owned outright. Himself. Independent.

The open door of the restaurant, over which he hung colored beads, reminding him of the colors of the world he had seen with his own eyes—the red of the shuhag he never saw his mother wear on her forehead and of the blood that he did; the orange of the sun that he had seen set in the west of three continents; the yellow of ghee and of McDonald's french fries which he had secretly come to love; the green of the trees on his mountain home and of Ireland's grassy hills, the blues of the Indian ocean and of Claire's eyes.

He stopped, opened his eyes, looked at Ganesh again, the ugly, large-nosed elephant man who reportedly made a wonderful lover.

Why were Claire's eyes entering his mind?

What did they have to do with doors, with open doors?

He closed his eyes again, tried to concentrate.

He saw Claire there, again, with the blue of her eyes through the words of the poem he had memorized as a student in Lucknow, when he was just beginning to learn about love, in his own body:

> Had I the heavens' embroidered cloths,
> Enwrought with golden and silver light,
> The blue and the dim and the dark cloths
> Of night and light and the half-light,
> I would spread the cloths under your feet:
> But I, being poor, have only my dreams;
> I have spread my dreams under your feet;
> Tread softly because you tread on my dreams.

He heard Brigid stirring in bed and opened his eyes again, and then shut them quickly out of a sense of guilt at having allowed Claire to enter his thoughts like this, during his meditation, on this day so obviously full of anxiety for Brigid that he could see it on her face already, through the dim blue light before dawn.

He skipped purple and went straight to white to complete his meditation, remembering the white on white embroidery his great-grandmother did, which she continued to do even up until the day of her death, the stitching so delicate that it might have been done by the tiny translucent spiders that lived in the crevices of the bark of the oldest trees in the forest.

He then sent a blessing to those spiders and those trees, and to his great-grandmother, his father's mother, and another to his mother's mother, also in the spiritworld, and to his own mother, and to all his aunts, and to all the mothers he knew, including Claire, and Brigid's mother, whom he had never met but who, he knew, could probably use some extra blessing on this day.

And he finished by giving light to Brigid, who was not a mother, and so lacked the wisdom of one. He prayed that the water surrounding her now in the shower would stay with her all day and into the night, as protection, as comfort, as something clear and pure and clean and white and full of wisdom.

TWENTY

Claire woke in her white bed, late on Monday morning, long after Michael had left for work. It was an overcast but windless day, she noticed as she moved from the bed to the window, which she always looked out, first thing upon waking, down at the river below. The ribbon of water looked still and glasslike under the low gray sky. Seagulls bobbed upon the water, their feet struggling underneath against the current. She sighed.

Seeing Miriam again yesterday had been difficult for Claire, in the way that holidays and reunions and turning points had always been hard for her, burdened as they are with multiple feelings of excitement and sadness and pride.

But Miriam was getting better. Dr. O'Brien had confirmed that. And there was love—yes, it was love—that she saw in both Dr. O'Brien's face and the nurses' faces for her daughter. It made her feel, oddly, like a better mother than she'd lately thought herself to be.

She'd always been like this, though. She'd always encouraged Miriam's sense of independence, sense of self. Claire remembered when Miriam was two and had started attending a French *crèche* in London—they'd known they would be moving to Paris, and they wanted her to be bilingual—and Miriam started saying phrases that Claire had not taught her—"My head itches" and *"C'est bête, ça!"* — and Claire had felt so proud. She felt she was succeeding as a mother by allowing Miriam to become a *person*.

She felt this now, too. Even though her daughter was very sick, and even though she was still in the hospital, and even though they didn't know when she would come home, Claire felt that she was a good mother.

Her own mother had not been able to do this. Claire knew, from years of therapy, that it was necessary for her to be an ocean away from her mother to feel separate from her. Yet now, with her mother dead, she was slowly allowing her back in. Listening to her again, like she did that night at the Schubert concerto, telling her that Miriam needed help.

What would her mother say now, she wondered, if she saw her, wrapped in a purple silk robe, staring absent-mindedly out the window in the middle of the day? *Get busy*, her mother would say. Make a pie. Go shopping—there's no decent food in the house. Plan a dinner party.

As Claire started to make the bed, this last suggestion struck her as an exceptionally good one. She could have a dinner party, she thought, and this would be a way of getting to know Brigid better, and Padmaj, too, and letting them get to know Michael.

It had been years—years!—since she'd had a dinner party with people whom she actually liked. They'd entertained, of course—a cocktail party when they first arrived in Dublin, dinners for international guests of the bank in Paris—but it hadn't been since London that she'd actually cooked a real meal for real friends.

She headed to the kitchen to look for the phone number of the Indian Treets restaurant, found it, and dialed before she changed her mind.

"Indian Treets," said Padmaj, in a slightly harried voice.

It was 12:30 now, she noticed, looking at the clock on the microwave glowing green, just thirty minutes away from the rush of lunch hour in Dublin.

"I'm sorry to bother you, Padmaj. It's Claire. Should I call back at another time?"

"Good day, my Poet lady! Do you need take away today?"

"No, Padmaj," she hesitated, hoping she was pronouncing his name correctly, wondering if she was making a mistake, thinking he was a friend. Then she thought of another way of approaching it. "I would like to get in touch with Brigid. Do you have her number?"

"Yes, certainly. But she is not at home at the moment."

Home? Were they living together? Already?

"But allow me to give it to you nevertheless. You could try to call her this afternoon. She would like that, Claire."

There was something in his voice as he said this that made Claire certain that she had not been mistaken—he did consider her a friend.

"Okay, Padmaj, I will."

***

Claire decided that her mother must indeed be communicating with her from beyond because as she got dressed she wanted, suddenly, to make a Kentucky bourbon pie, like her mother used to make.

She went to the kitchen again and searched the bookshelf for that red Betty Crocker cookbook. A piece of paper would be wedged between pages 96 and 97 in the pie section—between the pecan and pumpkin pie recipes.

As the leaves of the old book crackled, Claire heard her mother's voice. "Maybe if you'd done this before, your daughter wouldn't be sick right now."

Claire winced, wondering if it were true.

"No, it's not true. I'm an old bat and you're a good mother."

And then her mother laughed.

It had been a long time since Claire had heard her laugh.

Claire felt chills run down her arms. Chillbumps, her mother used to call them. A teenager from rural South Carolina, her mother had met Claire's father on a trip to visit cousins in Charleston, and married him soon after.

In the humid streets of Charleston the rest of her life, she longed for the smell of long grass being mowed on a late summer afternoon, the clicking sounds of her grandmother's knitting needles, and the taste of a warm pie on a cold afternoon.

The last, Claire decided, was something she could make happen— even here, in Ireland. This was, after all, where her mother's grandmother had come from in the late nineteenth century. As a girl of nineteen, she could see no way to make a living in the county of Galway, so she set off after her parents held an American wake for her. With knitting needles and wool she had spun herself and a yearning to find a place with the green sea like the one she held forever in her heart.

Claire remembered all this from a time before her mother starting criticizing, from when Claire was too small to reach her mother's waist and would hug her mother's legs as she cooked in the sunny Charleston kitchen. Her mother had told her all this when Claire was very young, and then, for some reason, had stopped telling. Perhaps, as a mother getting older, she found her grandmother's mourning for home too close and painful.

Claire checked to see what ingredients she already had—there was bourbon in the liquor cabinet, some salt and sugar and flour in the pantry, and enough butter. Then she tucked the recipe in her coat pocket, and headed to the market. First, she took a bus to the farmer's market on the edge of the city, where she picked up pecans, imported and expensive, then she went back to her neighborhood market to buy eggs, light and dark corn syrups, vanilla, and cream. At the last minute, she also bought a large bar of chocolate from the shelf. She'd always liked chocolate melted on the top, even if her mother said it wasn't authentic.

How authentic could you be when you are a poor Irish Catholic girl turned Protestant and American and married to an agnostic Jew? She laughed.

Her arms full of the two bags of groceries and her heart lighter than it had been only a while ago, Claire started walking back towards home.

Yes, it was, finally, becoming home. She hoped Miriam could feel it, too. She sent a little prayer to her daughter, a little white light, as her grandmother in South Carolina called it.

As she was about to cross the street, she saw Brigid coming down the road.

"Brigid!" Claire called, before she got close enough to notice that the woman had been crying.

"Claire…" Brigid almost moaned as they approached each other.

"Oh, dear, are you okay?" Claire asked, wishing she'd left her alone.

"No, not really," Brigid said, in a small voice. "I was just heading to see Padmaj at the restaurant, but he's probably still busy with lunch." Her voice cracked.

"Well," Claire offered, tentatively. "Would you like to come home with me? I was just about to make a Kentucky bourbon pie."

"A what?"

"It's an old family recipe. It's delicious."

"Well, I could use some bourbon," Brigid said, with half a smile.

"Come on, then. I was going to call you this afternoon."

"You were?" Brigid looked almost cheered.

"Yes. Ask Padmaj. I called him this morning looking for you. Come on, I don't want this cream to spoil."

"Okay then," said Brigid. "At least let me carry some of your load."

When Claire started walking side by side next to Brigid, she noticed for the first time that they were, despite all their differences, exactly the same height.

TWENTY-ONE

Claire's apartment, Brigid discovered, was exceedingly beautiful. Like Claire herself. It was in a newly refurbished building in Dublin. Brigid hadn't ever even been in a building like this in Dublin. Dark wooden beams lay against high white ceilings, and windows let the southern light fall in long rays upon the hardwood floors. Here and there were objects from travels, pillows covered with blue paisleys from Provence, an eight-sided ceramic box painted in reds and browns from Morocco, and a poster from a Chagall exhibit in London. Brigid felt a bit overwhelmed with it all.

"Are you sure you're okay?" Claire asked gently after setting the grocery bags down on the kitchen table and looking at Brigid, standing mute in the doorway. "You look like you're going to cry."

And Brigid did.

***

After Claire handed her a tissue and sat her down at the table and put on water for tea, she knelt beside Brigid, put her hands on Brigid's hands, and looked up at her. "What is it? Can you tell me?"

Brigid had been doing so much telling lately. She wasn't sure if she could. She sighed, a shaky sigh that signaled the end of tears and the beginning of speech.

The tea kettle rang out. Claire jumped and went to prepare the cups.

Brigid looked up at the groceries, still unpacked, and said, "Go on and make your pie."

"No, I couldn't." Claire handed her the tea.

"Yes, do. And I will tell you."

"You're sure?"

"Yes. I'm sure."

***

"I woke before dawn," she began. "Padmaj usually does, alone, to meditate, but today I got up early, too. I wanted to prepare myself."

Claire looked over from the eggs, brown sugar, and vanilla she was whisking. Before sleeping in that morning, she had, since meeting Padmaj, also been rising, most days, before dawn, to write in her journal. It was when the poems came. Poems about waking. Waking from a dreamless sleep, waking from nightmares, waking from a dream.

"My father called me yesterday. To tell me he was to be released from prison this morning. I hadn't seen him in fifteen years. When I was twenty, he was jailed as a suspected terrorist."

Claire poured half the nuts into a white bowl.

"As part of the peace process," Brigid continued, "they're letting out many of the prisoners who had never been tried, had been held all this time without proof."

"Can they do that?" Claire asked.

Brigid was struck by the fact that this had also been Padmaj's reaction. "They *do* do it. All the time," she answered.

Claire added sugar to the nuts and began to mash them with a pestle.

Brigid paused. She wasn't sure whether to tell Claire all of what she'd told Padmaj.

"Go on. Sorry for interrupting," Claire said.

Brigid decided against it. Focus on today, she told herself. "So, anyway, my father called and asked me to meet him when he was released. Which I did today."

Claire's wrist stopped its downward twist for a second, then continued.

"I was at the jail just before sunrise. The sky was the most amazing pink color. Do you know that saying, 'Red sky in morning, sailor's warning, red sky at night, sailor's delight'?"

Claire nodded. Her grandmother had said it.

"I wondered, standing there, if it were a warning for me. If I should not have come. I've wondered this every day since I've been here. If I should not have come when my mum called. I've never been able to trust her."

Brigid paused. She knew she never get through this if she veered too far away from the story. But then again, she thought, how much the story of the present ensnares us with the past. How much of the present is made understandable only with a knowledge of the past. Focus, she told herself.

"'Twas my mum who called me to tell me my father would be released. And so I came. I'm not sure why. Perhaps I came to make peace myself. I don't know. Fifteen years is a long time. I don't think I'd ever really thought about how long until I saw him. He was so gray, and stooped. He was thinner than I remembered. Older. An old man."

To the bowl of minced nuts and sugar, Claire added a cup of flour, a stick of butter, an egg yolk, vanilla and salt. She mixed it with her hands.

"He didn't even see me. He looked right at me but didn't see me. Maybe I wouldn't have known him, either, on the street, after all this time, but, even after everything..."

She paused again. Claire kept mixing.

"I still wanted him to *know* me. He's my father. That's what I felt when his eyes looked through me. I was a little girl again, hoping. My heart knew. My heart knew why I came. Why I came back. Why I am here."

Claire transferred the dough to the flour-covered counter and kneaded it.

Brigid began to cry again, quietly.

"So I called, 'Da, it's me,' and I waved, and he saw me, and it was then that I remembered. I saw a flash of anger in his eyes, and all the accusations that had piled up over the years, why hadn't I come earlier, what kind of daughter am I, and then I remembered why I stayed away. Why I left. And stayed away."

Claire rolled the dough into a circle.

"He's a mean man. A crazy man. And he hadn't changed at all. I saw that then."

Claire greased the pie pan with a stick of butter.

"He walked over to me, with a plastic bag in his hand. I was afraid of him. Other people might have seen a little hunched old man, it's what I saw when I first saw him, but as he came closer, I saw the fire in his eyes, and I was a child again. A wee scared child."

Claire lay the dough into the pan and began cutting the edges with a knife.

"And then as he came nearer to me," Brigid continued, "He said to me,

'Was it the double of my dream
The woman that by me lay....'

***

Claire stopped. She knew the poem. It was Yeats. The first two lines of "Towards Break of Day." Something about it haunted her. She felt an instinct to go find it now, to read it now, as one would a fortune. But she didn't want to interrupt Brigid.

"I knew he meant where's mum. I know him, still, after all this time. He's in me. I know what he means."

Claire turned back to the filling, now almost at room temperature, and added the rest of the nuts, the syrups, whiskey, flour and a pinch of salt.

"So I told him I didn't know where mum was. Probably drunk, was the answer, but I didn't say it," Brigid continued, as she looked at the bottle on the counter, then at the clock. It was long past noon.

"Do you want some?" Claire asked.

"Just a spot in my tea," Brigid answered, sheepishly. "Would you join me?"

Claire hesitated. She didn't want to seem judgmental, but there was something in her that wanted to be alert. "Sure," she said, pouring a teaspoonful into her cup.

"So I said to him," Brigid said, after sipping, "'*I'm* here, Da.'"

Claire poured the filling, wet and sweet and golden brown and glistening, into the pie shell.

Brigid finished the rest of her drink in one long gulp.

"And that was it. He cocked his head to one side, looked up to the pink sky, and walked away."

Claire put the pie into the hot oven.

"Will you stay till it's done?" Claire asked, trying to smile, wiping her hands on a towel.

Brigid suddenly felt very heavy. The last thing she wanted to do was eat. When she felt like this, she usually drank. Or slept. Or drank, then slept.

She decided to go home and do both.

***

Brigid was out the door only a moment when Claire ran to her volume of collected Yeats on the living room bookshelf, looked up the title in the index and turned to the poem. Its third line, "Dreamed, or did we halve a dream?" stopped her, and she put the book down and went into the bedroom to get her journal.

Yes, there it was, her poem from a few dawns ago:

> To have a dream is to half a dream,
> To wake the waker from the wake
> To come together with another
> To take from death what life can make.

She felt again that uncanny sense of poetry carrying knowledge, or memory, or something from the past that lived on still, not in our minds exactly, but in our feelings, in our bodies, in the way our bodies want or do not want.

In how we hunger.

Claire thought of Miriam then, which made her sit down on the wooden floor in the bright afternoon light of the great window. She felt her daughter's absence fully for the first time since the girl's departure, and Claire wept at all she had not done as a mother, all she could not do, would never do, for her. It was not in her.

Had it been in her own mother?

Just what is it we are missing, as American mothers, she wrote then in her journal, that makes us pull away from the past and try to start over, again and again, with each new generation, as if there could be found nothing, nothing useful from all that has come before?

In the middle of bright beams of winter sunlight coming through the window, warm and low, Claire was shivering.

Chillbumps, her mother called them.

Chillblaines, her grandmother had said.

She would, Claire vowed to herself, try to find out what it was that had made her own daughter fail to hunger, fail to eat what she had been given, while Claire herself was never satisfied, always hungry, always searching for that unknown thing around the corner, when she already had so very much.

She would go back, Claire decided, beginning now, to seek out the answers on this island of her mothers, to learn what still survived on the land, in its language, what could be used both as food and as healing, so that, as mother and daughter, they might finally be able to satisfy their hungers of both body and memory.

PART II

ONE

Claire did have that dinner party that late January night after all, as her mother had suggested, and many more in the time that followed. It was as if over the months that Miriam was in the hospital, Claire had been in a kind of treatment, too. She tried to cook regular evening meals for herself and Michael, to have fresh vegetables and fruits for them to eat, and to divide her days between the preparation of food and the reading and writing of poetry. The pinnacle of her week was Sunday, when she would cook a delicious meal for four: Brigid and Padmaj and Michael and herself. When the weather warmed in March, Padmaj decided to start closing the restaurant all day on Sundays, so he and Brigid could have one whole day together each week and so they could come over in the evening for more leisurely meals with Claire and Michael.

And so it was on an Easter Sunday night in April that the four of them were sitting around the large oak dining table finishing their meal. Claire had served a baby spinach salad with walnuts and raisins, and then a spring vegetable stew. Now she was cutting the ginger cheesecake she'd made—her first cheesecake ever—and wondering why she'd feared it would be so hard when actually it was quite easy.

"How is Miriam doing?" Padmaj asked, as, in time, they had become friends who trusted each other and could ask about difficult things.

"Well, we've got news." Michael began cautiously, while Claire's eyes lit up and she finished for him.

"She'll be coming home this week! Friday!"

"How wonderful!" Brigid and Padmaj said together.

"So, Brigid," Claire said, "I've been meaning to ask you, but I've been putting it off."

"Yes?"

"Would you take me to the Famine Museum this week? I've wanted to go, but it's been closed all winter, and I really want to go before—"

"Before Miriam comes home," Brigid said.

"Yes. After all the reading I've been doing about Irish history, I think it's important for me to go. Miriam has been composing a concerto about the famine, you know. In fact, it will be performed on Thursday night, before her release." The word "release" made Claire stop, remembering Brigid's father, but she forced herself to continue.

"I don't know if it will be possible for you both to come," Claire said, "but you're welcome."

"It'll be a busy week, then," Brigid said weakly, and Claire wondered if the word had conjured up her father for Brigid, too.

"If you'd rather not, that's okay. I understand," Claire said quickly.

"No, it's not that. Let me think. I think Wednesday would be my best day. I don't have any massage clients scheduled, and I can ask Meghan to teach my noon yoga class."

"Really?" Claire asked, lighting up again. "Oh, could you? It would be so wonderful!"

"Yes, of course."

"Thank you."

"And I'd like to come to the concert, too," Brigid added.

Padmaj nodded. "I, too, would like to come, of course, I am so sorry, but...."

Michael shook his head. "No, don't worry. There's no need to apologize." As often happened with couples, the women were closer friends and dominated most of the conversation when the four were together. This was all the more true because of Padmaj's quiet nature.

"I am very sorry, though," Padmaj repeated. "I know it is an important occasion for your daughter. I would like to extend my congratulations to her in person."

"How about Sunday, then?" Claire offered. "She'll be here next Sunday. I can't really believe it, but she will. And perhaps she'll play a little from the concert for you then," Claire smiled at Padmaj.

"I would be honored," he said.

Michael noticed that Padmaj's face had clouded over, and he said nothing more while they finished their dessert and tea.

The women continued talking, discussing what time to leave for Strokestown, how long it would take, what they should wear, if they should pack a lunch, and so on.

"It would be kind of ironic not to have a restaurant at the Famine Museum, anyway," Brigid laughed.

Padmaj blinked. Then he looked down at his hands.

"Maybe you wouldn't want to eat," Claire said quietly, thinking of Miriam.

"Nonsense!" chuckled Brigid in her usual exuberant way. "I'd think the Famine Museum should make a person fecking hungry!"

They all laughed, except for Padmaj.

Then the room became quiet.

Michael looked at Claire with the wrap-it-up look that married people give each other at dinner parties.

"Before you go," Claire suggested adroitly as she cleared the dishes, "I have a little gift for each of you."

She disappeared into the bedroom, and then came out with three brightly wrapped boxes.

"What is it?" Brigid beamed, like a child.

"Go ahead. Open them."

They fidgeted and muttered, pulling on the ribbons and ripping paper, until they discovered what was inside.

Within each box was an intricately painted egg, which Claire had spent weeks preparing, blowing out the insides, allowing them to dry, and then decorating them.

"You know we don't celebrate Easter," Claire explained, "but the egg is an ancient symbol of fertility and rebirth. Spring. You know, even our words Easter and estrogen and estrus come from the name of the ancient goddess Oestara, the goddess of spring and fertility."

"I didn't know that!" Brigid exclaimed. "I should have known that!"

Brigid looked down at her egg. On it were painted dozens of tiny green shamrocks in a swirl pattern from top to bottom along the curved edge of the egg. It made one almost dizzy to look at it.

"Here's something else you might not know," Claire grinned, obviously happy that her gifts were being appreciated. "The three leaves of the shamrock, before Christianity, represented the three mothers—virgin, mother, crone—and it was said that each person needs the care of three mothers to survive on earth."

"Well, I sure need more than the one I've got!" laughed Brigid.

"May I see yours?" Michael asked Padmaj. Michael met his hand with care as the man, so sad, it seemed to Michael, reached out his hand to show the egg. The entire egg had been painted to look like a lotus with hundreds of delicate white petals.

"Amazing!" Brigid exclaimed again.

"The lotus is also a symbol of fertility, right, Padmaj?" said Claire, and he nodded.

Claire continued. "It is a flower with both male and female characteristics, as it bears the bud, bloom and seed pod all together."

"The body is a blossom which ultimately turns to dust," Padmaj said quietly.

"How depressing!" said Brigid, who then looked at Padmaj's eyes, felt stupid, and realized she'd again had too much to drink.

"What is yours?" Brigid asked Michael, to divert attention away from herself.

"Well," Michael said. "It's a tree. And it says something along the roots. I can't quite read it." He squinted.

"Let me help you, old man," Claire joked.

She held the egg, the top half painted to look like branches, the bottom half like roots, and read the tiny black letters along one side: "Two who are one, and one who is three."

"What does it mean?" Brigid asked.

"Well," Claire explained carefully. "You may know that the ancient Hebrews worshipped in sacred groves of trees." Her eyes avoided Padmaj's.

"And the ancient Hebrew mystical text, the Kabbalah, is called the Tree of Life. These lines are from the Kabbalah. It's about the wisdom that comes from the mother and the father—'two who are one'—and what each child carries from the past and also makes anew—'one who is three.'"

Claire looked discreetly at Padmaj, who nodded to her.

Brigid noticed this, how Claire and Padmaj seemed to hold some understanding that she herself did not share. "What about you, Claire?" Brigid asked. "Where's your egg?"

"Oh, I've hidden it away...." Claire said, slyly.

"Well, we'd better go on now, so you two can start looking for it," Brigid laughed.

"Thank you again," Padmaj said, as they were gathering their coats. "And blessings to you this week with Miriam's homecoming."

Padmaj hugged Claire. It was the first time he had ever done so—she was usually the one to initiate the touch.

"I'll call you about Wednesday," Brigid called to Claire on their way to the elevator.

And the door shut, and the couples were alone.

TWO

Back at their house—for they had come, over the months, to think of it this way—Padmaj was quiet, lost in his thoughts. He lit the candle on the bedroom altar, while Brigid, trying to sober up from having had too much to drink, decided to take a shower.

She came out, hair wet and scraggly, wrapped in his old green robe.

"You okay?" she asked him, as he handed her a hot cup of tea.

They settled down into bed.

"I have...." he started, and then stopped. "I find myself remembering many things tonight."

"Are they sad things?"

"Yes."

"Do you want to talk about them?"

"Yes," he said, setting down the cup. "But first I would like this," he said, and took her cup, and kissed her, and placed himself, gently, but forcefully, on top of her.

He had never done this before—been so forthright. Sometimes, in fact, Brigid felt like a tiger compared to the quiet and polite way he approached her, physically.

"Oh my," she giggled, but soon enough, her breathing deepened, then quickened, to match his rhythms within her.

She glanced over his shoulder and noticed the statue of Durga riding a tiger and thought that perhaps the tiger is not only a predator but a kind of protection.

After, he said quietly, "Do you remember," holding her white hand in his dark hand, "when I told you I would someday be telling you my story?"

"Yes," she whispered.

"Now is the time."

"Okay," she said, and waited.

He stood up, nude.

"These trees," he said, pointing to the large painting above the altar, "are called Sinsyaru trees. They grow in my homeland forest. Their roots grow in the air, see?" he said, pointing to the long fingers that seemed to hang down from the branches.

"This is the way I was raised. Like these trees."

She did not know what he meant, but she was sober now, and quiet.

"My mother raised me in a tiny village of small women and trees."

He spread his arms wide. "All these trees, as far as you could see, they were my home. The women worked together and depended upon the trees. For everything. The trees were our food, our fuel, our baskets, our medicines, our clothing, our lives. The trees were our mothers. The women hung babies from the trees while they harvested."

Brigid's eyebrows raised.

"What Claire said about mothers is true, you know," he said, raising his voice a little. "We need many mothers in a lifetime. The mothers in my village knew this. And they also knew that not all mothers are human."

Brigid thought about the sea and air and green hills of her early childhood in County Clare, and nodded.

He continued. "One day when I was eight years old, men came from outside the village. They tried to convince us to cut down the trees. They said if we mined the mountain, we could make more money. They were asking us to kill our mothers."

Padmaj suddenly felt vulnerable and chilled, standing there with nothing on.

He got into bed beside Brigid and put his head against her chest.

"For money," he said, shaking his head, still uncomprehending.

"I was so afraid. These men were obviously willing to use force to convince our mothers to change their minds. It was my mother who came up with the idea of *chipko*. It is a word that means this," he said to her, drawing his arms around her hips and squeezing her.

"Hug?" she asked.

"But more," he said. "More force."

Brigid thought for a moment.

"Cling?" she asked.

"Cling," he tried it out on his lips, then continued. "This is what they did. The women clinged to the trees..."

"Clung," she corrected.

"Clung. The women clung to the trees. They were not letting go."

He became silent. He had never told this story before, had not even thought of it, as a story, in English. He found himself groping for words.

"What happened?" she asked, breathless from his words and his strong grip on her.

"It was night. Very dark. I was hiding with the other children. Our mothers had given us candy."

He looked at her to see if she remembered, and she nodded.

"They told us it was magical candy and would make us strong. They wanted us to stay hidden, so that in case something was happening to them we would not see."

He paused again.

She could hardly breathe.

"There was screaming. The mothers were screaming, and men were screaming, and even we heard some gunshots."

He dug his face into her belly.

"But then it got quiet."

He looked up at her.

"And then we heard footsteps."

He lay his face against her again.

"Our mothers were back."

They sighed, together.

"They had returned. They had won. Many had been beaten and were bleeding, including my mother, but they had saved the trees with their lives."

They sat together, quietly, for a long time. He could hear the steady heartbeat within Brigid's chest.

"Padmaj?"

"Yes?"

"Why were you sad tonight?"

"I don't know. So many memories of home. The ginger in the dessert Claire prepared. Miriam coming home. The look in Claire's eyes, a mother's eyes, missing her daughter. What she said about the three mothers. The sacred trees she talked about. And the lotus on the egg."

Brigid nodded, trying to understand, remembering how she felt, sometimes, in America, when Ireland would rise up out of the past and call to her. Call her home. Despite everything.

"Do you know what Padmaj means?" he asked.

"I never thought about it," she said, stroking his hair. "I didn't know it meant anything."

"Everything means something," he said.

She smiled. She was not sure if this were true, but that he did was one of the reasons she loved him.

"Lotus," he said.

"Lotus?"

"Padmaj means Lotus."

THREE

"You don't have to do that," Claire said, standing at the doorway to the kitchen as Michael rinsed the dessert plates.

"It's okay. I don't mind."

"I mean," she said, wrapping her arms around his hips from behind, "*don't* do that."

"Oh," he smiled. "What then should I *do*?" He turned, leaned down and kissed her. Their late honeymoon would be coming to an end this week, and he would be sorry to see it go. Of course, he had missed Miriam terribly, and of course, he was relieved that she was better, but this was something that he would miss: Claire's spontaneity, her affection, her sense of freedom from a watchful daughter's eye.

Claire had become his lover again.

***

Claire was not afraid. She had no sense that something was ending. In fact, these months of having Michael to herself had stirred a desire for another kind of beginning: she wanted to have another child.

She hadn't told Michael this. She knew he felt they were getting old. She knew he was looking forward to the time when Miriam would be away at college and they would be a couple again.

She was not. Maybe this is what was meant by the empty nest syndrome. Maybe. But, as she kissed him, as she tugged him into the bedroom, she did not care what this was called. She wanted him. And she wanted to be a mother again. It was as if the two desires were banks of a river, and her body was the water, flowing between them.

After, when Michael got up to use the bathroom and brush his teeth before bed, Claire smiled, resting her head against the pillow, and thinking about her egg inside, wondering if it might also be waiting.

"That egg," Michael said as he crawled back into bed beside her, and for a second she thought he'd been reading her thoughts.

"What?" she said, startled.

"The egg. The egg you gave me," he said. "It's beautiful."

"Oh," she said.

"Where did you get the idea for that?"

"From a book on ancient goddess myths at Indian Treets. It was on the table when I was waiting for lunch one day, and I picked it up, and there was something about it. I don't know. It spoke to me."

She did not tell him how Padmaj also had spoken to her, that day, for hours after the last lunch customer had left.

Claire noticed that Michael was starting to fall asleep, his breathing getting longer and deeper as he nuzzled against her shoulder.

Like a baby, she thought, remembering when Miriam would fall asleep in her arms after breastfeeding. The letting go. The trust that the mother would be there to hold you.

"I started thinking about mothering," she whispered to Michael, his face smooth and relaxed, like a baby. "Ever since Miriam got sick, and specifically since that day that Brigid told me that perhaps my family had been Catholic and converted, I've been thinking about history. I've been wondering what other changes have taken place.

"We see the world as it is now," she continued, almost inaudibly. "But what has it been? What has gone before? And how does it continue to affect us?"

Michael twitched. He was almost completely asleep.

"The power of the mother," she continued, "is that she passes on, through her body, the history of all that has come before."

His hand's hold on her hip loosened.

"I want to have another chance to pass on this history. I want to be a mother again."

His eyes popped open.

"What?"

"I want to get pregnant, Michael."

He rolled away from her and sighed. "Oh, Claire, I don't know."

"That passage from the Kabbalah. On your egg. That's what it meant."

Claire looked into Michael's eyes and said, "I want to make a home. I want to stop moving. I want to raise a child to stay in the same place, to nest in a tree. Miriam never had that, and look what happened.She reached into the pile of books on the table beside their bed. "

"But Claire, that doesn't make sense. Once my work is done here, I'll be transferred to another—"

"Michael," she smiled, showing him the book she had been reading to him. "It's your own people's book."

"I don't know, Claire."

"What do we ever really know, Michael?"

She knew he hated when she got like this.

"Be realistic, Claire. I'm forty-five. You're forty! What if something... the health of...."

"We can't keep living our lives like that. We have to have faith."

"Faith?" he asked. He didn't know what that meant. He knew only who he was, who she was, and that they loved each other. Beyond that was too much to know. Beyond that led to persecution, boundaries, wars.

"Love, Michael," she said, stroking his thick hair. "Love leads to desire. Acting on that desire takes faith."

He looked away and then said, "Can I think about it?"

"Yes."

"Good. Then I need to sleep now. I've got to work in the morning. You and these Sunday night dinner parties."

"Okay, sleep," she said. "But I'm not tired." She took her journal from her desk and shut the bedroom door quietly, went into the living room and sat in the big leather chair by the window.

The moon was full and almost directly overhead. It was midnight. She could see to write from the light of it. It lit her page.

The river glowed in the moonlight, too.

"Two who are one," she thought to herself.

"Perhaps I am two already," she wrote. "Perhaps your dad and me, we've made you, little one. Are you here?"

She looked up at the moon again and noticed a bright star to the right of it. She remembered Miriam's little voice singing, "Twinkle, twinkle, little star, how I wonder what you are." Miriam had always been a musical child, singing, dancing, and later, piano, then cello.

Claire remembered her pregnancy, still, in her body. It was like a song she could still hum by heart. She kept every moment—every waking, every feeding, every tantrum, every first word—in her memory, too. Maybe this is what it meant to be a mother: to remember. But what about the mothers who were forced to forget? Who had to turn things off, in their mind and body, because the pain was too great? How did that get registered in their mothering, how did that get passed down in the memory of their children? How do you remember a feeling that is not there?

She could do better. She had been a good mother to Miriam, but she could do better, she was sure of it.

She looked to the star by the moon and thought she saw a baby twinkling there. The promise of it filled her with hope.

"Are you coming, little one, from far away, like that star?" she wrote in her journal, and then, suddenly feeling the weight of Michael's ambivalence—ha! resistance was a better word—she felt afraid.

The image of the egg she'd given Brigid came to her. All the tiny shamrocks. Each with three leaves for three mothers.

She thought of Dr. O'Brien and the nurses in the treatment center whom Miriam had come to love over these months.

It was true. One needed many mothers to make it through this life. Claire turned again to her journal to write.

> Twinkle tiny,
> will you find me,
> will you find your mothers?
> For I am only one,
> and you must come so far.
> You will need others
> when you come
> to nest
> on this earth
> from your star.

FOUR

Padmaj, too, was awake in the night, like Claire. He could not sleep after telling his story to Brigid, conjuring up the memory of fear, bringing it here to his new home in a new language. It made him afraid, all over again, as he had been when a boy, and this made him rise from the bed, leaving Brigid sleeping, to go to the kitchen quietly to make tea. Then, the warm cup in his hands, he walked out the front door to sit on the porch and watch the full moon already tipping into the western sky.

They called it "Chandra," the moon, in India. A woman's name. He'd heard the Irish called a woman "Celine," which meant moon, too. So much they had in common, these two former British colonies. The least of which, he sometimes felt, was this: their former ruler.

The harp, for instance, existed in both places thousands of years before Britain was more than a flea-filled island of warring tribes and hairy men. The hand drum, too, had been used since ancient times in both lands. Perhaps, when Claire had spoken of Miriam and her concert, it was his knowledge of the old musical roots that the two countries shared that had triggered the nostalgia for India that night.

But it was not nostalgia, exactly.

He knew too much for it to be nostalgia; that was something to be saved for the next generations, those who might visit but never live in the motherland. No, as an emigrant he did not have the luxury of simple nostalgia.

Like Brigid, he had seen too much. He and Brigid shared this, as emigrants, which she was, still, Padmaj thought, even despite her return. She was, he could see, reluctant to reclaim the place as her home.

And they shared so much more, as well. Not only had they left their countries at exactly the same age, they had also both been left by their own fathers.

Padmaj had not told Brigid about his father yet. And as he began to remember what an astrologer had told his mother on a night like this, when Padmaj was still a spirit in his mother's womb and a star sat closely to the moon, he wondered if he ever would.

The story of his father was buried deep within him and could only be unearthed by someone with great patience, which right now would eliminate Brigid, who tended toward impatience with herself and others because she was so obviously still stirring in pain.

But the knowledge that Padmaj held about the histories they shared drew him to her nonetheless. It was as if he could experience, through her, a possible reunion with his own father, who was, like hers, an outcast. Like hers, driven by political passion. Like hers, a lover of poetry. Like hers, absent still.

It was not simply the partitioning of Pakistan from India that had driven his father from him. It had taken Padmaj years to understand this—years of reading history, years of education, years of travel. If he, like most of the people in his village, had never left, he would never have understood this, and he, like they, would still blame the Partition or Pakistan or even themselves, for the great pain in their lives.

He knew, though, that it had been more than simply prejudice or politics or nationhood or history that had driven his father to abandon them. It was, Padmaj had come to accept, a kind of character.

Brigid's father shared this character, too, he guessed, which is why he could have walked away from her that morning when she came, over years and continents, to meet him. There are certain people whose pain is so great, Padmaj thought, that they must separate themselves from others, either by abandonment or cruelty or killing. They must show the world, through their actions, how evil they feel inside, thereby forcing society to punish them, fulfilling their own prophecies that they are being mistreated, ostracized, persecuted, and shunned.

The only answer to this, Padmaj had learned from his mother, is great love.

"Cross the bridges hard to cross," his mother would often say, citing the *Veda*.

It was what had brought him here: the great love of his mother. It was she who first crossed the hard bridge of forgiving his father, continuing to love him with all her heart so that her son would not grow, as Brigid had, to have a hard pit of resentment where the fruit of one's heart should be. And then it was she who crossed the hardest bridge of all, in letting her son go, in encouraging him to go to school, to learn, to travel, to do what he would with his life.

And so, the restaurant, the walls of which he'd scraped and painted with his own hands fifteen years ago, became a testament to his mother's love, as he served people food for both their bellies and their spirits.

For in all his years, all the books and people and lands he had come to know, he was certain of one truth the world over: people hunger.

They hunger for food, and this drives them to sell what they should keep, to trade land and trees and even their bodies and spirits for something warm and quick to fill their bellies.

They hunger for spirit, especially when their bellies are full and their tongues are bored by a myriad of tastes and they know that they are still unfulfilled, still empty in the place that matters most: the soul.

Padmaj understood that most of the peoples of the globe could go on gorging their physical bodies endlessly, ignoring their spiritual needs because they were invisible.

But they weren't.

This is why, since that very first night he had met Claire's daughter, and ever after, when Brigid or Claire or Michael had given him news of Miriam, he had felt a special kinship with her. Miriam knew, as Padmaj did, that Ghandi had fasted in order to try to stop the violence escalating on both sides during the Partitioning of India. Miriam understood, as Padmaj did, the way that history had worked, the world over, to serve people's need for physical food at the expense of what could feed their spirits.

Trees. Music. Poetry. Love. The star that sits close to the moon.

He was remembering fully now what the astrologer had said. In a tiny darkened hut outside the village, the astrologer had shown his mother an open metal box in which a single candle burned.

"See the flame?" the astrologer had said to his mother. She nodded.

"See how it moves, never stays in one place, refusing to be physical, to be solid in form?" She nodded again.

He shut the box and then quickly opened it again. On the inside of the lid was a black ring, a perfect dark circle in the middle of the shiny square.

"This is like spirit," he said. "It refuses to be visible except when we try to shut it out. And then it manifests itself in dark circles, endless loops and scars upon the flesh."

His mother had told him this story so many times, Padmaj could almost swear he had been there, had seen the dark circle the flame made for himself, with his own eyes. But he had not yet been born.

"That child you carry," the astrologer had said to his mother, pointing to her belly, still flat, "will become a man of spirit. You must let him move freely or he will cast dark circles on everything he touches."

At the time, his mother had not even known she was pregnant, yet ten full moons later, she gave birth to her only child. And she had remembered what she had been told about him. And she passed it on to him.

His mother had indeed let him grow to be a man of spirit. She had allowed him to move freely wherever this spirit called him. Still, wherever he went, he could feel the shadow of his father within him, like a ring around his heart. It was what had drawn him to Brigid—

the recognition that she was a twin to him, each in its own wounded skin. It was also what found him wanting something permanent with her — the hope that Brigid would forever see in him the glowing flame and not the dark circle. That with her, he could be the man his mother had raised him to be and not the boy his father had left, blaming the nation that had reached independence at the same time as it had torn itself apart.

FIVE

Claire was as interested in discovering Ireland's history as Brigid was in forgetting it, Brigid mused as she drove into Dublin's center to pick up Claire that Wednesday morning. Like a younger sibling who had fallen deep asleep and did not hear the parents fighting late at night, Claire could imagine that the Irish past was glorious, heroic, somehow mythical. Brigid knew better. Brigid had witnessed the violence first-hand.

Yet still she was going.

The Famine Museum had not been here when she left for America. No one was even talking about the famine then, let alone opening museums and holding university lectures and listening to presidential speeches about it.

The famine, then, was something that had happened but did not exist except in what was missing. The letters from cousins in America and Australia, the empty countryside, the low numbers of women in the maternity wards—these were the legacy of the famine.

The production of Guinness had increased six hundred percent in the first few years after the famine, Brigid remembered reading somewhere, as she sipped bottled water to ease her headache from having drunk too much—again—the night before.

She was no longer catching babies, she told herself, so she could let go a bit in the evenings. But she knew this was an excuse. She knew she'd been drinking too much since coming back. She knew she would have to quit—soon.

It puzzled her, why this old desire for drunkenness had returned in her, now. She was loved, for the first time in her life.

What was she still craving?

This was the reason she had decided to go with Claire, to the museum. To see if the answer could be found, as Miriam thought it could be, in the past.

***

Brigid noticed that Claire was more quiet than usual as they drove west on N4, the highway toward Strokestown, in the center of the island. Brigid was usually the talkative one, but since hearing Padmaj's story, she had felt pensive, and Claire did not rush in to fill the gap that her silence created. They sat together, silent, in Padmaj's tiny car—at least the defroster was working, Brigid smiled, remembering that first night with him—as they watched the morning fog begin to lift, revealing shallow green hills, like a thin woman's hips and thighs and breasts, beside them.

It would be a warm day. The fog meant that the cool of the morning would be followed by a warm afternoon. Sun, even.

Brigid finished her bottle of water and then found she was hungry.

"You were wrong," she said to Claire.

"About what?"

"I *am* hungry. Just thinking about the famine already, I'm starving!"

They laughed.

Claire opened her bag and pulled out banana bread, still warm.

"You're amazing!" Brigid exclaimed as she pushed a chunk of the soft sweet bread into her mouth.

"I try," Claire said slyly.

It took them two hours, and by the time they navigated the final passage with the crazy map Claire had printed off the internet—in which the north was at the bottom and Dublin, to the east, was at the left—it was lunchtime, and Brigid was hungry again.

There was a restaurant in the museum building after all, as Brigid had predicted. Just a tiny kitchen and an outdoor eating area near the car park, still it tempted one before heading down the gravel path to the entrance.

Brigid knew that Claire probably wasn't hungry—she looked like she was coming down with something, in fact—but Brigid was starting to get the falling blood sugar characteristic of the day after a night of drinking, and she wanted to eat before looking at the exhibit.

"Okay, let's eat," Claire agreed, deciding to have a salad.

Brigid chose a quiche and a bowl of soup.

"Did you know the term 'soup kitchen' comes from the famine?" Brigid told Claire after they were settled at one of the outdoor tables surrounded by a rock wall fence.

"Really?"

"Yes. The British served people outdoors from huge vats of soup. They even hired a chef from France to come up with a suitable recipe."

Claire shook her head. It was then that Brigid remembered how Claire had told her that Miriam's first meal after the intravenous feeding had been soup.

"I don't know if that's really true," Brigid lied, wishing she could take back her chatter. "I don't know much. We didn't learn about this in school, really. I saw a documentary on the telly once, in the States. This will be all new for me, too." They sat together in silence. Claire did not finish her meal. Brigid cleared the table, throwing everything away in a large green bin by the fence.

***

A quiet continued to fall on them as they entered the cold stables that held the exhibits in the museum.

They were the only visitors that day — it was still too cold for most tourists, and since it was the week after Easter, the schools were closed.

A woman with large glasses handed them brochures through a bullet-proof plastic window, informed them that the tour was self-guided, and then went back to the novel she was reading.

"Shall we go together?" Brigid asked. "Or would you like to wander alone?"

Brigid knew that Claire would want to be alone — she was that kind of woman, an introspective, thinking woman who liked to take things in at her own pace. Brigid also feared she would babble too much and was only glad to separate to spare herself the embarrassment.

"Let's go alone and meet back in an hour," Brigid suggested.

Claire nodded, smiling faintly.

***

Brigid had seen drawings of the famine before — renditions of the dirty, monkey-faced Irish, done by British reporters of the time — but she had never seen photographs.

In the fourth room of the exhibit, Brigid found herself frozen before one black and white, but clear, photo of a family. They were inside their house, which had a dirt floor and no furniture except for one wooden cradle, which was empty. Surrounding the cradle were four children — all girls, or perhaps just dressed that way. One girl was lying down. Asleep? Dead? The other three children clung to their father, who looked vacantly into the empty cradle. In front of the cradle was a child's story book, lying upside down, and open.

Brigid remembered the books that had kept her company as a child. She searched the photo for evidence of other furniture — a bed, a chair — and found none. They had no food, and they had no furniture, but they had a cradle, and a book.

Brigid began to cry. Over the past ten years in America, she remembered crying only once. And yet she'd cried so many times since coming back. After seeing her mother for the first time. Then alone in her hotel room. After making love with Padmaj. And the night she told him her story. That day at Claire's, after she saw her father again. During Padmaj's story, only days before. And now.

Her eyes were drawn to the father in the photograph. It looked as if his children were holding him up. His face was—she had heard stories about this—hairy, fuzzy. This must have been why the British called them monkeys.

The sign below said this condition occurs in cases of extreme starvation.

Brigid had to turn away.

Inside her mind was a picture of her father, on the day he was released, gray and stooping and thin. How she'd simultaneously been repulsed by him and wanted to lean into him. Wanted, somehow, to hold him up. And to hold him.

She wondered where he was. Neither she nor her mother had heard from him since January—at least this was what her mother swore. Brigid felt he could be around every corner, waiting for her. It was why she drank, she realized. To feel far away. From him. From the fear of him that stalked her, like a tiger.

At the other side of the room, another photo caught her eye. It was a village in County Galway, just before the famine struck, with a few children, and at the far left, a girl, perhaps Miriam's age, looking uncannily like Claire. Thick, shoulder length, dark hair, pulled back by a ragged scarf, and a wide, white forehead above big, round eyes. Brigid imagined them blue, dark blue, like Claire's. And she had the full lips that Claire used so often to express herself without speaking—by smiling, frowning, pouting, biting.

Brigid had stopped crying and suddenly wanted to embrace Claire. What was that word Padmaj used? Chipko? Cling? That was how she felt now, about this woman who was her friend but something more. Like a cousin or a sister. One of her own. One of the ones who got away. Who escaped. Was still missing.

For Brigid found herself feeling strong somehow. The way Claire had been looking to her, for history, for a sense of belonging, home, the past—all this that Brigid had rejected, run from, tried to forget. This, Brigid realized, *was* in her, was something she carried by virtue of those mothers and fathers, like the people in these photos, who did not leave.

These were her people. These were Claire's people, too, but it would be harder for her to claim them, for she had been cut away from the land.

Unlike the trees that Padmaj's mothers saved, Claire was a tree that had been cleared.

And now, as Claire walked into the room with tears in her blue eyes and her beautiful mouth quivering, Brigid held out her arms to her. Remembering the shamrock-covered egg Claire had given her, Brigid thought, Welcome home, cousin. Welcome home.

SIX

The images of hunger haunted Claire, still, as she sat in the dark, between Brigid and Michael, biting her lip as the lights dimmed and the curtains parted that Thursday evening in the hospital auditorium.

Miriam stood by herself, lit by one beam of light in the center of the stage, dressed completely in black except for a silver Claddagh ring on her right hand, which Claire had given her and which shone as she struck the first note on her cello—a low, mournful sound. The sound made Claire see again the photographs of the children in the museum, their limbs like matchsticks and their bodies bloated.

Then Miriam was joined from backstage by three more musicians—two violins and a viola. Their rhythms were pastoral, nostalgic—and made Claire remember how she had imagined Ireland would be, before she came. A green land of leprechans and luck. Women, plump and soft like her grandmother, knitting in front of peat fires as redheaded children played nearby.

Claire thought of all this almost with a sense of shame now, as she pictured ragged waifs standing outside their crushed houses, roofs on fire, and imagined that this might have been her great-grandmother's final image of Ireland, not the idyllic image that grew so easily in the minds of her American-born descendants.

And yet, here she was, finally, back, facing the real history.

***

The music picked up, as a line from an Irish jig played against an American folk tune, in a jazzlike counter-rhythm.

Who was that great-grandmother who came from Ireland to settle in America? Claire asked herself. And what did it mean that Claire knew nothing about her history, except what Miriam had discovered, a birth record in a tiny western coastal town?

What did it even mean to be Irish, Claire wondered, when there is no memory of either the place or the person who came from there, no recipe handed down, no skill or trade or story?

Or song. Her child, born singing, almost grown, was on stage, proudly leading the quartet in making the music that she herself had written. Tomorrow, healed, she would come home.

***

A lack of memory, Claire realized, had not been a problem at home, in America. It had been an advantage, allowing people to come and go at will, to think of the whole world as a kind of home. A possible destination.

But, yesterday, in the museum, the bare feet, swollen bellies, dirt floors, and crushed homes—all this was what her great-grandmother had called home, what she had left, knowing she might never return.

Even a conversion had not saved her.

These conversions were increasingly common as the famine years approached, Claire had learned: landlords would grant privileges to those tenants who converted. And then, with the famine full on, people were asked to denounce Catholicism in order to obtain a bowl of soup at the workhouses.

It was a matter of survival, Claire understood, that had made these conversions necessary, whether for power or land or food. Still, it would have separated her great-grandmother from the vast majority of Catholic poor at the time.

Her great-grandmother had given up her faith, Claire knew this much. And this, in addition to her emigrant status, had separated her from Brigid's ancestors who had stayed—and who, Claire sometimes felt, were the true Irish. Real.

Whoever she had been in the past, Claire decided, her great-grandmother was continuing to reach forward into the present, forming Claire, and her daughter Miriam, and the next child she so desired.

***

Claire remembered the way Brigid had looked at her, in the car, on their way back to Dublin after the museum, when Claire had shared this desire with her.

"It would be great to be pregnant," Claire had told Brigid, "to give a child a real home."

Brigid had looked at her, clearly startled, her hazel eyes rimmed with red, eyebrows raised, so that they looked to Claire almost like raspberries with fuzzy leaves on top.

"I'm coming," Claire had explained, "to think of Ireland as home."

Brigid had looked back to the road and blinked.

"Miriam has been doing research on our family's genealogy, and she's found the birth record for my great-grandmother. It's in a town called Clifden, in County Galway. Do you know it?"

Brigid had nodded.

"We're going to go there, as a family, when Miriam comes home."

Brigid blinked again.

"And Michael and I thought, perhaps, in the summer, we'll rent a cottage and vacation there."

"'Tis beautiful," Brigid said.

"So you've been there?"

"Yes."

"Tell me! What's it like?"

Brigid had shaken her head. "Nothing I tell you will be true."

Sometimes Brigid's somber attitude came through full force and knocked Claire off balance. Claire, who could certainly be morose alone, hid it well in the presence of others, and was startled by the way Brigid did not.

"I just thought..."

"No, Claire, I'm sorry. I just meant that you should see it yourself. 'Tis a lovely place, really, and you should make it yours by going there. You should." Brigid had tried to smile.

"I've heard there are mountains," Claire tried to say something safe.

"The Twelve Bens."

"Where have I heard that before?" Claire wondered out loud.

Brigid had not answered.

***

The music stopped, then began again, slow. Almost whispering.

Claire felt a quivering in her spine, thinking back to that day in January when Brigid had first told her about her father, remembering the premonition she'd had after, reading the poem from Yeats.

Michael felt Claire shudder and took her hand, and Claire was grateful all over again, as she often was, for him, for his presence, his love. She smiled at him, and he smiled back as their daughter, almost healed, almost grown, continued to play.

***

The music murmured, and Claire thought about how she had closed down that day with Brigid, how she had been, ever since, afraid to ask about Brigid's father again.

Not that Brigid had wanted to talk about him, really.

Claire could tell that Brigid was afraid of him, too. That she was trying to forget that he was free, that he could reach her.

Claire felt it, too, the sense that he was, somehow, within her.

It was this, all of this—the hunger, the conversions and the refusals, the wakes and the departures, the sense of identity tied to a land, to a few remaining people who knew every nook and cranny of a hillside, remembered what had happened there, felt pride and shame, both—all this, Claire was beginning to understand, had made Brigid's father who he was.

Even so, something about Brigid's father still terrified Claire.

"Isn't that the purpose of terrorists?" Michael had asked her, one night, in bed, as she confessed her fears to him.

"I suppose," she'd said, "but I'm still afraid. Sometimes I have terrible dreams…"

"You eat too much before going to bed," he'd teased her.

She hadn't told him about the dreams. She'd been afraid she would help make them come true by saying them out loud.

The music was becoming jolly. It was disconcerting, the shift. Miriam had explained to her that this was the emigration, from the point of view of those leaving. The way they so easily could forget what they'd left behind. The effect was working, as slowly, another melody, lower, almost wailing, interwove itself into the swiftly moving dominant stream.

Michael put his arm around Claire, held her shoulder tight, as she found herself crying, quietly, releasing all the tension she'd felt—about Brigid's father, and Miriam's illness, and the desire to get pregnant, and the whole horrible history of the Irish, which she was coming to claim as her own.

She remembered, suddenly, an unexpected image from the museum, from a foreign country. Was it Pakistan? Bangladesh? The way a foreign government forced the local people to convert to new crops—for export—leaving their children hungry and the earth stripped while the foreign owners became rich in the process.

But this was not history.

It was happening now.

Claire had always before thought that these sorts of things happened in the past, or to other people. Coming to Ireland, claiming its history, had begun to open her to the realization that she herself played a role in this.

That each of us, every single one of us, is a part of all of this.

Claire thought of Padmaj. This might be something he would say. She decided to ask him about it. Soon.

***

124

The music changed again, slowed, became a comforting tune that seemed to float on water.

The water between the continents, Miriam had explained. Between Ireland and America.

And between Ireland and India, thought Claire.

The salty water between us. And within.

The sea. Our tears. The womb.

Suddenly Claire felt a twinge in her abdomen. She wondered if it could be the egg implanting, and this slowed her tears. She remembered how, with Miriam, she'd bled a little and cramped, and thought she'd had a light period, but later realized it had been the egg implanting itself after lingering for a few days in the fallopian tube.

The thought that this might be happening again filled her with a kind of hope, and she sighed, letting the tears flow away.

Miriam's piece really was quite wonderful, she smiled to herself, as the music began to wind down to a lullaby. Claire was proud of her daughter. She couldn't wait to tell her.

Gradually, as the concert ended, Claire began to imagine that the dread of the past—her own past, the world's past—and the anxiety it created in the present, might one day recede, for Claire and for Michael and for all their friends and family. She began to dream that history might someday be a source for them, as it had begun to be for Miriam, a source of beauty and justice and understanding, something that could sustain them in the present, not simply something to fear or fight or forget.

SEVEN

Brigid sat at the end of the aisle, next to Claire, took Claire's hand and squeezed it, lightly, briefly, as the curtains parted to reveal Miriam and the other musicians on stage.

But as the music started, Brigid felt her heart sink, hearing the awful syrupy tones of the kind of popular Irish music being bought and sold all over the States now as background filler in dentists' offices and coffee shops. She held her breath, trying not to sigh, hoping that Miriam was smarter than this.

She was.

The slow refrains gave way to a kind of jazzy duet, and Brigid remembered the way she'd loved jazz as a teenager, and the way she'd romanticized everything American. Ireland and America were like two lovers who met once in the night but never really saw each other in the light of day.

What a day.

**

After the long trip to Strokesberry the day before, Padmaj had left the house quietly that morning, to let Brigid sleep in, which she so loved to do.

And so when the phone rang in the kitchen, Brigid had not heard it at first. Instead it had become part of her dream, a dream in which a baby was calling to her.

"Mum, mum!" the baby—not a baby, really, but a toddler—was saying into the phone, the way children do. "Wake up, Mum!"

Brigid's first thought upon waking had been that Claire's declaration about wanting to get pregnant must have struck a deep chord in her somehow.

And then she'd realized that the phone was actually ringing, and she rushed to the kitchen in a white t-shirt and underwear.

"Hullo?"

"It's your Da," Brigid heard her mum whisper through the phone.

"What? What do you mean?"

"It's your Da," her mother had repeated. "He's here, with some blokes from the Real."

"Mum? I can hardly hear you. Can you speak up?"

Brigid could hear singing in the background—male voices, off key, and drunken.

"No!" her mother had said firmly, her anger flaring. "Look, I can't do it, not with them here. You've got to be the one to do it."

Brigid remembered her dream. Perhaps she herself was the baby, calling for her mother to do what she should do, what she had never been able to. Or maybe it was Brigid who was the mother now. She didn't know.

Brigid began to have the prickling sensation across her lower back that she used to have as her father crept into bed, waking her.

She was being awoken.

"Brigid, are you listening to me? Do you understand what I'm saying?"

Brigid knew. She knew that her father was with the organization again, and that he was planning something, and that they were using her mother's apartment, and that she'd promised to alert the authorities, and that all this was what her mother was whispering about.

It had been four months, long enough that she had begun to tell herself that her fear was all in her mind, that there was nothing to fear. But this, she now knew, had been an illusion, and what she'd feared would happen was happening, she knew all this in a flash, and so she said, "Yes, Mum, I understand."

***

The music stopped, then began again, slow. Almost whispering.

Claire shivered next to her, and Michael took Claire's hand.

Brigid was amazed again at how these two loved each other. She remembered back to the first time she saw them, in the elevator at the hospital, and the way they'd seemed so in love and so sad at the same time. Brigid had always thought love and sadness were opposites, but Claire and Michael were teaching her that they needn't be.

She wanted to love Padmaj like this. Despite her sadness.

***

As the music began to murmur at her, she remembered her turmoil, getting dressed that morning after the phone call, how she shook, buttoning her shirt, and then suddenly realized that she was ravenously hungry and that her period was late.

Was it possible?

It was true, Padmaj hadn't been all that careful. Brigid wondered now why. And she remembered the dream. She almost heard the baby's voice then again. She knew that mothers often had dreams of

128

premonition like this during pregnancy; she'd learned as a midwife to come to believe them. They were often uncanny in their ability to convey necessary information: an ectopic pregnancy, a need for more iron, a cord wrapped dangerously around the neck.

"Wake up, Mum!"

She was the mum, now, and she was waking up, she'd said to herself, as she'd started Padmaj's car with hands still shaking, and then, thinking better of it, had run back inside to drink a glass of milk and grab some nan before driving to work.

***

The music slowed, and Brigid knew this was the final movement. Claire had explained this to her in the car the day before, how the final movement would move into the sea between the countries.

The sea. "Ireland free from center to sea." How often Brigid had heard her father say they would drive the British into the sea, copying what the Palestinians said about the Jews in Israel. "*Éire soar ó lár go farriage.*" The fecking losers, the lot of them, thought Brigid, they couldn't even come up with their own slogans.

It cheered her a little to discover her anger again at her father, at his group, at the way they used history to their own, deadly advantage.

Michael's arm bumped her shoulder, startling her.

Brigid looked over, and Claire was crying, and Michael had put his arm around her, comforting her.

Brigid told herself again that she would call the authorities.

She had to talk to Padmaj, too, she told herself. About the pregnancy.

Somehow the two were linked, crazily, in her mind—the decision about whether to keep this baby and the decision about whether to turn her father in.

She was in that in-between state, she told herself, before the final, right decision is made, when one still considers the other possibility.

That was all. She was simply considering the other possibilities, fully, before making the right ones.

The concert ended, and she was clapping, knowing she was expected to stay to congratulate Miriam, but she suddenly felt ill, and wanted, so very badly, to run away.

To be alone.

Herself. Alone.

EIGHT

On Saturday, Claire lay in bed on before dawn thinking back on the day before, while Michael slept soundly next to her. She stretched her fingers out across her belly, imagining that it was slightly more rounded than it had been before. Then her hands lingered lower, and she remembered how wet she'd been during her pregnancy with Miriam, as if she had been ovulating for nine months straight. She grinned in the predawn dark, recalling her pregnant desire, and the way her orgasms had radiated out from her womb to her hips, and thighs, and knees.

Miriam had been home for close to twenty-four hours now, and today was Saturday, so no alarm would go off to wake Michael for work. She watched him, with love, as he lay there, so trusting and open, with the light beginning to turn lavender outside their window.

The alarm had gone off the morning before, even though they could have slept in, because Michael had forgotten and set it, as he always did, each weeknight. They'd lain in bed together after he turned off the alarm, the two of them, watching the sun slowly rise, throwing light across their white bed, on the last day they would wake alone as a couple in their apartment, each silently wondering what the day would bring.

Claire had found herself, as always, dreading the hospital itself, wishing she could stay home, have Michael pick her up and bring Miriam home, but she knew how this would look. If there was one thing she'd learned as his wife, it was how things would look.

A sadness had overtaken her then, as she thought back on the things Miriam had said about them while in treatment, about their lives, about their money and travel and rich nomad way of life. She'd never imagined she'd have a child who would grow to criticize her, to despise what she was. But then again, who did?

Her mother's voice returned to her as the morning sun filled the room.

"But then again, who does, dear?" her mother said, and Claire thought again of her own young desire to leave her parents' home, to go as soon as possible as far as possible with the first person who would take her.

It turned out that the first person was Michael. But what if it hadn't been? Who would she be now?

Maybe this was what Miriam was trying to figure out, too. Who she would be. On her own. And maybe, Claire admitted, the lack of a home to reject makes such a project almost impossible.

Besieged with too many emotions all at once, she decided to get up and start cleaning Miriam's room, which hadn't been entered in months.

She was ready to begin anew. She knew this. She knew that after cleaning all morning—from Miriam's room she would move on to the kitchen, and bathrooms, until she had cleaned the entire apartment—she would then go to the hospital with Michael, freshly showered, and smile, and forgive Miriam for what she had said about them, their wealth, and Michael's work.

"No, not forgive," her mother's voice had said.

Her mother was right. It was not about forgiveness. It was about listening. About hearing, and accepting that what a daughter can teach is as important as what a mother tries to make a daughter learn.

Claire knew that was why she was longing to get pregnant. So she could start over, not only for Miriam, but for herself, and for Michael, so they could stay in Ireland, let the child have a home all the way through its growing. Before leaving.

Her own great-grandmother had left Ireland for America, and perhaps if she hadn't, she and her daughter might never have lived, Claire thought, remembering the swollen bodies and hairy faces of the dead in the famine photos. Perhaps it was this that had put the desire in Claire, all these years, to run.

She'd felt it drain out of her, the desire for constant movement, last drop by drop, that day at the museum. She wanted, she'd realized, as Brigid had held her in the room filled with black and white photos and yellow afternoon light, to be like her. To know where she came from. She wanted to be able to go back and say, Here is where my people come from. And stay there. Even despite the pain.

She had never had that, a sense of home, in America. The last time Claire had visited Charleston, after her mother had died and Claire had gone, alone, to bury her, the city had nearly disappeared under strip malls and highways and chain bookstores.

Miriam was right; this was not a legacy.

The idea of a legacy had never meant anything to Claire. But now, as she lay in bed that Saturday morning after bringing Miriam home, she remembered the joy of the day before. They has all three had cooked a delicious meal together while listening to "The Carnival of Animals," Miriam's favorite music from childhood. And then they lit the Shabbat candles in the southern window at sunset as they sometimes did on special occasions. As they sat down to dinner that Friday night to celebrate their daughter's homecoming, Claire thought she might just be coming to understand what legacy might mean.

***

Michael stirred beside her.

"Is there enough milk for crêpes?" she asked him, knowing he'd been up in the night, eating cereal and fretting over missing work on Friday. There was a big meeting planned for Monday, and he'd missed the final meeting to go over preparations.

"Hmm?" he asked, half awake.

"I want to make crêpes," she said. "Like we used to. In Paris. Is there enough milk?"

"I think so," he mumbled, and rolled over.

"I'll get some if there isn't," she said, as she stood up.

At once her stomach lurched. She thought she might be sick. Then it faded.

So soon?

She'd heard morning sickness could be worse with subsequent pregnancies.

As she tied the knot around the waist of her robe, she remembered how the fullness of her breasts had been the first indication with Miriam.

She smiled to herself, wondering if there were enough milk. In the house. In her.

Perhaps soon there would be more than enough, she chuckled, as she got out the flour and sugar, butter and eggs.

Syrup? She searched the refrigerator, then the pantry. Damn.

Miriam came into the kitchen.

"What are you doing, Mom?"

Claire froze. It had been so long since hearing her voice, in their kitchen.

"Did I scare you?" Miriam asked, her long hair tied up in a knot at the back of her neck, her long beautiful neck bent slightly, in concern.

"No, sweetie, I was just…making crêpes. Or trying to. I can't find any syrup. It's been so long."

"We don't need syrup."

"We don't?" For a second, Claire worried that Miriam was going to say she wasn't hungry.

"No, see," Miriam said, confident, going to the refrigerator. "These raspberries will be delicious. We can add a bit of sugar to a few and make our own syrup, and then use the rest." She looked through the refrigerator again. "And look. Here's some ricotta cheese. That would make an excellent filling."

"Where did you learn all this?" asked Claire, beaming.

"In treatment. You know food is medicine. And there's really not enough protein in the crêpes as they are, and not enough fiber. You know, Mom, as a vegetarian, you really don't get enough protein, and you're looking kind of pale, so if we add the berries and the cheese, you'll have an excellent breakfast."

"Will I?" Claire asked, allowing Miriam to take over, allowing the possibility of a friendship growing between them. Everything was so different about her now.

"Sit down, mom. You don't look so good. I'll make everything. Oh, hi, Daddy," Miriam said, kissing Michael and ruffling her long fingers through his rumpled hair as he came into the room.

"And another thing. Before your coffee, Daddy, or your tea, Mom, you should have something smoother. Caffeine revs up your insulin production, which sets you up for a blood sugar roller coaster ride all day long."

Michael raised his eyebrows at Claire.

"I'll make a protein shake that we can all share."

"Oh..." Michael moaned.

"Come on, you'll like it."

Claire grinned. "I'm game," she said. "I'm all for what's new."

But even as it felt new, it also felt old. As if they were returning to something that very long ago had been lost, and only just now, after finding it, were they realizing how much they'd needed it to begin with.

NINE

Brigid woke early, long before dawn, and watched Padmaj sleeping. His hands were on top of the blanket, palms up, and he looked like he was doing the dead man's pose in yoga. She winced then in the dark when she thought of what he'd said when she asked him if he did yoga.

"What are you thinking? I am not some kind of Indian poster boy," he'd said teasingly, smiling.

"Do you go to Mass?" he'd asked then, with just a hint of edge to his voice.

"I'm sorry," she'd said, retreating into her shell.

"Wait," he said. "No, I'm sorry. I am only joking." He'd taken her face in his hands. "Do you know what yoga means?"

"Union?"

"Precisely," he'd smiled, pushing her over and kissing her. "Let us pray."

How little she knew about this man. How he surprised her with his smile and his laughter, the way he could take his soft hands and place them upon her and soften her. She felt herself resisting it, the sense that he could be trusted. She had never trusted anyone, not really.

There had been Mattie. She had come closest. She could still cry if she let herself remember the phone call she'd made in late January.

"I think I'm staying," she'd said over the crackling wires, after calling her own number and letting it ring for forty minutes before Mattie came over to pick it up.

"I've been giving the boys a bath!" Mattie laughed. "I had to get them out of the tub and let the water go down so they couldn't get back in and drown! I left them shivering in their robes over there! It's still snowing here. Can you believe it? You just about drove me crazy with all this ringing!"

"Mattie, I'm calling to tell you I'm staying."

Mattie was quiet. Then she asked, "Did you get things straight with your mama?"

"No."

"You see your dad?"

"No, but..."

"So you stay on then. Get what you need to get done."

Brigid imagined the hurt in Mattie's face. They'd been like mother and daughter for eight years, through all the babies, through her daughter-in-law's illness and death, through raising the boys together. It was like asking someone for a divorce over the phone.

Brigid wanted to tell her about Padmaj, but that would have been like admitting an affair.

"You still there, Brig?"

"I think you should call the BIA and ask for a new midwife," Brigid said, finally.

"Nonsense. I can take care of Grace's baby. And that's the only one. So far. You might be back in time for the next one."

"I don't know, Mattie."

"I'll pay this phone bill. To keep the phone working. You call me when you need me. Or when you know when you're coming back. Okay?"

She was not a woman to argue with.

"Okay. Tell everyone hi. And I miss them. And you. I miss you."

"Take care of yourself, girl."

"I'll try."

Take care of yourself, Brigid muttered to herself as she slipped quietly out of bed in the dark. I'm an unwed mother living on a tourist visa in my own land where my father is a fecking active terrorist agent. I'm taking some bloody good care of myself.

"You all right?" Padmaj whispered. She'd never before risen earlier than he had.

"Yes, I'm fine. Go back to sleep." And, thankfully, he did.

She dressed in the kitchen, drinking cold leftover tea and nan and running her fingers through her hair before writing Padmaj a note.

I can't tell you where I'm going, but I'll be back. I love you.

Everything she'd written was true.

She couldn't tell him where she was going because she didn't exactly know. Her first instinct was to go back to her mother's to see if her father were still there. Or to find out if her mother knew where he'd gone. After that, she didn't know. She just knew she had to see him one more time.

Second, she would be back.

Because, third, she did love him. She didn't know if she would keep this baby, she didn't even really know for sure if there was a baby, but every midwife's bone in her body told her it was so. The swollen breasts. The hunger. The sleepiness. Even the spotting, at the time when her period was due, which many women mistook for a light period. So while she knew she loved Padmaj, it remained to be seen whether she would love this baby. His baby.

She knew that his answer would be yes. Yes, she should keep the baby. Yes, he would love the baby. Yes, he loved her, too.

But that was why she had to go find her father. To be the kind of woman who was deserving of all this love.

***

She parked the car illegally in front of her mother's building and almost retched from the smell of the bar on the ground floor. They had only closed in the last hour or so, and the sidewalk was still wet with beer and the human waste that collects when people are gathering to forget their separate memories together.

"Mum," Brigid said quietly into the intercom after buzzing her mother's apartment. "It's me. Can you send the lift for me?" There was apology in her voice, from knowing she was waking her mother, and from knowing what she meant to do.

No answer came except the far away sound of the elevator heading down to the first floor.

Brigid could see from the elevator that her mother's apartment door was open, but the apartment was quiet. Two whiskey glasses still sat on the kitchen table, beside an overflowing ashtray, and her mother's robe was draped across one chair.

"Mum?" she called into the bedroom, her voice barely above a whisper.

"Shhh," her father hissed in her ear from behind. "She's still sleeping. What are you doing here at this hour? It's hardly even morning."

"Da!" Brigid jumped. "I didn't know you were here!"

"Didn't you?"

"No," she said as she looked down. She'd never been able to lie to her father.

"Isn't that why your mum called you? So you could turn me in?"

Her face flushed.

"Well, go ahead, girlie. Pick up the phone. I'll sit here and make my coffee while they're on their way."

"Da, I just want to talk to you."

"I had a lot of time for talking when I was sitting in the H block, rotting away, and you never came to see me then."

"Da, I was little…"

"You're not little now," he said, sucking on the short end of a cigarette and looking down across her body in a way that made her feel like the rubbish on the street outside.

"It's been a long time," she said, "but I came back. I came back to see you. Don't you remember? I was there when you were released. Didn't you *see* me?"

"'The double of my dream,'" he responded, and she knew he remembered.

She wanted to ask him why he walked away.

Instead she sat down, suddenly dizzy from the smoke and his closeness and the lingering smell of whiskey in the room.

He came over to her and reached out his left hand. It was white, and clean. She held her breath. He touched her hair. It was the first time in—how many years? Her mind was counting backwards, ten, fifteen, twenty. Was I fifteen or was I ten?

"'Nothing that we love over-much,'" he said to her, softly, "'Is ponderable to our touch.'"

She jumped up and ran to the kitchen sink where, through the window facing east, the sun had just snuck up above the horizon, its first rays hitting her eyes as she closed them upon the light, upon her retching. "What the feck is going on out here?" she heard her mother say from the kitchen doorway.

"That's what I'm trying to find out," her father said. "This one here takes it upon herself to visit at the rosy finger…"

Brigid retched again, a dry heave of nothing.

"Brigid Mary, are you drunk?" her mother said.

Brigid shook her head and wiped her mouth with the back of her hand, still facing the window, her eyes still closed.

"Brig, why are you here?" her mother asked, again.

As Brigid turned around and saw the blush of lovemaking still on her mother's cheeks, her father in his boxer shorts standing protectively close to her mother, one hand on her mother's shoulder while the other was lighting another cigarette. Her mother was avoiding both their eyes. Brigid knew then that her mother's phone call had been a mistake, made when she was too drunk to think clearly about what she truly wanted, or perhaps made before she'd gotten too drunk to forget about what was the right thing to do. Brigid knew she was truly alone.

She could not ask her father about his plans, nor hope that he might try to alter them. She could not ask her mother for more information, which she most certainly had been given, as proof that she was loved and trusted again, nor hope that her mother herself would turn him in.

She would have to do it herself.

"What's wrong?"

Claire was frozen, holding a wooden spoon, dripping with red sauce, in her hand.

"Sweetheart, are you okay?" Michael asked again, taking the spoon from her and laying it on the small blue Moroccan bowl near the stove that served as a spoon rest. She remembered, as he did so, how he would take Miriam from her and lay her in her cradle, gently, like that, after the baby had fallen asleep in Claire's arms in the rocking chair, and then guide Claire slowly back to bed.

"I think my period's starting," she whispered.

"Oh honey," he said, and put his arms around her, gently.

"No," she said. She didn't want to be comforted.

"Are you in pain?"

Claire nodded. "I'll go get some pills."

"Do you want me to cancel dinner?"

"No," she said again. "I'll just lie down for a while until they arrive."

"Do you want me to do anything?" Michael asked, trying to be helpful, looking at the countertops covered with a huge pan of lasagna, bowls of asparagus and salad, and two of her now famous Kentucky bourbon pies.

"Just put the lasagna in the oven and wake me when they come."

Claire went into the bathroom and inserted a tampon, changed her underwear, and took two pain pills. The effect would numb her cramps and also give her the faraway feeling that she longed to have.

She cried then because she was definitely, unmistakably bleeding.

Her period had only been three days late, but she had felt so sure.

She really had wanted a baby.

She had fantasized about Brigid being the midwife, sharing the experience with her, becoming closer in the process.

There was a knock on the bathroom door.

"Mom," Miriam said softly. "Are you okay?"

Claire opened the door.

"Yes, sweetie." She looked into her daughter's worried eyes, recalled her vow to be more honest, to reflect back to Miriam the sense of responsibility that she'd learned during her daughter's illness. "Well, no." They moved to sit on the bed, covered in a soft white down comforter.

"I was hoping I was pregnant," Claire confessed.

"Oh, Mom." Miriam hugged her. "I didn't know."

Claire felt the tears falling again.

"Did you know," Claire asked her, "that I used to cry when my period came and I was trying to get pregnant with you?"

"You did? I didn't know that."

"I did. And I was feeling… I don't know. The same kind of presence, maybe, that I felt before you came. As if you were waiting for me, and I was failing you."

"Oh, Mom."

"Is that crazy?"

Miriam smiled, her dark eyes sparkling. "You're asking *me* what's crazy?"

They laughed together then, in the way they used to, when Miriam was a girl, and then Miriam tucked her mother into bed, as Claire used to do, kissing her on the nose and saying, "Curl up quiet, honey, sleep like a bunny, and wake in the morn like a rose."

***

Claire woke in a darkened room to sounds of Miriam greeting Brigid and Padmaj in the living room, and Michael filling drink orders in the kitchen, but she did not move.

She was suddenly remembering something Brigid had told her on their way out of the concert on Thursday night.

Michael had gone backstage to see Miriam, and Claire and Brigid had gone to the restroom, and from her stall Claire had been bubbling over about the concert and their plans to go to Galway.

"I wanted to go right away, but Michael has this important meeting out of town next week, which he can't miss."

"Where?" Brigid had asked.

"Belfast."

"Where?"

"Belfast, I told you."

"But where?" They were washing their hands now, and Brigid's face was getting flushed.

"I don't know exactly where. Why are you getting so upset?"

Brigid had not answered.

"Sweetie," Michael rapped on the bedroom door. "Padmaj and Brigid are here."

Claire stood up to wash her hands and wipe her mascara with a tissue while calling, "I'll be right there."

She wanted to take Brigid aside, tell her about the bleeding and her sadness and ask her about that weird conversation after the concert. But when she entered the living room, Miriam was lifting her bow to play. Padmaj and Michael were settled on each end of the couch. Brigid was in the leather chair by the window. They were all sitting so attentively and fire was blazing so sweetly that Claire simply smiled and sat on the couch between the two men as Miriam began to play.

It was the final movement from her concert—the part about the sea between the worlds—the womb, the separation of one generation from the next, what keeps us from each other and makes life possible at the same time.

Claire began to cry again, and then Brigid did, too. Padmaj was looking into the fire in the way that men do when they are in the presence of others but would rather be alone.

Michael's mind was on work. He was leaving early in the morning and he wished that the three of them could have had a nice dinner, quiet, before he left for the meeting. He really had too much on his mind to be the only clear thinking one in the room.

Except for Miriam. She was so clear she was shining. The bow, back and forth, as if it were spanning the exhausting space between the continents, between the old world and the new. She was so beautiful. The best thing he'd ever done. Besides marry her mother. They were his two best things.

"Honey, that was just beautiful," he said, when the piece came to a close. The others were silent. "I can hear it in a totally different way when you play it as a soloist."

"Thank you, Daddy," Miriam said.

"The concert must have been spectacular," said Padmaj.

"It was," Claire said, smiling, wiping her eyes.

"Thank you all," Miriam said, putting the instrument away, a bit nervous from the strange silence of one dinner guest.

Padmaj tried to bring Brigid into the conversation. "Brigid told me it was—what was the word you used?—rememberable?"

Miriam laughed, not at Padmaj, but at the word. "That's perfect! That's exactly it! It's about the ability to remember!"

"I don't know if I am using the correct word," he said.

"It doesn't matter. We know exactly what you mean," Claire said and took his hand. "Come on, let's go eat." She led the men into the dining room, leaving Brigid and Miriam alone in the firelight.

Brigid said, very quietly, "You are a gifted composer."

"Thank you."

"No, I'm not just being polite. I mean it." There were still tears in Brigid's eyes. "You have captured something about Ireland. The way it is like a mother who has spread herself too thin, scattered her children all over in the hopes of placing them in better homes than she could provide."

"Thank you," Miriam said again. "It means a lot to me that you think so. My mom thinks so much of you."

"You're lucky to have such a mum."

"I know. I mean, I'm learning that more and more each day."

"Why is she so sad tonight?" Brigid asked, quietly.

"She got her period."

"Oh."

"Come on, you two," Claire called. "Time to eat."

No one was very hungry, but they did their best to have small portions of each delicious dish.

And since none of them really wanted to talk about what was on their minds—Claire and the ghost of a baby, Michael and the meeting, Miriam and her lack of hunger, Brigid and her father, Padmaj and Brigid's silence—they all spoke about the meal.

"What is in the lasagna, Claire? That spice, what is it?" Padmaj asked.

"My secret ingredient. Nutmeg," Claire smiled. "I add it to the ricotta."

"Fabulous."

"Mmm, yes," the others agreed.

Finally, after everyone had had a piece of the pie and coffee and dinner drinks had been poured, Miriam excused herself, saying she had homework. Claire said to Brigid, "Why don't you come help me with the dishes and the men can go sit in the living room?"

Once alone in the kitchen, the two women embraced.

Claire wanted Brigid to tell her she would get pregnant again, soon, that it wasn't too late, and Brigid knew what Claire wanted to hear.

"It's all right," Brigid said. "It's not too late. Don't worry. You're a wonderful mother. I'm sure there's a baby hovering nearby, just dreaming of being your child."

"You think so?"

"I am certain of it."

And Claire believed her.

ELEVEN

Padmaj couldn't help but notice that Brigid had not been herself all evening; she'd not had anything to drink, nor said anything much at all.

"Are you feeling okay?" he asked her, putting his hand on her knee in the car on the way home. "Ever since..." he began to say, but did not want to pry, and began again. "For some time now, you've been distracted."

"I know," she said. "I guess I'm sick."

"Sick?"

"I don't know. Maybe."

She was not answering the question, and he knew it, so he let her be. He feared that all of this had something to do with her father, but he also feared that, if pressed, she would retreat further. Even leave. And so he left her alone.

***

Alone. And lost. Brigid was lost in memory. One long memory that was her life, dozens of images from across decades, some from before she was even born, a messy deck of cards being shuffled in her mind as she prepared to deal the next hand.

Her sister Terri as a teenager, coming to Brigid's little flat, with her long brown hair matted against her head and her eyes red. "Brig, I'm hearing voices. What am I going to do?" Terri had held her palms up for Brigid to see, as if the answer could be read there by clearer eyes.

"Don't go getting yourself knocked up, whatever you do," their mother's voice telling them across the kitchen table in Dublin, as they were reaching puberty. "What happened to me don't have to happen to the lot of you, making your life miserable like mine." She held the empty glass up in her right hand. "Pour me another, would you, Terri?" she said to Brigid's sister, shaking the ice cubes.

Brigid and her sister in bed at night, still in their house in Miltown Malbay, their father at the doorway, as they whispered a Hail Mary under the covers to keep him away.

"Nobody'll love you the way I love you," her father's voice, from under the sheets, as she stared at the ceiling, repeating to herself, "Full of grace, full of grace, the Lord is with thee."

"Blessed is the fruit of thy womb," the nuns chanted at the end of the chapel rows, each Wednesday, while Brigid stared at her hands on the wooden pew in front of her.

Her sister's hands, begging to surrender.
Her mother's hands, begging to forget.
Her father's hands, begging to enter.
Her own hands, begging to be blessed.

***

"Stop the car," she said to Padmaj.
He did.
"Do you remember what I told you about my father? About my father and my sister and me?"
He nodded.
"No one knows that."
He nodded again.
"You must never tell anyone."
He stopped nodding.
"You must promise."
He breathed in, held it.
"Please," she begged.
He sighed, nodding. "I will promise—"
"Wait. There's more. Do you know where I went when I took the car yesterday?"
"No, but—"
"Hush. You don't know. I never told you. You don't know."
He tried to see the light in her eyes, but they were dark.
"You don't know anything," she said, through clenched teeth. "You must promise me."
"Are you in trouble, my love?" He was on the verge of tears.
"Whatever you say, say nothing."
"Nothing?"
"Say nothing."
"Nothing."
She took a deep breath, blew out. "Okay." She looked through the passenger window at the rain. A plan was taking shape in her mind. This was not hard. Now that she had begun, she was not as afraid as she feared she would be.
But she could not tell Padmaj more than he already knew. She did not want to make trouble for him.
It was for this reason that she knew she would be leaving. To save him from trouble.
This was why she had made him promise to be silent. The less he told, the better. The less he knew, the better still.
This was why she did not tell him she was leaving.

***

But he knew.

He knew as she showered before bed and he lit the candle in front of the altar and prayed for her safety.

He knew as they made love for the last time and she cried, and he wiped her tears with his soft hands, and held her.

He knew as she lay in bed next to him, waiting for his breathing to deepen, signaling that he had fallen asleep.

He knew as he woke to hear her gathering a few things in the dark before she tiptoed to the front door.

He knew as he saw the moon, still hanging in the pale blue frame of their western window, in the dawn's light.

He knew.

She was gone.

TWELVE

Claire was dreaming, a deep dream of the high green of her childhood summers that she missed and the low white of her college winters that she escaped and the smooth yellow of her early married days in Morocco, when the sun and the heat of her husband's body were like one hot thing, melted together, meant for her pleasure.

***

Michael was on the morning train to Belfast, looking through his notes for the meeting, when an image of Claire's body, young again, in the Moroccan desert light, came to him, and he adjusted himself in the seat, suddenly filled with desire for her.

***

Claire had been up most of the night, feeling too warm and restless, but now, after Miriam and Michael had kissed her goodbye at dawn, she was back in bed sleeping soundly and did not see the bright morning light coming in through the window. Instead in her dream the light and heat of the sun's rays became a flaming sword that hit her eyes, and she tossed and tried to avoid it, but it bounced and came to meet her on the other side.

"Oh," she cried out loud, to the empty apartment.

***

Michael thought he heard her cry and turned around, instinctively, even though he was miles and miles away on a street in Belfast, on his way from the train station to his meeting.

He stood, on the sidewalk, in his favorite blue suit, the one Claire had told him to wear for good luck, and wished that he had been kinder to her the night before. He had been relieved when her period arrived; he thought they should take some time to focus on Miriam before trying to have another child, which he wasn't exactly against, just wary of rushing into too soon.

***

Padmaj came rushing into Claire's dream, saying, "Come to Kashmir, don't stay on that side of the fence," as he tried to help her climb the barbed wire fence in between them. Behind her a dragon breathed wands of fire.

In her fear she kicked Padmaj in the mouth, and he began to bleed.

***

As Michael approached the bank building, he saw a man in a brown suit whose face reminded him of Brigid's.

The man approached him. He was bleeding, near his mouth, as if he had just recently shaved, too quickly, and cut himself.

"Matthew," he said.

"My name's not Matthew," Michael said, and walked away.

***

"My name's not Matthew!" Claire heard in her dream. Michael was yelling it, from the other side of the fence, where he stood with Padmaj.

"My name's not Matthew! My name's not Matthew!"

And Miriam was there suddenly, between Padmaj and Michael, and she was thin again, saying, "Mommy, I'm not hungry."

Claire's legs were bleeding from having been cut by the barbed wire, and red liquid was running down her thighs.

"Take, and eat, for this is the body of Christ," a voice said from above, and she fell.

***

Just before Michael opened the door to the executive meeting room in the bank, he had a sudden sensation of heat in his hands.

It was as if the room were on fire inside, and he knew better than to touch the metal doorknob.

***

Claire was falling, falling, and the fence was falling away in front of her eyes, the wires coming together in the form of millions of the letter H. Miriam was a child again, and Claire was teaching her letters. Teaching her to read.

"What starts with H?"

Home.

History.

Hunger.

Heaven.
Heart.

***

Michael heard the explosion just as the bank president stood to open his mouth to greet him, so that for a second it was as if the noise had come from the mouth of the man himself, and Michael thought, How did he come to have such a loud voice?

***

And before Claire woke, the millions of tiny letters piled upon each other to become one gigantic H, a dolmen of four huge stones with one balanced between, standing still and solid for millennia, what will not topple, will not fall, even as kingdoms do, even as governments do, even as people do.
Everything.
Falls.

***

The blast made Michael fall to his knees, and then on his hands, but he felt nothing, he only stared at his hands, and they were so small, suddenly, and too finely made, delicate and fragile, like a spider's web, which could be blown away in the wind.

***

Claire woke to the sound of her daughter's voice, calling, "Mother!" as she entered the room.
Claire stared at her, still partly in the dream, and then looked at the clock—almost noon. She wondered what Miriam was doing home from school, and then noticed that Miriam was crying.
"Where's Daddy?" Miriam wept.
Claire's dream rose before her and she could not breathe.
She did not know what to say to the girl.
She knew.
He was gone.

THIRTEEN

Brigid's departure did not alter Padmaj's morning routine, except that as he showered, as he lit the candle at the altar, as he drove into the city, as he unlocked the front door to the restaurant, his mind was walking in circles through a forest, noisy with dripping leaves after a rainstorm but absent of animal life.

The trees had been his mothers, his comfort, all his life. And now, in Ireland, this land where wild trees had first been destroyed by invaders and then later replanted in gardens by them, he needed the trees of his childhood to accompany him on this walk.

At the top of each loop, he asked the question, would she be back. And as he headed down the eastern side, the hidden morning sun would answer no, no, no. And at the bottom of the circle, he would nod and say, yes, I know, for he never really expected her to stay. He had hoped, but hope is a delicate thing, as that hermit poet knew.

As, in his mind, he started back up toward the top of the wheel he was walking, he allowed himself to hope, just briefly, and the hope became a brook, and he let it flow, despite what the hermit poet had warned about rushing brooks, so that by the time he was starting the circle again, he was also arriving at the question again, would she be back, and then he was off, going around and around again.

He did this as he boiled the water for tea and peeled the eggplants for baigan bharta and set out the water glasses, two for every table. He did this as he paid bills and greeted a few early customers. He saw no reason to stop the wandering in his mind as long as he could attend to his daily routine, and so he let the aching in his heart play itself out like a mantra.

The early customers ate and left, and the restaurant, Padmaj suddenly realized, was completely empty in the middle of lunch hour. Just as he was thinking this thought, a customer came in, a middle aged professor from Trinity, and said, "Isn't it awful?" and the loop in Padmaj's mind stopped dead.

For a second, Padmaj wondered if he meant the emptiness of the restaurant.

"What do you mean?" he asked.

"The bombings. Haven't you heard?"

And while Padmaj wanted to know more, wanted to shake his head and say, no, I haven't heard, tell me, he couldn't, for the path he had been circling all morning suddenly disappeared and he realized that she was not coming back.

What this man was telling him, he knew, meant that she would not be back.

"I have not heard," said Padmaj, slowly, carefully, afraid he would reveal the awful grief that had begun within him.

"There's been a bombing in Belfast, and another, moments later, in Jerusalem. The IRA and PLO are thought to have planned them together. Both took place in banks where meetings about the..."

"Banks?" Padmaj interrupted.

"Yes."

"Were people hurt?"

"Many, yes. Killed."

Padmaj understood then that Brigid must have known about this. He had suspected it the night before, with her phone call and her making him swear to secrecy, but he had not pressed her, he had not allowed himself to imagine that she might actually know something specific.

"Are you okay?" the customer was saying, but Padmaj could not hear him, for there was a ringing, an insistent ringing, and then someone was calling his name.

"Sir?" the customer was saying, "Do you want to answer the phone?"

Padmaj turned his head toward the phone and saw the cook waving to him in the doorway to the kitchen, saying in Urdu, "Padmaj! Padmaj! The phone is ringing!" and as Padmaj walked slowly to the phone, the customer said, "I'll be back another day," and the cook retreated, muttering to himself, and so Padmaj was alone when, through the popping of wires, he heard his mother's voice for the first time in months.

"Hello? Padmaj? Dear? Can you hear me?"

"Yes, Mama. I am here." He began to weep.

"Bhabha?" she called him, by his childhood name. "Are you all right? We've been listening to the news reports all day."

"Mama, I'm..."

"It is so good to hear your voice. I couldn't get through for a very long time."

"Ma...."

"Oh dear, Bhabha. Tell me. What is wrong?"

"I don't know." It occurred to him that Brigid had made the phone call from the phone booth for a reason.

"I am fine," he said, all at once recovering a sense of clarity. "I am. Do not worry. Belfast is far, far away from here. I am not hurt."

"But someone you know?" she asked, with a mother's perception.

"I do not know."

"You must find out."

"Yes, I will."

"And then come home."

The suggestion would have struck him as absurd five years ago, one year ago, certainly one month ago when Brigid was there with him, even a day ago, an hour ago, but now, it seemed right. He had saved enough money to keep up the payments rent on his house and the restaurant, and even to pay the cook and the two waiters for a while.

And while up until that moment, racism had been a low kind of humming in the background as immigrants trickled in to the country, terrorist attacks always heightened people's fears of newcomers, which meant that the hum would soon rise to a scream.

"Do not worry, Mama. I will come home."

"Oh, I am so glad, Bhabha! Wait till I tell Auntie and Uncle!"

"I need a few days. I have a friend here. Her husband may have been hurt," he found himself blurting because his mother's joy built a bubble around him that made him feel, for an instant, safe.

"Oh, Padmaj," she said.

"I cannot say anything more now. I will call you when I get to the Delhi airport."

"Don't you want me to have Uncle Niren pick you up?"

"No. Don't worry. I will see you soon."

"Be careful, Bhabha."

"I will, Mama. I love you."

"I love you, too."

FOURTEEN

Claire and Miriam sat stunned in front of the television like the rest of the world, and at first it was a comfort, the sense that one could be there without leaving the safety of home, but after a while, the endless looping of the same video footage and the same text read by the same announcers, over and over, began to take on a surreal aspect, as if they were not really real, the television was not real, they were all pieces in some large chess game that had gotten stuck repeating the same play, over and over.

"That's enough," Claire said, standing up and turning off the television with the remote. "We've got to find out something," she said and then it occurred to her that she could try Michael's cell phone number. She went to the kitchen to dial, her numbers tracing the pattern automatically as they had so many times before, but instead of a ring, she heard a high pitched tone and then a recording, "This line is inoperable. Please try back later or contact your service representative for more information."

"What's it saying, Mom?" Miriam asked.

Claire held the phone at arm's length but did not let go, as she used to do when Miriam was a toddler in the midst of a tantrum, kicking and biting but needing not to be abandoned.

"It says the phone's not working."

"Oh, Mom," Miriam cried.

Claire took her into her arms. "Honey, shh, it doesn't mean anything. Come on. Come on. Let's sit down."

As they went to sit at the kitchen table, the phone, still in Claire's hand, rang out, and she jumped.

"Hello?" Her heart filled with hope. Let it be him, let it be him, her mind chanted like a mantra.

"Mrs. Levin?" It was someone who knew Michael.

"Yes?"

"This is Fred Prescott, at the bank."

"Yes?"

"I'm sorry to tell you this, but we've just gotten word. You need to come down to the bank."

"I don't think I can do that." Claire was being absolutely honest, as if all the layers of appearance had finally been peeled away and she was suddenly a raw, skinless self.

"Well, then," the voice said. "Well, then, I will come to you. What is your address?"

"17 Bachelor's Walk."

The irony of the name of the street rendered the caller silent. He struggled for something to say. "Why, you're just across the bridge."

"Yes, Michael chose it so he could be close to home," Claire said.

The voice found this disconcerting. "I'll be right there," he said.

***

Claire wondered, as she put on a light green linen dress and sandals and ran a brush through her hair to get ready for the man from the bank, why she was feeling so calm. It was as if her mind were out somewhere, perhaps beside a round blue lake that reflected a clear, clear sky, and she could simply sit on the edge and hear nothing, feel nothing, say nothing, as if she were simply part of the surface of the world and had nothing at all to do with the muddiness of what lay below.

"Who was it, Mommy?" Miriam interrupted her, as she was brushing her hair.

"A man from daddy's bank. He's on his way over."

"Oh, no."

"Here, here. Come here," she said, and she wrapped her arms around the girl, taking comfort in the touch, as the skin that touched her daughter became soft warm parts that were earnestly wishing this were not happening while the rest of her stayed hard and clear knowing it most certainly was.

The doorbell rang and Claire loosened herself from Miriam, becoming wholly cold again, and let the visitor in.

Claire remembered his face from a cocktail party and wondered why he had been chosen for this task. She would learn later that all of the top executives had been killed in the blast.

"I am sorry to tell you, Mrs. Levin," he began, and she floated away, he was not even using her name, he did not even know her well enough to know her name, and here he was, telling her that her husband was, as she already well knew, she had almost seen it herself, she knew he was, yes, that was the word he had used, dead.

Miriam began to cry again and Claire put her arm around her.

"If there's anything I can do. Or the bank can do," he was saying.

"Can you bring him back?" Claire said, in a strong voice.

The man was startled. He was a bachelor, could only imagine what she was going through, no, not even that, not even imagine, he could not imagine—

"No," he said.

"Well, then, thank you for coming," Claire said, trying very hard to be polite. "Excuse me if I don't see you out."

"Yes, of course," he said, and backed away, as one would leave a bomb that might at any moment go off.

***

Later, when Claire had lain next to Miriam in her bedroom, and had rubbed the sobbing girl's back until she fell asleep, the pillow wet with tears, Claire went to the large window in the living room overlooking the River Liffey where the sun was in its afternoon descent.

Fred Prescott had said, ducking his head back in the door, that the bank would be arranging a memorial service, which would take place on Wednesday morning, and if she had any requests, songs or readings or speakers or such, she could call him at the bank.

Claire knew, somewhere deep within, that there was a small gray ball of pain, the size of a pin now, but growing. It would be an orange by morning. By the time of the memorial service, it would be a boulder, almost too heavy to carry, and soon, it would knock her over and she would not get up, not for a long, long while.

She would have to have someone to help her when this happened.

But there was no one to call. Michael's parents were both dead. Her own mother was dead. Her father was in a nursing home, and, most days, did not remember her except as she was at eight, reciting poems after dinner.

Poems.

As the sun hit the horizon in the west, she realized that Brigid's father... She did not let herself finish the thought.

Padmaj.

Claire could call him. He would come.

This thought wound itself, like the soft woolen yarn her grandmother used to make socks and sweaters, around the solid ball within her and held it, warm and tight in the twilight.

Miriam cried out in her sleep as the phone rang again, and as Claire rushed back to the darkened kitchen to answer it, she heard the words in her head, from farther away now, Let it be him, Let it be him, and the clear part of her supposed that it would be a long time before they would become too far away to hear.

"Claire?"

"Yes?"

"It's Padmaj."

"I was just..."

"Do you want me to come over?"

"Yes."

"I am coming."

Claire put the phone down carefully, as if it might split apart and break. She wrote a note for Miriam, then went to the girl's bedroom, taped the note to the inside of the door, and closed it. With a mother's perception, she knew Miriam would not wake until morning.

Claire went to the closet, got a dark green jacket, and went down to wait.

FIFTEEN

After saying goodbye to his mother, Padmaj sat down in a chair at one of the tables in the empty restaurant and felt as if he could not move.

The sense of loneliness, which had begun with his father when he was young, and which had been growing, ever since leaving his mother, and his motherland—this unease which had started to recede when Brigid first arrived, had now returned full force. Once again, he found himself feeling as if he were standing on sea, not land, as if the earth underneath him had been washed away, as if everything were constantly changing and shifting underfoot.

He remembered how he had the sense that Claire, too, lived on water, the first time he had seen her. And like him, she, too, used language to stay afloat across continents. And then last night—was it only last night, he asked himself, for the day already seemed to have lasted a thousand years, yes, it was only last night—as Miriam played the cello piece, how it put him in mind again of water, of the groundlessness of moving from one place to another, as he had ever since he left his mother.

He sat there in the middle of the empty restaurant, thinking of this, for a long time, until finally the cook came and asked him what was wrong, and why there weren't any customers today.

Padmaj could not speak. He felt that he might say something, even in speaking to this dear old man who was from his own land, who spoke in his own father's tongue, that might betray Brigid. So he shook his head.

"That call was from my mother. She is sick," he lied. "She wants me to come home."

The cook was very sympathetic, which made Padmaj feel guilty for having lied to him.

"I will be going to India. I will pay you and the others while I am gone, but the restaurant will be closed. Today. I am closing it today."

Padmaj was grateful that there were no customers, for he suddenly felt the need to flee.

"Now," he said. "I must go now."

The cook offered to freeze the dishes that he was preparing, but Padmaj felt nervous.

"Here, take the keys. Lock up. Straight away. I must go." And he left.

***

His house, upon entering, echoed as it used to do before Brigid's presence. He walked to the kitchen. It was long past lunchtime but he had not eaten. He opened the refrigerator and stared. He was not hungry. He walked to the bathroom. The towel Brigid used the night before was still hanging there, slightly damp, and he put his face into it, hoping that her smell might remain.

He was standing like this, his face in a damp green towel, when the image of Claire came to him. He needed to reach her. He needed to find out what had happened, to Michael, to her, to see if she needed help, if she wanted him to be with her.

They were both alone now, he knew this.

He went to the kitchen and dialed the number Brigid had written on a piece of paper taped to the wall.

***

"Claire?"

"Yes?"

"It's Padmaj."

"I was just…"

"Do you want me to come over?" he blurted. The thought again that Brigid had made her phone call from the public phone, not from home, not from the restaurant, came back to him. He did not want her to say anything more on the phone.

"Yes," she said. Her voice sounded like crushed glass. Like something broken.

"I am coming." He hung up.

He was standing on the front step, about to lock the door, when the phone rang again.

He rushed back to the kitchen, and in his mind he found himself hoping it was her, saying Brigid, Brigid, Brigid, with each step he took, but in his heart, which was pounding, he discovered he was also holding Claire, and their two names merged in the middle and became a deep sound, like a gong he heard once in a temple dedicated to Kali, clagong, clagong.

Padmaj answered the phone. "Hullo?"

"Padmaj, what is going on?" said the cook, in Urdu, through the phone, breathless.

"What do you mean?"

"Some Irish thugs were just here, tearing the place up, looking for you. They wanted to know where you were. I told them you were going to see your mother, who was sick. They were very upset. Padmaj, what is happening?"

160

Before Padmaj could answer, there was a loud knock on the door.

"Thank you for calling," he said in a soft voice. "Goodbye."

The knocking at the door continued, insistently.

"I am coming," he called.

Two detectives were there, at the door, and more, uniformed guardai, were in back, near several cars, lining the street.

"Padmaj Devi?" the tallest officer asked.

"Yes?" he said, trying to smile.

"We have a few questions we want to ask you. Do you mind coming with us?"

"Not at all," he said, politely, and for a moment, he was simply a waiter again, a gracious and kind immigrant whose only wish was to serve delicious food, to make people feel satisfied and happy. Not a suspect in an international terrorist plot which had killed two hundred and thirty-two people in Belfast and six hundred and seven in Jerusalem and injured thousands. Not a foreigner with ties to an ex-convict who was now missing and wanted, dead or alive.

SIXTEEN

Claire paced back and forth on the sidewalk in front of her apartment, wrapping her green jacket tightly around her, as the temperature dropped and sky over the Liffey's source eventually lost all its pink. It was not until it was completely dark and she could no longer feel her feet, as if she were walking on stumps, that she had to give up waiting.

Walking back into her apartment, she was struck by the quiet. Waiting for Padmaj had given her something to do, something to look forward to, and now that this was gone, she was finally, eight hours after knowing that Michael was dead, allowing the feeling to seep into her heart.

Tears fell silently at first, and then when she reached the apartment, she let out a wail and ran to her bed, still unmade since the morning, and curled into a ball under the white covers and wept.

All night long, she imagined Michael's warm skin next to her, the smell of his body, the sound of his voice. She patted the emptiness of the half of the bed where he never again would be, where she would never touch or smell or taste or hear him again. Tears fell and she rubbed the wetness into the sheets and pretended it was him.

It was into this damp pool of warm sheets that Miriam crawled, at daybreak, saying, "Mommy," and they held each other while the sun rose over the Liffey.

***

At first Miriam and Claire had stayed in the bed, the way they had when Miriam was a newborn, neither of them eating, not wanting to leave the warmth of the other's presence, sleeping day and night, losing all sense of time, sometimes looking into each other's eyes, sometimes watching the other sleep, sometimes crying together, sometimes, so as not to wake the other, crying quietly, alone.

But before dawn on Wednesday, Claire slipped out of bed and gotten into the shower and felt, for the first time, a bit of hunger.

She was defrosting a bagel in the microwave and making tea when Miriam walked in to the kitchen.

"Mom," Miriam said. She reminded Claire of a toddler, just beginning to walk and talk.

"Yes, honey?"

"I've been thinking."

"Yes?"

"I think, today, after the service, I'm going to go back into the hospital."

Claire did not move. The microwave beeped.

Miriam continued. "I've been hearing that voice again."

The doctor had explained this to Claire, that anorexia was connected, perhaps, to other dissociative disorders, where, in certain advanced stages, the person heard voices and felt controlled by them.

Claire nodded, not wanting to break Miriam's trust by speaking.

"The doctor said that if this happened, I should go back."

Claire continued to nod. She did not want the girl to leave. She was all she had. But she knew this was exactly why Miriam needed to go.

Claire made herself smile. "I'm proud of you, honey. I think you're making the right decision." It was what Michael would have wanted her to say.

The tea kettle started to whistle.

"Do you want tea?" Claire asked.

Miriam shook her head. "I think I'll make myself a protein shake."

Claire smiled again. She could tell Miriam was not hungry, and she knew that these protein shakes were a way of trying to start the day off right. For a moment she had the sensation that Michael was in the room with them.

"You're a good mother," she heard him say. "Look how she takes care of herself, even when she's in great pain."

"I don't know," Claire whispered to him as she dipped her tea bag in and out of the steaming water. "I don't know how I'm going to do this without you."

***

Wednesday was the first really warm spring day. Miriam wore a blue dress with small white flowers that Michael had bought her for the concert only the week before. Already it fit her more loosely than it had then, Claire noticed as she watched Miriam blowing her hair dry in the bathroom.

After her shower, Claire went to the closet to get the black dress that Michael had given her for her last birthday, but she found that her hands were suddenly shaking so hard that she accidentally ripped the dress in the back, near the neck.

***

To mend it, she went to look for a safety pin in her desk drawer, and there, she also found, by chance, the note Michael had written when he gave her the dress.

"40 is sexy."

This she folded and tucked into her bra, imagining that he would smile at that, from wherever he was.

Neither Claire nor Miriam cried during the memorial service. It was a very public affair, with television cameras and heads of state and hundreds of people they had never met before. They sat in the cathedral—Claire was struck by the irony of it, having it in a Catholic cathedral—holding hands and not moving. A cameraman even got a close-up shot of their hands, which appeared around the world on that evening's news.

When it was over, they walked out together, nodding silently to whomever spoke to them, and then embracing each other, on the sidewalk, under the bright blue Irish sky.

Miriam would walk to the hospital now; it had been arranged that morning. She would go alone. She knew how Claire hated hospitals, and she knew her mother could not face one alone, without her father. Claire had promised to call every morning. It would give them both a reason to get out of bed.

As Claire watched Miriam walk away, the white flowers fading on the dark blue dress as she made her way down the street, she saw her pass someone, about a block and a half away, and pause, and speak, and then keep walking.

The man looked toward Claire then, and lifted one hand, in a tentative wave.

It was Padmaj.

Claire had the impression that he was afraid and would come no closer, so she started walking toward him.

As she approached him, her mind registered several things at once: he seemed pale, he had a huge gash from his lip to his left ear, and there were tears in his eyes.

"My Poet lady," he said, his voice cracking, as she let herself fall into his open arms.

The muscles of his back were smooth, different than she was used to, and the difference underlined her grief for Michael and her need for Padmaj's comfort.

"I am so sorry, so sorry," he said.

"Where were you?" she said, quietly, into his chest. "What happened to you?"

"My Claire," he said, shaking his head and stroking her hair gently back from her face as he looked into her eyes. "I did not want to leave you like that, my Claire, my Claire," he repeated. "I am sorry. I am here now. I am here."

She clung to him, and he did not back away.

Finally, she said, "Take me away," and he did.

SEVENTEEN

They sat together in his car, with the motor running, both looking forward on the one-way Dublin street, not speaking.

Padmaj guessed that Claire did not want to go back to her apartment, without Miriam there, without Michael.

But he could not imagine taking her back to his house. He had not been back since they had come to question him, and he knew that it would be disheveled from their search. They had told him that they had found Brigid's things there, and they had brought the items before him as evidence, making him hold them as they beat him, as they tried to get him to say where she was, what she knew, what he knew.

Two of his ribs and his cheekbone had been broken.

He had, as he had promised, said nothing.

***

"Where should we go, my lady?" he said to Claire, finally.

Her lips curved into a slight smile. She wanted so badly to touch his cheek, to know what had happened, to know where Brigid was, where he had been, but she said nothing.

"Head west," she said, and he did.

***

They drove without speaking for hours, following the sun's course. The entire day passed like this, each of them lost in their own thoughts of what they were missing, what the other had lost, as they aimed toward the westernmost edge of the country. At one point in the afternoon, they came to an intersection of three roads where a train was crossing. The road they had been on was ending, and they had to make a decision. If they went south, they would go to County Clare. North would bring them into County Galway.

Padmaj looked at Claire, and he reached out and took her hand as the train receded into the distance.

"Galway," she whispered, looking away, and he headed in that direction.

***

He kept going as far as the road would take him. He would have taken her to America, if he could have. Instead they stopped at the westernmost point of the island, the closest one could get to America in all of Europe. The region was called Connemara, and it was the land where Claire's great-grandmother had been born.

The road literally ended at a cliff. Padmaj turned off the motor.

Claire opened the door and stepped out. He followed. They walked to the edge. Only a mile behind them was a white cascade where the salmon leapt on their way to spawn, and in front of them, there was the great green sea, and sinking into that sea, the golden sun.

For a moment he had the impression that she was going to jump, so he pulled her toward him. It was the third time he had ever moved to touch her. The first had been that night in her apartment, the night before the bombing. The second had been that morning, as she cried in his arms on the crowded Dublin street. And now this.

The evening wind blew her hair into her face, and he reached to gather it and hold it back. He wanted to see the deep blue of her eyes, which matched the color of the spring flowers on the cliffside behind her.

He was looking through her like this, at the tears falling from the blue of her eyes and the flowers behind, as he leaned closer and kissed her, his eyes open.

His lips were soft and full. She pressed herself against him, afraid that if he let go, she would fall into the water. Rocking like the waves against the shore, what she felt there, against his younger, smoother body, was safe and warm, a temporary home on the water. She moved her whole body closer to it.

***

As night fell across the western shore, the waterfall in the distance behind them glowed in bright starlight and the two of them fell against the damp rock, holding tight to each other, murmuring, sometimes tasting the salty spray of the water as the wind turned, sometimes tasting each other's tears, as his legs met the memory of blood on her legs, as her face met the memory of blood on his face, and wet, in the dark, their bodies merged, skin to skin, and then within, and they clung to each other and cried out in pleasure and sorrow against the cliffed green ground.

PART III

ONE

If Ireland were a woman curled on her side with her back to Britain, the island's west would be her belly, soft and rounded, with the counties of Galway and Clare forming the two sides of her birth canal, where the waters of Galway Bay flow warm into her womb.

It was upon the stony hip beneath this womb that Brigid had been born, and it was there that she returned, pregnant and alone alone, and on the run from her father and history. She was exactly the same girl as she had been when she lived there, as anyone could have seen who looked closely into her hazel eyes that sparkled only a bit less than they had when she would climb the rocks of the Burren with her sister and pretend they were dragons on a mission for the lovely Findabair who had escaped her mother Maeve.

All the mothers of this island, Brigid had thought, even as a child at play, had taken on too much of Maeve, the warrior queen who would slay anything that came into sight. Their strength was legendary, it was true, and it had indeed helped them to survive wave upon wave of invasion from foreign men, but it was hard, too hard, to be the daughter of such a woman, either in legend or life.

And so Brigid and her younger sister Terri had, as children, pretended to be dragons who saved Maeve's daughter by whisking her away to the Burren where she would live for ever and ever among the ancient stones and moss and flowers swept in from the great north by white glaciers and frozen winds. It was here that Brigid finally, as an adult, returned to face the love that her parents had demanded, the loyal love that, in legend, had ended in Findabair's suicide.

Brigid arrived at the Burren late that Wednesday night wearing the same clothes she had dressed in on Monday, before dawn, while Padmaj lay still sleeping. She carried only a small woolen bag that held one change of clothes, slung over her shoulder, and in her pocket was only cash, no identification, nothing that could link her to the events of that day. She had bought her train tickets in cash, going first north to Sligo for one night, then south to Cahir, then finally west to Galway, to throw any keen observers at the train stations off the track. At Sligo, she had cut her hair in the train station restroom and bleached it with hydrogen peroxide. She looked younger, harder, like a German tourist, uninterested in conversation or company. And so, walking the back roads of the Burren from Galway to the place she had been born, no one slowed to ask if she wanted a ride or needed directions. She was a stranger to them, just as she felt herself to be.

"Would you like a bit of soup and hot tea in your room?" asked the tiny woman innkeeper with gray eyes.

A small black and white television was on behind the reception desk in the lobby, and Brigid tried not to look at it. She'd overheard conversations about the bombings, but this would be the first pictures she saw.

"Yes, thanks," Brigid had said quietly, trying to make sounds that could be mistaken for American, and looking down.

These were the only words that she had spoken in days that had not been strictly commercial transactions. It made her, just for a moment, long to stay.

"Do you know how long you'll be staying?"

Brigid looked up. Behind the woman's gray eyes, she saw a stretcher carrying a covered body being loaded away from a burning building, surrounded by other buildings in crumbles.

It would be dangerous to stay in any place too long.

"Just one night," Brigid said, decisively, and picked up her key and headed upstairs to her room.

***

It was a moonless spring night, but warm, and she sat next to the open window after showering, dressed in a clean t-shirt, eating her soup and crackers and tea, listening to the hissing of wind across the stone.

She remembered the sound of the wind in the desert, how it had scared her at first, sometimes knocking at her windows like a visitor, other times moaning like a woman in labor. After a while, though, she had become used to it. It became a companion, making her nights alone, year after year, bearable.

She was alone as she always had been, and once again she turned to the sound of the wind.

She slept badly that night, as the past finally returned, catching up with her, after years of staying away.

In her dreams, she dialed the same telephone number that she had in the red booth on that rainy night before the bombings, but instead of a switchboard operator, Brigid heard her sister's voice, calling out to her.

"Brig!" her sister cried. "Help me."

And then the line went dead.

And so Brigid ran, all the way from Dublin across the island to the west, following the echo of her sister's voice in the dark, chasing and falling across the limestone rocks, trying to find Terri, knowing she was in terrible trouble, trying to escape their father.

But her sister could not be found.

Finally Brigid reached the ocean, and the voice disappeared into the water.

Her sister was gone, and Brigid was too late.

***

Brigid woke, crying, and feeling as she had many times since her pregnancy began that the baby within her might be her dead sister, or perhaps her father, who could now also be dead for all Brigid knew, one or the other of them coming back, to live again, within her own body. The possibility that she might give birth to another version of their madness made her sick.

She rose from bed in the dark to splash water on her face, to wipe the nightmares away. As she looked into the mirror, she thought she saw, just for a second, the faces of her sister and mother and father behind her. Then the cool water was on her face, and they were gone.

She knew what the legends said about descendants. The whole Irish state had been founded on the idea that each generation held a direct line from the ancient past, which it carried like a flaming sword and committed to keeping ablaze.

This was why she had left for America: to be in a country where people changed their names, forgot the past and moved on, where history was what you said it was, and where it was mostly used as background for some story that newscasters called a "recent development."

She did not want to keep the torch of the Irish, which her mother and father had passed to her and that now burned within her, lit any longer. The image of the body being carried away from the burning building came back to her. She wanted to find a way to put the fire out.

***

In the morning, she returned her key to the woman at the front desk, thanked her kindly for last night's meal, and began to walk west.

She knew what she was looking for, and she knew it could be found in the sea.

It took her most of the morning to reach it.

She waded in at Doolin, the water cold, the huge cliffs to the south standing as witnesses, black and green.

She spread her fingers wide, as her ancestors had before her, during the famine, to search for the ocean's dark weed.

They had eaten it to stay alive.

She would place it inside her to give way to death.

When enough had been collected, she laid it out on a rock to dry, and napped beside it.

The sun warmed the baby within her.

Upon waking, Brigid gathered the seaweed into her bag and then, again, she began to walk.

She stepped into the first inn she found, asked for a room, and went to her room around back which faced the afternoon sun, low on its descent.

She undressed, placed the seaweed within her, and then lay down, upon the bed, to sleep again, and to wait for bleeding.

TWO

Padmaj felt Claire waking with a start next to him in bed, then watched as she rose to take the cell phone from her purse into the bathroom and gently shut the door.

Damp and tired the night before, they had checked into Poyle's Hotel in the center of Clifden and, unused to the way the sun's rays hit the western shore, both of them had slept later than usual in the morning.

Padmaj lay in the blue hotel room, still darkened by the heavy curtains, and listened to the sound of Claire's voice, hearing only its smooth tone but not her words, as she talked to her daughter. He was hungry for the sound of her voice. She had said almost nothing to him since they had been together. He realized, with a sharp sensation in his heart, that he had grown used to Brigid's constant chatter, that Brigid was still there, in his mind, even as he had made love to Claire.

Claire came out of the bathroom in a white bathrobe supplied by the hotel. "I'm sorry," she said, placing her cell phone back in her purse. "I didn't mean to wake you."

"You didn't." Padmaj sat up and turned a light on. "How is Miriam?"

"Remarkably well, actually. It's an amazing thing as a mother when you realize your child can be quite fine without you."

"But you must miss her," Padmaj said, thinking of his own mother.

"Yes, of course, but that's about me." She sat down next to him on the bed, but not too close. "I've always believed that it's a parent's job to let your child grow, to grow away from you."

"Yes, my mother said that, too."

"And you miss the child forever, but you mustn't let that become a hindrance, something that keeps them from being who they are meant to be."

He looked at her and said softly, "My mother wants me to come home."

Claire nodded. "How long has it been?" she asked.

"Twenty years."

***

Twenty years. Saying the words out loud sent Padmaj back in time, and before he knew it, he was telling the story to Claire.

"One May day after my graduation from college, when I had been planning to remain in the States and work as a waiter for the summer until starting started graduate school, I received a phone call from my aunt. She said to me, 'Come back and stay. We need you.' My uncle was sick with cancer. This uncle was more than an uncle to me. He was my mother's brother and he had taken care of my mother like a husband ever since my own father had left."

He stopped. There was so much to remember. So much that had never been told.

"Returning home at the age of twenty-two, as the plane circled the mountains of green trees, I noticed the bare spots near the top, and I thought of my father, who must have been just beginning to go bald. It had been many years since I had seen him."

From the plane, he couldn't see where India ended and Pakistan began, he explained to Claire, and yet, this border had defined who he was all his life.

"They had been children together, my mother and father," he continued, "in the village, before independence. They had played together as children, and later kissed and vowed to marry, to have many children, and to live together forever."

"But they only had you?" Claire asked.

He nodded. "My father, at the age of thirteen, had to leave with his family during partition. Almost all the Muslim families in the area had to leave. He only came back many years later, at the age of thirty, for the funeral of his grandmother, who had been, even in 1947, too old to leave."

Padmaj paused. "They reunited the night of the grandmother's funeral, the two childhood friends."

"And that's how you came along?"

He nodded. "He promised my mother that night that he would stay. She was an old woman by then, at the age of twenty-nine, by village standards. She had never married, had stayed quietly loyal to her childhood love all her life. He promised that he would stay, the night that I was conceived, but he didn't."

"And he never come back?" Claire asked.

"Only a few times, bringing gifts for me, for the first few years, but he never stayed long.

He could not be the only one of his kind to come back and stay. I understand that now, as an adult."

"But it was hard to understand it then."

"Yes."

"And it's been twenty years since you went home?"

"Yes."

"Why so long?"

Padmaj took a deep breath. "While I was away at school Lucknow, my mother had moved to a house along a larger road, where my uncle and aunt owned a little grocery store. It was here I stayed for a year when my uncle was sick. One morning at dawn, my mother woke me and handed him a white envelope with my name written across the top. Inside the envelope were hundreds of thousands of rupees.

"'What is this'?" I asked her.

"'Go,' she said to me. My uncle was better now. The chemotherapy had worked. The cancer was in remission. The store would be fine without him, she said.

"I started to ask her where she got the money, but she put her fingers on my lips. Her look said what every eldest son had always heard from his mother in this land — 'You are my favorite, my first, my best. Go. Succeed. Do whatever it takes to be in your own mind the treasure you already are in my heart. Go, even when you hear my heart breaking. Go, Bhabha. Go.' And so I did."

"How did you end up in Ireland?" Claire asked.

"I called an Indian friend from college who was working in Dublin for a computer company, told him I had some savings, was thinking about opening a restaurant, and I asked what the climate was like."

"'Cold, man,' he said."

Claire and Padmaj laughed.

"'I mean the climate for immigrants,'" I explained to him.

"'Cold, man,' he repeated."

This time Padmaj and Claire didn't laugh. They thought of Brigid, and her father. They thought of themselves.

"My friend convinced me to come. He said there were loads of people here from British Africa, Nigeria, Kenya. He said they dying for something other than fish and potatoes, to eat."

Claire smiled.

And so, for the last twenty years, Padmaj told Claire, he had built a successful business, was learning Irish as a requirement for becoming an Irish citizen, and had built a strong clientele, mostly professors and students from Trinity, and immigrants from British Africa, or tourists from the United States or France, people who wanted something other than salt and butter on their vegetables.

He had taken his application for citizenship very seriously. He'd studied government in college, listened with his whole body when the professors spoke of democracy, Western individualism, equal rights.

"I meditated upon these ideas," he told Claire, "and in my mind, I saw a kind of path, a kind of daily way of being, that could be, I imagined, what the sixteenth teaching of the *Gita* meant by 'perform your action here.' Here. In this land of saints and scholars, I felt I was doing this, bringing these spiritual and philosophical principles into action."

He paused.

"All I ever wanted to do was contribute," he said to Claire.

***

Contribute. This was a word his father had used, once.

"Your mother," his father had said. "She is a remarkable woman. She does more than just live. She lives to contribute."

Padmaj, as a boy, had tried to guess the meaning of this word by looking deeply into his father's eyes, filling with tears.

"I cannot stay, son," he had said, taking the boy's little hand, which was clinging to the sleeve of his father's thick white cotton dhoti. "This nation will not allow me to contribute. One day you will understand this."

His father kissed his hand. And then he left.

"Come back and stay, daddyji!" little Padmaj cried to the empty doorway.

But there was no response.

And so he tucked this word away. It was the only inheritance he had from his father. Contribute.

***

"All I ever wanted to do was contribute," he said again. "And now I must be leaving."

THREE

Claire looked into his eyes fully for the first time since embracing in the night, and she felt again that same spark within her that his dark eyes had kindled since the first day they had met. It made her feel guilty to admit this, even silently, to herself. But the loss of Michael had caused a kind of clarity of heart that she had desired before but had not quite been able to achieve.

She wanted to cling to him. But she knew, as well, that she had not really begun to mourn Michael, that in part, she had made love to Padmaj as a way of making love to Michael's ghost, as a way of tricking her body into believing that he was not really gone.

"My mother is worried about me."

"She should be." Claire reached out and lightly touched his cheek. "And you will not likely be safe again until…"

They had not said Brigid's name, but it hung, in the air, between them.

"Will you go soon?" she asked, pressing her hands against the mattress to guard against the sensation that she was falling.

"I have a plane ticket for this evening."

She took in a large breath, held it. His independence of spirit, which she was only just beginning to see, seemed to strengthen her.

"Would you like to come with me?" he asked.

She blew out, slowly, between her teeth, as if in the early stages of labor.

"Yes," she said, and smiled, but her eyes were sad. "But I can't. I should stay in Ireland in case Miriam needs me, and I also have to be alone, I think, for a while."

"I was sure that is what you would say," he said, a bit stiffly, as if he had prepared this response in advance. "But I wanted to ask you anyway."

"Thank you," she said, also polite.

The longer they were awake in the daylight, the more obvious their strangeness to each other became.

"My lady," Padmaj said finally. "What will you *do*?"

And as Claire looked into his strange eyes, her own eyes filled with tears. She knew that they were not tears for Padmaj's departure, but for herself, and for Michael, for the way that Michael had always protected her, fed her well, given her a sense of safety and shelter, no matter where they roamed. And that all of this was now over.

She looked down as the tears fell.

"My lady," he said again. "Claire. I fear I cannot leave you like this."

"You will promise me you will take care of yourself?" he asked, touching the peachy curve of her cheek.

"Yes, of course," she said, pulling away from him. "I will be fine," she said. "I will stay here. Well, not here, exactly, but I'll find a place, something nice, nearby. I've wanted to come here anyway, and I really don't want to go back. So I will stay here."

She got up suddenly and said she was going to take a shower.

And then quietly, he left to return to his mother.

***

After having tea and a dry scone in a small café, Claire asked a woman on the street where she might find a clothing boutique. She still had on the black dress from the memorial service, and her hair was a bit wild from having dried in the windy western air.

The woman looked her up and down and let the American accent register, and then directed her to the most expensive shop in town, which Claire found quite reasonable.

She bought a light woolen sweater, several matching sets of slacks and tops and two linen dresses, as well as three pairs of shoes and four matching sets of bras and panties. Claire chose one outfit to wear out of the store and then asked for an extra bag for the clothes she had been wearing.

She carried these two bags — one with the old clothes and one with the new — to the realtor's office around the corner and asked for a small house with a good view and handed him a credit card for the down payment and first month's rent.

"It's too far to walk," the realtor said. "Do you have a car?"

Even with Michael's death and Miriam's return to the hospital and Padmaj's leaving and the newness of everything, Claire had been feeling that she was doing quite well, following her plan as she was, and she'd been quite proud of herself. But when the realtor asked this, and when she found her mouth beginning to form the words to say, "I cannot drive. I don't know how to drive," she also found her heart finally opening and the tears of the past four days threatening to come pouring forth in front of this short, round man with thick, dark hair and blue eyes like hers.

"Could you drive me there?" she asked, biting her lower lip, and he was so touched, inexplicably, by the change in her face that he had the sudden urge to take her in his arms, to hold her, to caress her, and make her laugh.

"Yes, of course," he said, blushing, bumbling, gathering his keys. "Allow me," he said, picking up her paper bags and leading her to his car.

FOUR

Brigid waited in that little room by the western sea for the blood to start so she could begin again, but it never came. She felt as if the past lay within her, unwilling to leave. Finally, after days of mild cramping and a slight fever, Brigid woke on a Sunday morning, with church bells ringing, remembering the Sunday afternoons she had spent on the Burren as a child, with fantasies of being alone, of living where no one could touch her or hurt her, where no one asked her to do what she knew would end in bloodshed and death.

She had structured her entire life around this fantasy, becoming obstinately single, leaving loneliness like breadcrumbs for the fears that trailed behind her to follow. Now, with the child in her as a reminder of the impossibility of being alone, she began to move away from her own childhood for the first time.

***

Day after day as the spring turned to summer, Brigid walked the Cliffs of Moher, watching the white waves crashing against black rocks that rose hundreds of feet above, and practiced over and over again her decision not to jump.

There was something soothing in the way the rhythm of the water combined with her footsteps as together Brigid and the land vowed again and again to keep themselves in one place.

She felt herself grow heavier with each step, more bound to the earth. In May, the kittiwakes, thousands of them, gray and small and cutely roundish, flew among the cliffs to lay their eggs in the nests below, while Brigid, just beginning to feel round herself, watched, far away from the tourists, upon her perch of a damp green blanket of grass, dangerously close to the edge. Again and again she saw the females lay two eggs into each nest, and then sit down to wait.

***

As a midwife, Brigid was well aware of what was happening inside her. She knew that deep in our mother's womb, we, too, form an egg. Round and round and round, the cells multiply until we become a sphere, a circle, a globe.

During the day, she sat cross legged as in meditation and watched the birds as they waited with their eggs. It gave her the sense that she was not alone. And for once, the feeling comforted her.

But at night, by herself in her room, she would dream. In her dreams, her pregnant self was giving birth to herself as a child again, and it terrified her to think that her story, with its suffering and solitude, might repeat itself like this, never ending.

Upon waking, she would force herself to remember the photographs of embryos she had studied in school, how, even as we started as circles, soon we began to fold in on ourselves, our cells diving deep into the center of our planet, in a moment of splitting that saves us from lives of endless repetition.

We are formed, she reminded herself as she stroked her belly, by what looks, at first, like destruction.

***

By July, her dreams had changed, and she was no longer afraid that the baby would be a copy of herself, but instead she feared something wholly other, a monster, like her father, and her dreams were filled with fish, and lizards, large heads, big dark eyes, and spines that curved upward into a terrifying tail.

Still, each day she continued to walk the cliffs, as the summer fogs rolled in and the moss spread thick along the ridges and she said to herself, over and over, I am here, I am here, I am here.

And the life inside her continued to grow.

***

One day in early September, walking the same path she had for more than a season, she felt something else within.

The baby was taking its first kicks, rustling in its own watery nest, just as thousands of new birds were now doing—the kittiwakes she had come to love, as well as the quills and gulls and puffins—all along the cliffs below.

The movement within startled her, and she stopped walking, closed her eyes and touched her belly, softly, as if to listen more closely with her fingers.

***

The legs and arms that kicked within her had begun, she knew, as plump branches coming from the trunk of the body's tree. And then the stumps became limbs, reaching out as the cells reproduced themselves, encouraging each other to grow, grow, grow. It was then,

Brigid knew, when we have grown arms and legs, a way to move and kick and embrace each other, that we begin to look human.

She saw in her mind how next the fingers and toes were formed. At first, these looked like paddles, like baseball gloves, like spoons. And then, once again, as at the beginning, came a kind of death, as the cells between the fingers and the toes started to destroy themselves.

"The death of these cells enables the separation that makes everything humanly possible," she remembered her mentor in nursing school telling her once.

"Touch," the beautiful older woman professor had said to her. "The use of tools. Writing. Art. All recorded memory of what has come and gone. The fashioning with our hands of what may someday be."

The woman had been like a mother to Brigid, believing in her and showing her an alternative to her own mother, revealing to her the art that nursing could be.

"I have indeed had many mothers," Brigid said to herself, as a large bird, a great black backed quill, threatened almost to extinction, swooped overhead on its way back home.

Her eyes followed the dark bird's flight to its nest, where she fed her three small fledglings, perched high between one element and the other, and their precariousness made Brigid slightly dizzy.

She closed her eyes again.

This was a *child* within her. Not herself, not a mere copy or a continuation of history, nor her father, her mother, her sister or a monster.

"We don't have to live on the cliffs any longer," she whispered to the baby. "I will take you back in. I will build you a proper nest. Let's go there, together, and make ourselves a home."

FIVE

Claire stayed in her new home, a little white cottage a half hour's drive from Clifden, all through the spring and summer. Her days were punctuated by morning phone calls to Miriam who had moved into a group home run by the treatment center, and afternoon walks beside the blue lakes and black marshes and yellow and brown hills all around.

Some days she pretended Michael was working—he had spent more time at work than with her over the course of their marriage, after all—and there would be a smooth space within her that would believe the lie and even begin to plan what to cook him for dinner. And then there would be the jagged timeless stretches spent in bed, except for the daily phone call to Miriam, when Claire forced herself to stand shaking outside in the chilly foggy morning air to clear her tears for the conversation. But most days were simply spent with the rhythm of walking, and the spirit of Michael along as company, as he listened with her to the wind over the landscape of her ancestry.

The green stripes of potato beds were like lines of poetry, she would tell him, scars that still remained on the land, divided as it was by rock walls into tiny squares of swampy marsh and steep rock, telling the tales of its history. It was this very land that her people had loved fiercely, she told him, even when it starved them, even when they had to choose—as his people had, too—between leaving it and staying behind, and dying.

She understood all this now, for the first time, through her body.

For it was within her body now, this knowledge that she carried, a growing belief in the spirit of the material world, a faith in rocks and lakes and eyes, a sense that what we see and what we hold in our minds are not separate. All that she had taken as solid, as ground, as matter, Claire was coming to understand, held mind and memory and imagination in it, too, just as she had always known language could.

Days she walked the land; nights she slept and dreamt of him; and at dawn, she woke to use language to translate what they were telling her about their history. How the wind spoke of hunger. How the sky sang songs, in Michael's voice, of what still survived beyond memory. And how the light could paint pictures of what was to come.

Language became more than a link between mind and matter, then, in her poems. It became a way of remembering Michael, and all that they had had, and all that they had never had, and all they were now, she felt, together becoming.

***

One day in early September, Claire veered off her regular course, venturing into some dark green trees, with thick waxy leaves and a smooth bark like myrtle. Something about them reminded her of Padmaj.

"*Etrange*," she said to herself out loud, and the smell of the restaurant came back to her, cumin and pepper and cardamom, right there under the shade of the trees.

"Excuse me?" a small voice said.

Claire jumped.

A little nun in a black and white habit peered out from behind a spice colored trunk.

"Did you say something?" the older woman asked, smiling.

"I didn't know anyone was here..." Claire apologized.

"Oh yes," the sister said. "There are many of us here." She looked down at Claire's belly, which was round like teddy bear's, and said, "Do you need help?"

Claire had become so good at pretending that what was happening within her was not happening that at first she did not know what the nun meant.

"Have you come to the sisters for help?" she asked gently.

"I..."

"Come with me," and a small white hand extended itself from under the dark robe and took Claire's hand.

The nun, whose name was Sister Marie, told Claire as they walked through the trees that many women came to the abbey in her condition, that there was no shame in asking for help, and that they could help her in whatever way she needed.

It had been so long since Claire had a conversation with someone other than the realtor or a shopkeeper that she found herself weeping.

Sister Marie patted her shoulder.

"Yes, yes, I know," she said lovingly, and Claire let herself be embraced for the first time since Padmaj had left.

Sister Marie continued to lead her through the woods, and then suddenly there rose a chapel in a Gothic style, splendidly out of place.

"Welcome to Kylemore Abbey," said Sister Marie.

***

Later, after Claire was served tea and soda bread and the sisters' famous homemade Clare jam in a room warmed by a fireplace and crowded with women of various ages and styles of dress, Sister Marie approached her again to ask if she would be staying the night.

Claire started to say that she had her own place, but then thought better of it. "Yes," she said. "You are quite kind."

"Dinner is served at seven," Sister Marie said. "Would you like to lie down for a while now?"

And Claire was sighing, somewhere deep within, at being taken care of again, and tears came again to her as she nodded her head yes and followed the sister to a room.

***

That night, just as Claire was about to fall asleep, Sister Marie knocked quietly at her door.

"I wondered," Sister Marie said, "if I could speak with you."

Claire let her in.

Sister Marie perched on a wooden chair and said, "Have you decided what to do with the child?"

Claire looked down at her belly and said no.

"Does the father know?"

Claire could not be certain who the father was; although she hoped it was Michael, she knew it could also be Padmaj.

Claire shook her head again.

"Do you have the means to care for it?"

This question took Claire by surprise. She'd never thought of it in this way before.

"Yes," she said. "I do."

It was actually quite simple. She was the mother. That was the most important thing. She knew she could care for this child. She knew how to be a good mother. So she would.

Sister Marie's eyebrows raised. This was the first woman she'd ever met who had answered affirmatively to this question. This was usually the question that clinched the mother's decision to offer the baby for adoption into a good and deserving home.

"You do?" the nun asked.

"Yes," Claire smiled. "I do."

They sat silently for a moment.

"Then, why, may I ask, are you here?"

Claire looked at her with large round blue eyes. "You led me here," she said. Claire had spent so much time alone that she had forgotten how clear and simple she had become in her interactions with others after Michael's death.

The nun shook her head. "So you don't need our help?"

"Oh yes," Claire said, beaming, "You've helped me tremendously."

"We have?"

"Yes." Claire paused, then said, "May I ask you a question?"

"Certainly."

"What are those trees we passed through on our way here? They are so strange."

"Those trees," Sister Marie sighed, as her eyes lit up and she settled back into her chair, thrilled to be able to speak of her passion. "Are the yew. It is said that, in Celtic legend, trees hold within them both myth and history, both sacred magic and practical wisdom, all that we need for this life. And the next." She looked up, briefly, as if acknowledging where she, at least, would be.

"The yew tree," she continued, "has roots that grow crooked underground. They are tangled and knotted, an arthritic map of fingers that reach out, hungrily, waiting to begin again."

The image made Claire imagine Michael's body, reaching across Ireland, touching her on its western shore, through Padmaj, that first night here. She remembered the desire that ran through her then, like a tap root connected to a much larger source.

Sister Marie seemed to read her thoughts, for she said, "It is said, in Celtic legend, that from the mouth of every dead person buried under the ground, a new root of a yew tree sprouts."

Claire's hands wandered down to caress her belly.

"What looks like death is actually a new beginning."

Claire looked up, suddenly feeling the baby move within.

"The yew, then, is a tree of new beginnings, of what springs fresh from each ending, from the death of our families, our friends and our neighbors. It is a kind of hope and rebirth, this belief that the dead are still speaking, that trees grow from their mouths, that the branches of the trees are their hands, that the leaves of the trees are their fingers, propelling us toward each other, generation after generation, again and again."

And as she spoke, Claire remembered the Easter night in early spring that she had written alongside the River Liffey, the sky lit by the full moon and a nearby star, and wished for a child.

This child.

And then Brigid's last words reached out to her from the last time they were together: "There's a baby hovering nearby, just dreaming of being your child."

Perhaps this was Michael's child, after all, the one Claire had wished for, with Michael, the one she had thought she would never have.

"One more thing," Sister Marie said, interrupting Claire's thoughts. "It is said that every new yew is a child of the one great mother tree."

"Two who are one, and one who is three," Claire said to herself, quietly, closing her eyes. How much they all shared, these disparate peoples of the ancient sacred groves: the inhabitants of Palestine, the mountain villagers of the Himalayas, and the scattered Irish, even the ones whose seeds had fallen as far as America.

"I can see you are tired," said Sister Marie, heading to the door. "So I'll be leaving you. Sleep well now."

Suddenly exhausted by the day and already upon the edge of sleep, still Claire heard Sister Marie say as she closed the door, "All the children are her branches."

SIX

Brigid walked back slowly to her room at the inn on that September day, realizing for the first time that she needed to have someone help her give birth to this baby. She couldn't do it alone. She had known midwives who had tried, and often the outcome was not successful. Brigid decided that perhaps becoming a mother meant giving up a bit of one's pride.

And so she decided to ask for help.

She went to the phone in her room and dialed a number she had not dialed in a long time, one she knew by heart.

The phone rang only once, more quickly that Brigid had expected, and then the voice she longed for answered.

"Hello?"

"Mattie?"

"Brigid, is that you?"

"Yes, Mattie, it's me," Brigid said, her voice like a child's.

"Sweetie, are you okay?"

"I'm pregnant, Mattie."

Mattie was quiet. Then she said, "How far along are you?"

"Five months."

"Goodness, girl, you worked fast!" Mattie chuckled. Why didn't you tell me earlier?"

"It took me a while to decide." Brigid found herself unable to say the words, sensing that the baby was listening.

Mattie was quiet again.

"Mattie, I think I need your help."

"Are you sure this is Brigid O'Connell? Mattie laughed. "The Brigid O'Connell I know won't ever ask for help!"

"I know," Brigid frowned.

"Well then, let me see," Mattie paused, counting in her head. "You remember that girl, Grace?"

"Yes."

"She's due any day now. I've got to stay for a while to help her get her rhythm once the baby comes. But it's the strangest thing. There weren't any more babies after you left. It's like you took the charm of those rabbits with you when you went."

Brigid remembered the rabbit tracks in the snow, the way they darted back and forth, like dancing. The memory made her think of the way Padmaj's slim dark fingers intertwined with her small white ones as they held hands, as if in prayer, while making love.

"So I can come after I'm sure Grace is okay," Mattie said, interrupting Brigid's reverie. "Probably by the end of next month."

"Do you think you can get someone to take care of the boys, though?" Brigid asked. It was hard for her to ask for help, and she found herself trying to find excuses for why Mattie shouldn't come.

"Oh, you don't know! My son met a real nice woman and they got married and the boys live with them now!"

"That's great, Mattie, but don't you miss them?"

"Actually," Mattie giggled, "They're all living in your house right here! I was just over here watching them after school till Renée gets home from work."

Brigid smiled.

"Brigid?"

"Yes?"

"How are things with your mama and daddy?"

"I haven't seen them in a long while," Brigid admitted. She paused, trying to get her mind to form the story, but it wouldn't come, so she simply said, "It's complicated."

"Girl," Mattie sighed. "Look. It's no more complicated than it's gonna be to get an old desert Indian on a plane across that big ocean for the first time in her life!"

"I'll send you the ticket," Brigid said.

"I'm not talking about that," Mattie said. "I'm talking about doing something you never did before."

Brigid was quiet. Some deep part of her knew that Mattie was right, and that becoming a mother would mean going through her own past first, unpacking it like a suitcase and putting all her belongings away, then finding a place to stay so the baby would know where its home was.

"If I can come all the way over there, you can do what you need to do, too," Mattie said.

"I don't know."

"Yes, you do."

Brigid shook her head.

"You're a mama now. You gotta have the courage of a mama. Okay? Promise?"

Brigid thought of the promises she'd forced Padmaj to make and wondered where he was now. And if he still loved her.

"Promise me?"

"I promise," Brigid said.

"Okay, then. Send me a ticket for the night of Halloween. I've always wanted to fly like a witch on a Halloween night."

Brigid laughed, knowing that there were people who might call Brigid and Mattie witches.

"And Mattie?"

"Hmm?"

"Thank you."

"You're welcome. Take good care of yourself now. And remember your promise."

"I will."

SEVEN

Early the next morning, as her little white cottage with the thatched roof came into view, Claire suddenly had the sensation that she was no longer standing on land, as if the great greyblue lake beside the house had swallowed her whole body, and water, not air, filled her chest with each breath.

Until then, she admitted to herself, she had not really believed that Michael was gone. For the past five months, she had used her poetry, her poetic sense of the world, to deal with her pain as best she could. And while the poems she wrote during that time were important—they had at least kept her *feeling*—they were not the whole story.

So arriving at the steps of the little house, she took off her shoes before entering, as one does before swimming, and then went straight to her bed and stripped it, hanging the sheets over the windows and mirrors, making for herself a dark wet pool in which to mourn.

She unplugged the phone and the stove and the refrigerator—she wanted no artificial humming to distract her from the sound of her tears—and then sat down on the wooden floor in the center of the house, to write.

***

For seven days she did not move, she did not wash, she did not speak, and only ate and slept sporadically, staying right where she was on the floor, filling page after page with the story of her life, sometimes tossing with dreams of Michael and Miriam and the unknown baby growing within, and then waking to begin again.

Sometimes she felt she was going mad. She would hear the wind knocking at the door in the night and feel it was death upon the earth, coming for all of them.

In the dark she would see shadows and shapes in the corners of the room and have to press her hands against her eyes to try to stop the fearful visions.

One morning, she swore she could smell something burning. After checking once, it took all her strength to resist the urge to stand and check the stove again and again, certain that someone had plugged it in while she was sleeping and left a body of a small animal in there, perhaps a rabbit, to burn.

After four days of sitting and writing, she felt hands upon her shoulders at dusk, and remembered that this same sensation had come to her upon her confirmation at thirteen. Then, full of faith, she had believed it was the Holy Ghost. Now, full of guilt about the night with Padmaj, she feared it was an evil spirit come to punish her. She stayed awake, all that night, afraid if she surrendered to sleep she might not return.

At dawn on the sixth day, she tasted in her mouth the distinct and sweet memory of her wedding cake, and she knew then that what she had shared with Padmaj and Michael, both, was neither holy nor evil, but simply love.

The love between Claire and Michael, their passion, their promise, their dreams and desires and silences and misgivings—all this she tasted fully then. Their love for the daughter they had created and raised together. His love for his work, his individual spirit that propelled him to leave her, daily, to reach out to the world, to participate in it, despite its painful history.

And her love for her friends, Brigid and Padmaj, and the community she had been trying to make with them.

It was the story of all this love that Claire wrote out clearly on the sixth day of her mourning.

On the seventh day, her body finally gave in to sleep, resting deeply from dawn to dusk.

She woke at sunset to pink rays streaming in through the sheets that covered the windows of the little cottage, so that the whole place seemed to glow like the inside of a rose.

At first, Claire thought she was asleep, and she sat, disoriented, in a kind of timeless pink dream, on the floor. And then she remembered, from the last day of Michael's mourning for his mother, what she next needed to do.

She went to the sink and filled a round bowl with water, took it to the front door, opened the door wide to reveal the sunset on Europe's western shoulder. Then Claire poured droplets of water over each of her hands three times. When she was done, she set the bowl down on the front step and went back inside, leaving the door open.

As the sky's light turned from pink to orange, Claire walked to the bedroom closet and pulled out a brown paper bag. Without looking inside, she put on slippers and a jacket and stepped back over the bowl of water to take the bag down to the edge of the lake.

Once there, she got down on her knees and began to dig into the soft black soil with her hands.

The sun's last bit of ruby light fell below the edge of the clear blue lake, revealing one white star that twinkled in the east.

When the hole was large enough for her to lay her belly in, Claire opened the bag and took its contents out.

Inside were the clothes she had worn to the memorial service for Michael, the black dress he'd given her for her birthday, even her shoes and hose and underthings, and the note from him that she had tucked into her bra, and, finally, the egg she'd painted for him, adorned with roots and trunks and the branches of intertwining trees, which she'd carried in her purse to his memorial service and had saved, ever since.

She laid each object in the ground, gently, and as she did so, she no longer felt afraid. Nor did she feel she was burying the past, but it was as if Michael were there, with her, planting a new future.

Once everything was in place, she used the back of her hands to push dirt into the hole, and then she lay her body down beside it, her round belly cradled low against the earth.And then, for the first time in seven days, she allowed herself to make a sound. Wordlessly, and with her face against the cool dirt, she began to hum. It was like a prayer, her song, but she was not asking for anything. She was, with her voice and her body, mixing together the present and history and committing herself to the care and the memory of them both.

The moon began slowly to rise in the east, coming to meet the star that had been waiting for it.

And then Claire rose, too, and prepared to return home, to give birth to the promise that, in this, her motherland, had long ago been planted.

EIGHT

Holding to the promise she'd made to Mattie, Brigid took the morning bus back from Ennis to Dublin to try to find her parents. For her baby. For herself. For all of them.

She arrived at noon on a breezy but extraordinarily sunny autumn day and, though she was slightly dizzy from hunger, she feared losing her courage if she tarried so she walked straight from the bus station to her mother's apartment and rang the bell.

"Hullo?" her mother's voice was fuzzy through the intercom.

"Mum? It's me, Brigid."

"Well, welcome back, stranger," her mother said, a bit coldly.

Her father must be still missing, Brigid thought, which would account for her mother's mood, the tone of abandonment.

"Can I come up, Mum?"

There was no answer, but the bell dinged and the door to the lift opened.

***

The apartment looked cleaner than it had. It almost sparkled in the bright sunlight.

"How do you like my new things?" her mother asked, spreading her arms wide. The kitchen table was new, and so was the cabinetry, and fresh flooring had even been installed. Brigid peered into the living room, which had been redone in hardwood floors and had new furniture.

Brigid shook her head.

"I can't believe it," she said.

"Well, I bloody well deserved it," said her mother, leading Brigid into the living room. "You should have seen how the Guardai ripped up this place. They destroyed everything, looking for evidence. Even the walls are feckin new because they tore them down looking for guns or whatever."

Brigid was speechless, wondering what had been done to her other friends' places. Padmaj. Claire and Michael.

"They found nothing, by the way," her mother said, with a touch of pride.

Brigid heard the pride and felt it lingering within herself, a false kind of smugness at pretending that what her father did had nothing to do with her.

She was ready to give this up.

Lost in her thoughts, Brigid took off her coat and laid it on the couch, and her mother shrieked.

"Bloody Mary, Queen of Heaven! What the hell happened to you?"

"Well, mum," Brigid said quietly. "I'm pregnant."

"I can see that! And pretty far along, too!"

"Five months."

"Jayzuz! Why didn't you tell me?"

"I…" Brigid found her old walls rising, and then took a breath, and sat down on the new couch.

Her mother sat next to her, but said nothing, only waited for Brigid to speak.

Something about her mother reminded Brigid of Claire. Maybe there was something about being a mother that made a person able to be quiet, to wait.

"I dunno, mum," Brigid said. "I dunno why I didn't come to you earlier. About everything. I'm sorry. I should have told you."

"No, Brigid Mary, you don't have to apologize. I'm the one who needs to apologize."

Brigid had never heard these words from her mother before.

"After they destroyed my place, I went mad. I spent days and nights on the streets, drinking, I've never…"

Her mother looked out the window.

"Finally, I ended up in a shelter run by some sisters and they helped me get dried out." She laughed.

"I did it, Brig," her mother said, looking expectantly at Brigid as if she were the child and Brigid the mother. "I'm a dry drunk. Look," she said, pointing to the pin on her sweater. "Three months clean and sober."

Brigid's eyes filled with tears. She opened her mouth to speak.

"Shh," said her mother. "I need to say something else to you. Brigid, I honestly don't know if your father was involved with those terrible bombings, but I do know that one of the people killed was the husband of your friend, Claire. The Guardai told me when they were looking for you. They wondered if you were involved somehow because of the connection and I told them no, but they didn't believe me, I was drunk all the time then, who would believe me…."

Brigid couldn't speak.

"They still haven't found your father. And when you went missing, too, they thought you might be in it together, but I knew it wasn't true. I knew if you had known anything, you would have turned your father in. And rightly so. Bad cess to the lot of 'em."

"Oh, Mum," Brigid cried, realizing fully for the first time that she had indeed had a part in it, in the death of Michael, in all the deaths.

"I'm so sorry, Brigid," said her mother. "I'm so sorry for everything. For staying with your father, for believing all his lies, for all the years of drinking, for your sister…." Her mother finally broke down in tears.

The two women, both mothers now, held each other, clung to each other, as their hands hung against each other's backs, not wanting to let go. It was the first time they had touched in years.

Brigid sobbed like a wee child who has dreamt that she has lost her mother and then wakes with relief to find her mother there, holding her, in the dark of night.

And still she longed to touch the other mothers she needed to complete her shamrock. Mattie would come soon, she told herself. And she needed, more than ever, to find Claire.

NINE

Claire found herself, on the morning of the autumn equinox in September, finally ready to blow out the candle that had been burning in the window of her little Connemara home. As the smoke still lingered behind her in the air, she walked out its white western door for the final time.

She kept walking through the morning, one bag in her hand, all the way to the Clifden bus station. Then she walked aboard the noon bus heading east, and then, once in Dublin, she walked straight from the bus station to meet her daughter for the first time since Michael's memorial service in the spring.

Miriam opened the door and exclaimed, "Mom! Why didn't you tell me?"

Claire was not sure what to say. She'd tried, over and over in the past months, to tell Miriam about the baby. But now here she was—her daughter, in person, waiting for her words.

Claire opened her mouth and one only word came out: "Baby." Then Claire took her daughter in her arms, and said, "I'm so sorry I was away so long. I'm sorry you had to go through all this alone."

Miriam took her mother's hand and led her into the house and down the hall to the kitchen. There, she sat Claire down at the table, handed her a glass of grape juice, and said, "Mom, I'm not the one who's been alone."

Claire looked into the glass she had been given and began to cry.

"I've been here," Miriam said, "with counselors who love me and understand me, and other people also on their roads toward healing." She waved her arms to gesture around the group home.

"It's *you* I've been worried about," Miriam said to Claire. "I've been worried about you, out there in the west, all alone."

Claire looked into her daughter's eyes and could not help but see her own mother, her long worry.

"But I see now you have not been completely alone," Miriam said, gently.

Claire nodded.

They sat quietly for a moment and then Miriam said, "Let's eat. Are you hungry?"

And Claire said yes.

***

Miriam served her mother a dinner she had lovingly made with her own hands, a salad of romaine lettuce with hard boiled eggs and homemade blue cheese dressing, steaming hot brown rice and lentils spiced with cumin and paprika, and a luscious dessert of crême brulée, Claire's favorite.

They ate together in the large dining room of the group home, which was uncharacteristically quiet because the residents had arranged to go out for pizza so that Miriam could have dinner with her mother, alone.

Miriam smiled proudly as her mother delighted over each dish, and then, as both of them scraped their round bowls to get the last bit of the creamy sweet dessert, Claire said, "That was the best meal I've ever eaten."

Miriam laughed. Her mother often said this when she was satisfied by a good meal, but this time, Miriam felt she had truly meant it.

"Mom," Miriam said. "I've got some news for you."

"Oh?" Claire's eyes widened.

"I've been accepted to the University of Chicago School of Music for next year. They have one of the best international music programs in the world, and there's a large Irish community in Chicago. Daddy helped me with the application in January, before I went into the hospital."

Claire was quiet.

"The letter came in the mail just last week," Miriam continued, her voice diminishing. "But now that daddy's gone, I don't know. I'm not sure I can do this alone. I thought maybe you might want to go with me—to Chicago."

"Miriam," Claire said, tears in her eyes. "That's wonderful news. It really is. I'm sorry. I was just surprised, that's all. You'd never told me."

Her mother reached out and took Miriam's hand.

"I'm proud of you," she said. "And you know what?"

"What?"

"Your dad would be proud of you, too."

Miriam smiled. "You think so?"

"I know so."

Then Miriam led her mother to the living room, settled her on the couch and said, "I have something I'd like to play for you." She went to the stereo and put in a CD.

Claire expected that it would be a recording of a new piece Miriam had written, something fresh and unusual. But instead what came out was sad and familiar.

It was the Carpenter's song, "Hurting Each Other," which, Claire suddenly remembered, she used to play over and over again at night when they had lived in London, when Miriam was a toddler and Michael's work started taking him away from them, making him come home later and later in the evenings.

Claire had completely forgotten about this.

Over time, she had become used to Michael's long work hours, and Miriam had moved out of the toddler stage, and this song had become a forgotten memory. But here now, with Michael really gone and their daughter, grown, in front of her, Claire began to cry. There was so much she had forgotten. So much she needed, still, to remember.

***

Miriam wiped the tears from her own eyes and then reached her hand out to Claire as the next track began, and together they danced, arm in arm, as Miriam sang to her mother.

"On the day that you were born
the angels got together ..."

When the song was over, it was quiet and they sat down on the floor and began to speak to each other, mother and daughter, healing and healed, growing and grown.

"Do you remember," Miriam began, "when we used to dance to this record when I was little, in London?"

"Yes," Claire answered.

"I think it was then that I decided to be a musician," Miriam said.

"Really?"

"Yes, I remember thinking that if music could move my mother like that—you would cry during the first song, and then be happy, and dance with me, and smile, during the second—then music must be magical, and I wanted to be part of that magic."

Claire nodded. "But you were always musical," she said. "Remember the story of how you were born singing?"

"Tell me again."

"Well, after we first brought you home from the hospital, I would sit up at night to breastfeed you in that old wooden rocking chair in our bedroom, and when you finally fell asleep, you would sing."

"How?"

"It was a beautiful, deep sound, something like chanting. Your daddy would look over at us from the bed, and we would stay awake for a long time listening to you singing like that, until finally he would say, 'Claire, you need your sleep,' and take you from my arms,

207

and lay you gently in your cradle in our room, and I would crawl, exhausted, next to him in bed."

They sat quietly together, remembering.

"Daddy took good care of us," Miriam said.

"Yes," Claire said. "He did."

"Mom?" Miriam asked.

"Yes?"

"How do you feel about having this baby without him?"

Claire touched her belly and said, "I guess I hope it's a boy. Like him."

"Would you raise him Jewish?" Miriam asked.

The questioned stunned Claire. It hadn't occurred to her.

"I don't know. Why?"

"Well," Miriam began, "After daddy's memorial service, I was on my way to the hospital, and I saw a synagogue. I'd never seen one before in Dublin, and it struck me. Why hadn't I seen one before? So I walked in. And I started talking to the rabbi there, that very day."

"Why didn't you tell me this earlier?"

"There were some things you didn't tell me, either."

"Point taken," Claire said. "Go on."

"Well, I discovered that there are actually *four* synagogues in Dublin, and we hadn't even been to even one, so I visited them all once I moved to the group home. I went to Friday night services until I found one on Zion Road where I felt comfortable. Did you know there's been a Jewish community in Ireland for hundreds of years? That the president of Israel in the 1980s was Irish?"

Claire shook her head.

"And did you know that after the Second World War, many of the remaining Jews in Ireland were forced by the Catholic Church into converting?"

Claire stared at her daughter, amazed by her and reminded of the sense Claire had had, while in Connemara, had she and Michael had indeed shared one history.

"I've also been attending a Kabbalah study group," Miriam continued. "Do you remember the egg you made for daddy?"

"I didn't even know you knew about that!" Claire exclaimed.

"Daddy told me about it after I came home from the hospital. He really loved it. It made him so happy."

"It did?"

"Yes. Didn't he tell you?"

Claire nodded. You're telling me now, she said to Michael. You're telling me now.

"Mom?"

"Yes?"

"So, do you think you will you raise the baby Jewish?"

Claire was quiet. Finally, she said, "In this past year, I've come to see all of us—me, Daddy, you—all our histories, all our religions, all our languages, all our cultures..."

Miriam listened carefully.

"As branches of one mother tree," Claire said.

Miriam's eyes widened as she asked her mother, "Did you know that the Kabbalah is also called The Tree of Life?"

"Yes, I..." Claire started to say.

"Wait here," Miriam interrupted and ran upstairs to her bedroom. When she came back down, she read to Claire from the Kabbalah.

Claire sat quietly for a while, then took her daughter's hand and said, "Honey, I don't have all the answers to your questions right now. I don't know if I can go with you to Chicago, and I don't know exactly how I will raise this baby. But I know we'll find a way to figure it out together. Okay, honey? Do you think you can believe in me?"

Miriam smiled. "Don't be silly, mother. Don't you remember? You told me that's why you wanted a daughter—so we could go through life with faith in each other."

And Claire said, "I remember."

TEN

Brigid's memories came flooding back to her as she made her way from her mother Rose's flat to Claire's apartment across the river in the twilight of that late September evening.

She felt Padmaj's arm on hers again, opening the glass door to the building, she saw his wide smile and dark almond-shaped eyes, she tasted his mouth again, while waiting for the elevator, cinnamon and clove.

She heard Miriam's cello playing as she knocked on the apartment door, and felt the heat of the fire burning within, as it did that last night here. She saw the pattern on Michael's sweater, blue and gray zigzags in the dark room, and then heard Claire's footsteps across the wooden floor.

As Claire opened the door, Brigid was struck by Claire's belly, a ripe melon sitting high up, just beneath her breasts, and Brigid remembered her last words to her on that night, about a baby hovering nearby.

"Brigid, you're pregnant!" Claire sang out, her smile wide, even after all she had been through.

"So are you," Brigid said, in shock, trying to register the news of both death and life at the same time.

Claire embraced her, and their bellies fit together, Brigid's low and wide, Claire's high and hard, as both babies kicked at once, and the women laughed.

"Oh, I've missed you!" Claire said, clinging to her.

"Me, too," Brigid said, crying. She remembered the first time she had been in Claire's apartment, how easily tears had come in Claire's presence, as she had cried about her father even then. And now. Again.

"Now, now," Claire said, taking her hand. "Come in, come in. No need to cry. Come in."

They sat side by side on the couch in the living room, lit by the fireplace beside them.

Brigid was quiet, counting in her mind just as Mattie had the day before. "We must have both been pregnant the last time we saw each other," she said. "But you were spotting, remember?"

Claire nodded, her mouth slightly curved down.

"That happens a lot," Brigid said, sounding like a midwife again. "Nothing to worry about." Suddenly she was not just accepting, but happy about the babies. Her baby, and Claire's baby, too. They would be mothers, together. "Oh, it's so good to see you again!"

Claire was quiet.

In the silence, Brigid gathered her courage and said, "Claire, I just today heard about Michael."

Claire said nothing.

"Claire, I am so sorry. Claire." Brigid was repeating Claire's name, as if to get clarity from it, as if to get clear, as Padmaj would say.

Brigid looked up toward the mantle above the fire and noticed a framed photograph of the three of them—Claire, Michael, and Miriam. She knew that somehow she must force herself to form the words that might bind the wounds that Claire and Miriam had survived, wounds for which she felt she was, ultimately, responsible.

So Brigid asked, "How is Miriam?"

The sounds tasted like iron in her mouth.

"She's been staying in a home run by the treatment center," Claire said.

"Oh." Brigid wanted to flee. This was too much, that Claire had lost her husband and now had two children—one of them so sick she still needed treatment—to raise alone. It made Brigid feel fresh sorrow for her own mother again.

"No, it's okay. Miriam's fine," Claire said, interrupting Brigid's thoughts. "I certainly couldn't have taken good care of her these past months. I needed to be someplace new. I went to Connemara after all. I've only just returned."

Brigid remembered those first months after her father had left, how her own mother, too, had gone to a new place to try to escape her memories, and how sad and cold her mother had been, lashing out at her daughters for the emptiness she'd felt.

"I'm sorry," Brigid said. She meant it, for Claire, and for her mother.

"Brigid. Brigid," Claire said, as she reached out to touch Brigid's face, putting her hands on her friend's freckled wet cheeks. Something about the gesture reminded Brigid of Padmaj, his ability to care for others even in the midst of his own sorrow.

"I'm so sorry," Brigid sobbed. "I'm so sorry about everything."

And for the second time that day, Brigid was embraced by a mother again.

ELEVEN

Although Claire hadn't hesitated to invite Brigid over when she called late that afternoon, Claire became increasingly anxious as she waited for Brigid to arrive. She couldn't decide whether to tell her about the night with Padmaj. She was sure that she wanted Brigid to be a part of her life, she wanted her to be her midwife, just as they had planned when she was trying to get pregnant in April. And she also wanted Brigid to be her friend, she was the only friend she had, really, and Claire wanted even more —

There was a knock at the door.

Claire just couldn't tell her.

It was that simple.

She felt herself smiling, too wide, falsely, to cover her nervousness, as she opened the door. Standing before her was a pregnant Brigid, plump and pink cheeked and with shorter hair.

"Brigid, you're pregnant!" Claire blurted.

"So are you," Brigid said, quietly.

Claire wondered if she could tell when a pregnancy had started, whether a difference of a few weeks would show, and so she hugged her, and didn't let go, hoping to hide herself from Brigid's measuring gaze.

***

Later, when they were settled on the couch in the living room, Brigid asked, "How is Miriam?"

"She's been in a treatment home," Claire said quickly, glad to switch the topic of conversation away from pregnancy.

"Oh."

"No, it's okay. She's fine. I certainly couldn't have taken good care of her these past months. I needed to be someplace new. I went to Connemara after all. I've only just returned."

Brigid looked down. Tears fell into her lap as she said, "I'm sorry."

Claire reached out to touch Brigid's face, saying "Brigid, Brigid." I'll forgive you if you forgive me, she said to herself. I'm sorry, please, one day, when you know, please forgive me, don't leave again. Don't leave.

"I'm so sorry," Brigid cried, echoing Claire's own words inside. "I'm so sorry about everything."

***

They sat holding each other for a long while, and then Brigid said what Claire had feared hearing from her for months.

"Claire. I'm so sorry about Michael. If only I..."

"Hush," Claire said. She was not ready to hear what Brigid might say next. "Stop. You are not your father. You are not responsible for what he may have done."

Brigid shook with grief.

"Look at me," Claire said. "We've both been through so much. We've learned so much. But it's not over. There are things we still need to do, together. Please. We need each other. Will you stay? Will you stay with me? So we can have our babies together?"

"Oh, Claire."

"Please."

"Yes. Yes, of course. I'll stay."

TWELVE

As the weeks passed, Brigid and Claire increasingly found that there was more and more between them that had not been said. They began, like a couple in a troubled marriage, to talk only when Miriam was visiting them. And when they were alone, they retreated into silence.

It was during one of these three-way conversations that Brigid discovered that Padmaj was in India.

Since she had fled to the Burren, she had tried not to think of him, not to miss him, out of her own guilt at leaving, at not telling him about the baby. She had, with her father, become good at this kind of forgetting.

"I called him," Brigid overheard Claire telling Miriam one day in early October in the kitchen. "But he hasn't returned my call. Maybe he didn't get the message."

Brigid was hungry to know when Padmaj had left, what he had said about her, whether Claire thought he would be back, but she said nothing.

At some level Brigid felt as if she had no right to him, no claim to him, until she came to terms with why she had left in the first place, until she came to terms with her father.

This was the other topic that kept the women silent.

Brigid suspected that Miriam knew about her connection to Michael's death, but they had never spoken about it.

And so, when the phone rang one Monday morning in mid-October, Brigid's first thought was that she was grateful Miriam was not there as she heard Claire's voice saying into the phone, "Mr. O'Connell?"

This was a mistake, Brigid thought. She should never have agreed to stay with Claire. She had been selfish, too hungry for Claire's forgiveness.

"Yes, she's here," Claire was saying, her face pale, as Brigid walked into the kitchen.

Claire handed her the phone and stood there, watching.

"Hello?"

"Your mum gave me this number."

Brigid looked into Claire's blue eyes, wide, unblinking.

"I want to see you," Brigid's father said.

Claire was close enough to hear his voice through the phone, and she nodded to Brigid.

Brigid shook her head, felt terrified, sick to her stomach.

Claire continued to nod.

"Okay," Brigid said, shaking.

"Where should I meet you?"

"Here," Claire whispered.

Brigid shook her head.

Claire nodded, bit on the inside of her cheek.

"Here," Claire repeated.

"Brigid? Are you there?"

"Yes, Da, I'm here. I…"

"Now," Claire said, her eyes clear and firm.

"You can come here," Brigid said, quietly, and gave him the address and then hung up the phone.

"Now call the police," Claire said to her.

Brigid did not move.

"Or I will. It's time."

Brigid picked up the phone again. She knew Claire was right. She did not feel any less frightened, nor any more certain that she ever had—about her father, about what he deserved, about what she herself deserved as a result of her role in all of it. But she would do it. Now. Whether or not she was ready.

Claire was ready. She had, in the six weeks that Brigid had been staying with her, been able to observe how clearly frightened Brigid was, as Brigid's formerly boisterous, flirtatious self had faded, leaving simply a scared girl in its wake. Claire found herself feeling motherly toward her, not angry, not even jealous of the love that she knew Brigid still, quietly, held for Padmaj.

Brigid hung up the phone in the kitchen and stared blankly at the gray October skies watching through the window.

Claire needed, she decided, to help Brigid with this. They had already shared so much.

"Now call the police," Claire said to her.

Brigid did not move.

"Or I will. It's time."

Brigid picked up the phone again, her hands shaking, as she dialed the number of the police station and asked the switchboard operator for the head detective on the case.

"It's Brigid O'Connell," she said when the detective came on the line. "Bobby O'Connell has just contacted me. He's on his way to meet me."

Claire heard the detective saying something, then Brigid said, "17 Bachelor's Walk. The name on the door is Curtain/O'Connell."

Claire felt, as she listened, as if the present were clicking into place, as if death were finally starting to withdraw its fingers from their hair. They had, just the day before, put their two names on the nameplate beside the front door intercom.

The detective said something else, which Brigid responded to with a firm, "Yes," and then the conversation was over.

"I'm going to get dressed," Brigid said and retreated into Miriam's bedroom which was now hers.

Claire went to the dining room window, which faced west. She imagined she could see all the way back to Connemara, as if a line stretched out across the body of Ireland, as if a new border were being drawn. Not a border between nations, but a border in time. What was happening now had been set in place long ago, even before Claire or Brigid's births, before their memory. And yet it had continued to follow them, through the generations, demanding to be acknowledged, asking for an answer that was not silence or violence or fear.

They were responding now.

***

There was a knock on the door.

Claire started from the dining room to answer it, and Brigid rushed out from her bedroom, her hair flatter from brushing, her face drained of color.

They arrived together.

The man on the other side was an old man, thin and fearful looking, with red and silver hair, curly like Brigid's, and eyes the color of a churning sea. But whatever apprehension he had within him fled when he spoke, as he attempted to drive his fear into others.

"My Two Marys!" he said, his voice echoing in the white hallway, as he stared at the bellies of the two women.

"Your mother told me *you* were with child," he said to Brigid, "but I see there were two immaculate conceptions upon this house."

Claire moved to guide him into the apartment. She hoped the neighbors were not home. She wanted whatever was going to happen to happen without innocent people nearby.

"I'm Claire Curtain," she said to him. "Please come in."

"What a beautiful Irish name," he said. "And a beautiful woman to match it."

"Would you like some tea?" she said to him, calling upon her reserves of politeness.

"Yes, I would, thank you," he said.

"I'll make it. Please, sit down. I know you and Brigid have much to talk about," she said as she headed into the kitchen.

***

Back in the kitchen, collecting cups and saucers from the cabinet, Claire found herself shaking. She had imagined, of course, many times, alone in her cottage in Connemara, venting her rage at this man who had taken Michael from her, and Padmaj, and Brigid, too. He had wiped out the life they had been making together, and she had retreated west, to heal, to escape from the memory of all she had lost.

She remembered the photos at the Famine Museum, pictures of whole families from Connemara, trying to leave but dying of hunger on the way, lying unburied on the roadside.

She had felt that urge within her, too, the desire to run, planted within her body as the great-grandchild of a woman who had gotten away.

But it was this impulse to run that had kept Brigid in fear of her father. They were the same, Claire realized now, as she heard voices rising in the next room. Rage and fear were the same force, set in motion long ago.

And now, as she looked one last time through the window toward the west before heading back into the living room with the tray of tea, she felt neither rage nor fear.

She was finally coming to rest.

FOURTEEN

Brigid's hands were trembling as she pointed the gun toward her father.

"Brigid! Stop!" Claire said, coming back into the room.

Brigid turned. Her vision of Claire was blurry from the tears in her eyes, and her own face was warm and ruddy.

Claire put the tray with the cups of tea down gently on the coffee table between Brigid and her father, then stood between them.

"You don't have to do that," she said quietly to Brigid.

Brigid was unnerved by Claire's calm. Where was her fear? Where was her anger? Hadn't she lost as much as Brigid?

"We've spent our whole lives running from each other," Claire said to Brigid, her voice strong and unwavering.

"We've spent our whole lives angry at each other," she said to Brigid's father.

Then she looked back and forth at both of them.

"No longer. We must refuse to do either any longer."

Brigid found herself releasing the gun's weight, letting her hands go limp, as Claire came to her, took the gun, and placed it next to the tea on the table.

Claire stood with her arm around Brigid as they faced the father. "We are not angry at you," she said. "We are not afraid of you either."

Claire looked into his eyes. "You have lost as much as we have," she said. "Even if you don't know it."

Brigid felt Claire hold her shoulders a bit tighter, then watched as she looked back toward her father to speak.

"It ends here."

Brigid felt as if she were back on the Burren, as if her sister were alive again, as if they were finally, together, facing the demon that had pursued them all their lives.

"You're a traitor to your nation," Bobby O'Connell said to them through clenched teeth.

Claire took a deep breath and responded slowly, saying, "It has never been just about a nation."

Something in the way she said it gave Brigid a vision of Padmaj, at dawn, sitting in front of his altar, his eyes upon the trees.

The door burst open then, and military police filled the room, as they led Brigid and Claire away to another room, disposed of the gun, shouting, and pinning Bobby O'Connell to the ground.

***

This was true justice, Brigid thought later, what Claire had helped her find the courage to do—what, together, they had done.

Not giving in to fear or revenge, but taking an unblinking look at the source of our pain, a look that takes patience and that, in time, gives us the promise of facing our history, and ourselves, and others, and assures us that we and our children might have the power to begin again.

PART IV

ONE

Claire heard her cell phone ring in the early morning hours of the first day of November and thought it might be Padmaj. No one else but Miriam had the number, and she was right there, in the apartment, along with Brigid. They were all up late, eating the warmed fry bread that Mattie had brought with her all the way from New Mexico.

By the time Claire got the phone out of her purse in the bedroom, it had stopped ringing. She pressed the button for incoming number retrieval. Yes. An international call.

She stood for a moment, looking out at the dark river through the bedroom window, listening to the women's voices in the next room. How would Padmaj fit into all this when he returned? If he returned.

She went back to join the others lest her absence would raise questions.

"Wrong number," she said as she entered the living room.

***

Late that night, Claire couldn't sleep, so she slipped out of bed, got her journal from her desk, walked quietly through the living room so as not to wake Brigid who had fallen asleep on the couch, and headed to the kitchen.

There, a light was already on.

Mattie sat at the table, drinking coffee.

"Can't sleep because of the time change," Mattie whispered. "I hope I didn't wake you."

"No," Claire said softly. "I often get up before dawn to write."

"Go right ahead. Don't mind me."

"Actually," Claire said, pouring herself a glass of orange juice, "I'd like to talk to you." She had liked Mattie immediately, was glad that Brigid had asked her to come to help with the final stage of their pregnancies and with the delivery of the babies, which was now only eight weeks away.

As the light gradually glowed more brightly through the windows, Claire found herself sitting down next to Mattie and telling her the whole story—of Miriam's illness, and Padmaj's restaurant, and her friendship with Padmaj and Brigid, and then Michael's death and Brigid's disappearance, and then, even, the story of her night with Padmaj.

"I have written over and over again about that night, in poems," she said to Mattie. "It is always with me. I felt such passion."

Mattie nodded.

"I loved Michael more than I've ever loved anyone. I still do. What I felt for Padmaj that night, I'm sure, in no way diminished what I felt for Michael. In a strange way my love for Michael grew. I feel, somehow, that they might both be the fathers to this baby. But I don't know what I should do. Should I tell Brigid? The silence between us is starting to become suffocating."

Claire glanced back toward the living room, then continued.

"I've been thinking about going back to America. Miriam will start college at the University of Chicago in September, and my father is in a nursing home, and we don't know how long…"

Claire shook her head. "One of the reasons I wanted this baby in the first place was so that I could give it a home, so that I could learn to stay."

Mattie nodded again. She had heard people on the reservation saying the same thing, had seen how they would come back after years of being away to raise their children in the presence of their parents and grandparents.

"It was my daughter who forced me to look at my own history, and it was Brigid who gave me my first lessons, but it was Michael's death—how do I explain this?"

Claire looked out the window, as the sky was beginning to glow the resolute greyblue of a Dublin dawn.

"In America, I'd never thought about history. I knew I was part Irish, but I had never thought about what it meant. After Michael's memorial service, when Padmaj drove me to Connemara, I realized that even though my ancestors are no longer there—the lore in my family is that only the ones who left survived—the land is still there. I learned for the first time that the land holds a kind of wisdom, both physically, but also, spiritually, and it was this that Michael and I had always been missing."

She paused, breathless from saying all this out loud for the first time. It was different than writing about it.

And then she said softly, "It was this sense of always missing something that Miriam's illness and Michael's death finally forced me to face."

Finally, Claire asked, "What do you think I should do?"

Mattie looked into her cup, long empty.

"Let me get a refill," Mattie said. "I can't think without something warm in my hand."

After Mattie sat back down, she began slowly. "First off, it's not all up to you. That's the first thing to realize. So much of what happens in life, almost all of it, actually, is not a matter of acting, but working in response to others in the world."

Claire was listening closely.

"You don't know who the father is, really," she said. "So that's out of your hands. And you don't know if Padmaj is coming back. You can't control that. And you can't predict what will happen between all of you, if he does come back. Or even how he will feel about you."

Claire felt herself spinning.

"But there is one thing you can be sure of."

"What?"

"The feelings you feel are the whole point."

Claire blinked at her.

"What do you mean?"

"All this has not been about Padmaj really, or about what Brigid's reaction might be if she learns about the night the two of you shared."

Mattie paused. Claire looked down.

"The important thing to come out of all this are the feelings that have been awakened in you. I've seen the change in Brigid, and in the way she is now with her mother."

Mattie looked at Claire and smiled. "And I know you know this as a mother yourself. I saw it last night in Miriam's eyes, how she knows that you see her, you love her—but you recognize her as a separate being from you. You delight in the woman she is becoming. You are her mother. But that is not all you are."

Claire nodded. She was beginning to see what Mattie meant.

"This is the whole purpose of love, or can be, for those of us who are vulnerable enough to be open to it," Mattie continued. "It's not just about loving the other person—but about what we allow their love to awaken in us."

Claire nodded again.

"Love is like teaching," Mattie said. "The point is not really who the teacher is, but what the student learns."

Claire stared at Mattie with wide eyes. "Padmaj once said almost the same thing to me."

"What was that?"

"'A human being can have as his teacher only another human being, for gods and goddesses we have never seen.'"

"Can I ask you a question, Claire?"

"Of course."

"What do *you* think all this has taught you?" Mattie asked gently, as she looked into Claire's eyes, which were radiant, and fully lit from behind with the bright morning sun.

Claire sat thinking for a while.

"I have learned two things," she said finally.

Mattie waited.

"I have learned that our actions, no matter how small, contribute to the whole."

Mattie nodded.

"And I have learned that it is better to be still than to move too quickly to action. I have learned, I guess, a kind of patience."

Mattie reached out and patted Claire's hand. "There's your answer."

TWO

Padmaj had not had anything to drink the entire time he'd been in India, so the beer he had in the bar behind the international checkpoint while waiting to board his plane back to Ireland was making him fairly tipsy fairly. He needed it, though, the beer, after being led to a side room and strip-searched upon check-in, all his bags unpacked, his clothes and shoes put through an x-ray machine, his naked body touched by gloved hands and swept by electrical wands.

His uncle had warned him of this.

"Don't go," his uncle had said the day he bought his plane ticket.

His uncle's reaction betrayed his long-held suspicion of westerners and his anxiety about the recent rumors about imminent terrorist attacks.

"You are safe here, Bhabha," his uncle had said, touching his nephew's cheek. "Remember what they did to you there. What, are you trying to commit sati?"

It had stung, his uncle's use of the term for the self-immolation of widows, outlawed by the British in 1829 but still practiced in some areas.

It conjured up his mother's long shame, as an unmarried Hindu mother whose Muslim lover had refused to marry her.

His father had not married her, but he loved her, still.

His mother had told Padmaj this only that morning, when she came to his bedside at dawn before Padmaj left for the Lucknow airport. She showed him a recent letter, written in the tight looping hand of his father, as proof of their enduring connection.

"It is why," his mother had said to him, "I cannot come with you to your new home. I still have hope that your father and I will be together, in this land."

Padmaj looked down at the letter in his hands, thinking that because of this man, he had had no father as a child. And now, as a man, he would have no mother with him, either. It was then that Padmaj noticed that his father had signed it "love."

Love, Padmaj said to himself in the airport bar as he finished his beer. He used to think he knew what that word meant, when he was younger. When it was abstract. A dream. The events of the past year had made it concrete for him, and clouded its meaning.

***

As the immigration authorities let him board the plane, Padmaj remembered how Brigid had told him of her relief when, as a young woman, she'd been allowed to leave Ireland for the first time, and to leave her father behind.

"It was grace," she told him. "I thought to myself, This is what grace feels like. It feels like leaving."

Love is an absence, Padmaj thought.

And grace feels like leaving.

These were yet two more things the two of them, Padmaj and Brigid, held in common, he thought now, as his plane taxied down the runway.

They were soul twins.

And this was why, he knew, he needed to find her.

And to make a new home.

***

Padmaj's first thought, when he had seen the pictures on international CNN of Brigid's father being brought in after his capture, was that her father was indeed, as Brigid had described, an old man. His hands were tied behind his back but his head was held high, as he looked straight into the cameras for all the world to see. Old. But still proud.

The television announcer had said that Bobby O'Connell's daughter had turned him in. Padmaj had felt his heart stop, when he heard it.

To think that she could have done so six months ago—before the bombings, before all the deaths, before that night with Claire.

What might have been avoided, if she had?

***

As the plane circled the mountains east of Delhi to gain altitude before heading north, Padmaj shook his head.

What he saw, out the window, were the mountains of his childhood, the same ones he'd seen from this angle at his return decades ago, when their tops were just beginning to go bald. And now.

Now they were completely bare.

The mountains existed as they had during his childhood only in his memory now. All the forests had been sold, their trees clearcut for lumber, and the mining for limestone had begun—mining which made the land's new owners wealthy beyond imagining— while at the same time dislocating its people and stripping its soil and even drying up the nearby rivers and the waterfall for which his beloved village had been named.

***

His mother had not tried to stop him, after she gave him the news.

"If you must go, Bhabha, then go," she said. "Go to see it for yourself." She was heeding the warning she had been given, when pregnant with him, to let him go wherever he wanted. As she had his whole life—even when she feared what he would think of her as a result.

He had hired a car the next morning and gave the driver directions to the old village.

It was not there.

The open air fires where the mothers had cooked, the huts where they had slept, the trees, their branches, even the tiny spiders that had lived in the trees—they were all gone.

Padmaj could not even get out of the car, just waved to the driver to keep going, until, two miles down the road, he croaked, "Stop."

He opened the car door quickly and stepped out onto the road, looking around him in disbelief and right there, in front of the mosque where his grandmother and generations of his father's people had worshipped and which now stood in ruins, its domed roof caved in and the walls crumbling, Padmaj vomited on the ground while the driver waited, the meter still ticking.

***

Later, when the driver dropped him off at the tiny apartment in Lucknow that his mother and aunt and uncle shared, he went to bed and did not wake for three days.

When he woke, it was to the sound of his aunt's voice calling him, "Padmaj, dear, your friend's father has just been captured. Come see. It's on the telly."

He watched the images, listened to the story without speaking, and then went straight to the phone and bought a one-way ticket to Dublin.

"I am leaving in two weeks," he said to the three elders, watching him.

"Don't go," his uncle had said.

The women said nothing.

They knew it was time for him to make a new home.

231

THREE

Brigid was at home, alone, the afternoon of the second day of November, listening to music in the living room. here was a light knock on the door, and it took her a minute to rise her wide, earthbound frame to go to answer it.

Standing there, with a medium-sized black bag over his shoulder, was Padmaj.

He looked at her body.

"Brigid," he said, his voice reverent. "You're going to be a mother."

Brigid grinned to think of her father at this very same door, as if their home were a place where men regularly came to have surprise encounters with pregnancy.

It seemed a long time ago. All of it. Her return to Ireland. Her father's release from jail. Her leaving Padmaj. The bombings. The time she spent alone in the Burren. The day when she finally let the pain of her childhood go free from her heart.

She smiled. "Yes."

"Then that means I am going to be a father," he said, bewildered, shaking his head.

"Yes, I suppose it does," she said, gently. "Come in. You look tired."

***

"I have just now come back," he said, looking around the apartment as the memories of that last night here came back to him — the fireplace, Michael's presence, Miriam's music, Brigid's silence, Claire's eyes — but he saw all this dimly, as if they had taken place in a dream and now he was fully awake. The room was so bright.

"May I make you some tea?" Brigid offered, as he knew she always did when she was uncertain about what to do next.

"Yes, thank you," he said. He had not expected her to be at Claire's apartment, and he nervously put his fingers through his hair as followed her to the kitchen. Did she know about the night with Claire? They had always been twins to each other, as if a wall in the shape of the number eight looped around them and bound them both, making them similar but somehow still separate from each other.

She turned to face him when they reached the kitchen and then laughed, "Aren't you going to put your bag down, at least?"

He did, and then put his hands in his pockets to stop their shaking.

She put the tea kettle on the stove and said, "Claire should be back with Mattie any time now. They went together to see the obstetrician. Claire's been having some spotting as she did at the beginning, and a little pain, which can be worrisome late in pregnancy."

It was then that she saw on his face that this was news to him.

"You did not know?"

He shook his head.

She felt her old defensive humor returning and joked, "Well, two surprises on the way for you, then," and there was something in his eyes that told her that something had changed within him.

But she was trying to learn to be quiet, and so she sat down at the kitchen table with the cups of tea, carefully, afraid of the pain that was in his eyes, and she waited for him to speak.

He sat down, too.

"Brigid, I did not know you were pregnant when I left. I would not have left you if I had known."

She smiled. She still loved him—that she always knew. But what she realized now was that she could love him in an even deeper way than she had before. Because he was the father of her child. Yes. But also because he had helped her begin to move toward the calm that she felt within herself now. The peace.

"I was the one who left *you*, Padmaj, remember?" she said, still smiling, remembering all this about him—his graciousness, his sense of honor, his inability to place blame.

But there was something different about him, too. A sadness in his eyes.

Just then the front door opened and Mattie and Claire returned.

FOUR

Claire saw the back of his head first, the thick dark hair, and then his black bag, and then Brigid and Padmaj walked out together to the living room to greet them.

Claire felt awkwardly large and self-conscious about what his reaction to her would be.

"My lady," he said, quietly.

Claire was not sure what to say.

"I called you," she said, and then he put his arms around her and held her.

He felt different, she realized with relief as she leaned against him, with Mattie and Brigid looking on. That wave that had crashed over them that night had long ago subsided and left something else in its wake.

"Claire? Padmaj?" Brigid said to them from across the room, "Is there something you're not telling me?"

Padmaj and Claire looked at her, and they stepped apart.

There was hurt in Brigid's voice, but not anger.

"If there is, you should tell me," Brigid began to cry, and Mattie walked over to her. "We should be honest with each other. I will understand. After all I did to both of you…"

Claire left Padmaj and walked over to Brigid and Mattie, and the three women embraced.

"Nothing is as important to me as you are," Brigid said, looking into Claire's eyes.

"I know. It's why I couldn't bring myself to say anything."

Mattie kissed each woman on the cheek and whispered, "I know you can do this," before heading to her bedroom and leaving them alone.

Padmaj sat down on the couch and put his face in his hands.

The two pregnant women went to sit on either side of him, and they put their hands on his back.

The women did not speak.

They waited.

Finally Padmaj spoke.

"When I was a child in my mother's village they used to say that the ancestors live in the trees and help give birth to the next generation."

Claire thought of the yew trees outside of Kylemore Abbey.

Brigid thought of the birds along the Cliffs of Moher.

Then his voice became cold, and his eyes lost their light. "But my trees are dead. I went home this time and found the forests destroyed, the trees felled and the rivers and waterfalls dry."

He put his face in his hands again.

"And now I have come here to find the two women I love are going to be mothers in a new land."

He paused, and then turned and knelt to face them both.

"I used to be certain of what I knew," he said. "But after what I have seen, I am no longer sure."

His eyes finally filled with tears.

"I do know I do not want to come between you. I want your children to have what I had as a child. I will help you in whatever way I can, but you are the mothers. It is you who should hold the power."

Brigid reached out to take Claire's hand.

"We have crossed many oceans to be together on this land," Padmaj said to them. "But it is the same earth that lies beneath us all. The same earth. And you are the mothers now."

FIVE

Brigid opened the door to Padmaj's house and found destruction everywhere.

She had offered, shortly after Padmaj returned, to go back to the house and to clean it for him.

"No, that is ridiculous," he said. "I cannot ask you to do that."

"You are not asking," she said. "I am offering."

He had looked at her closely, his brown eyes turning down at the edges, and said nothing.

"Please, Padmaj. It is a gift. For me, as well as for you. Let me give this."

He nodded, slowly, then he took her in his arms and said, "Whatever you need from me, I will always give."

Her belly, large and low, was cradled between them, as she leaned to put her head against his chest. "I know that. I have always known that," she said as he held her.

And then she left.

For what she needed was to be alone. To do this, alone. To make amends with him and with herself by cleaning, and arranging, and sorting, and fixing things in the material world. She had always been able to act in the world in ways that were healing. This is why she had become a nurse, why midwifery was an art in her hands, and why she would be a constant and able mother all her life.

During the search, the police had taken everything out of the closets and cabinets and drawers, and clothes and dishes and cooking utensils lay strewn about. And there were, just as her mother had described, huge gaping holes in the walls where they had inserted lights and metal detectors to look for guns and dynamite and written records.

But there was no record of Brigid's presence. All of that had been taken away, placed in plastic bags, and labeled as evidence in the event that would be needed in the trial.

It was not. In the end, the case against Bobby O'Connell had been so overwhelming that neither Brigid nor her mother had been asked to testify. The trial had been exceptionally speedy, for he had pled guilty, testified readily, and helped to bring in all those whom he knew for certain had been involved in decades of bombings.

Her father had even, upon the witness stand, repeated Claire's words when the prosecutor asked him why, now, he was confessing.

"I realized, finally," he said, "It has never been just about a nation."

But all this meant that Brigid had never spoken. She had allowed Padmaj to swear to her innocence and lack of knowledge while he was being tortured, she had let Claire speak on her behalf before turning her father in to the police, and she had let the lawyers present the story to the jury in her absence.

So this, now, was her testimony.

***

She began with the kitchen. She washed all the dishes and pots and silverware and glasses, lovingly, by hand, letting the hot water almost scald her skin as she remembered drinking tea in the bedroom, sharing picnic brunches on the rolling green hills surrounding the house on Sunday mornings, and standing in the kitchen for glasses of cold water after lovemaking in the middle of the night. She let each scene enter her, as she washed it, remembered it tenderly, allowing the salt of her tears to mix with the soap in the water to scrub the memory clean.

She was like her mother in this, she realized, wanting to start over, begin anew, even after great pain, even after loss. They had not, she and her mother, surrendered like her sister. Brigid refused to give up. Even after Padmaj and Claire told her about their night together. Hope was something solid to her, like glass or ceramic. Fragile but real.

Once everything was put away in the kitchen, she moved to the living room. She had brought plaster and paint to repair the walls, remembering what her mother had said about the way they had torn apart her apartment.

Brigid began to feel overheated from her work, though it was early November, and cold in the house. Her body had become an incubator for the baby during the pregnancy, her feet always sweating, her sex wet, her face constantly flushed and vivid.

She shut the blinds in order to have privacy, and then she took her shoes and socks and pants and sweater off and began to work on the walls in her t-shirt and underwear.

First, she smoothed the cracked plaster on the walls with sandpaper, grating away at the hard and uneven edges the gashes had created. Her knuckles turned red from the scraping, but she did not mind the pain. It mixed with the rhythm of the coarse sounds, back and forth, in her mind, and she felt herself being sanded, too. There had been a hard edge, she admitted, that she'd built within to protect herself from her father, which still lingered. It was what had kept her from fully opening to Padmaj, or to anyone, any man, all her life. With women she had been able to steer clear of it, and she had let Mattie, and then Claire, into her heart. But she was ready, now, she decided, to let this edge be cut away, to be rounded and softened, so that she could give herself fully to Padmaj and to their coming child, who, she hoped, would not be their only one.

When the scraping was done, she mixed the plaster and applied it to the open wounds of the walls, laying it on heavy and thick. She thought of the white creamy substance that newborn babies carried on their skin, a protection against the waters of the womb within. How she loved to touch and smell the vernix, in those first moments after birth, on her fingers. How she loved to see the mothers, and the fathers too, rubbing it into the babies' skin, making the children soft and moist for their long, dry journey on land. We need both, she thought, both protection against the ocean within that can overwhelm us and against the aridity of the earth's atmosphere. To strike a balance between these was what it meant to close the wounds, what it meant to be healthy.

After finishing the plastering, she decided to take a break to let it dry and, wrapping a saffron blanket around herself, went to sit outside to eat her sandwich. The hunger she had felt within her at the beginning of the pregnancy was tapering off, as the baby took up more and more space, and half of what she used to eat could now make her feel full. She sat on the front porch steps and watched the evening come.

The sky was a salmon pink in the west, with streaks of turquoise and sienna, as if someone had taken a paintbrush to the air. She thought of her homes in the west, first the childhood home in Miltown Malbay where, she imagined, the dried brown blood upon her legs as a child would have been the source for the sienna. Then she thought of the desert in the American west, and the Native women selling turquoise jewelry in the square at Santa Fe, making a living out of their survival, just as Brigid herself had done. But it was from her last home in the west—the small room she'd had at the inn near the Cliffs of Moher—that the salmon color came, the color of those beings who struggle to return home before dying, to mate and to give their faith to hope in the next generation. These were the colors of her life, and she could look upon them now and claim them all without shame or humiliation.

She rose to go back in to paint the walls, but the plaster had not yet dried, so she decided to wait. She had learned this skill from the babies. Waiting was the element that brought life, safely. It had taken her a long time to learn this. Her instinct had been for closure, for quick fixes, for completion. She'd learned her lesson, finally, when she'd lost a life from not waiting, sending the mother to the hospital in the middle of a breech birth, where the mother died from hemorrhaging after a caesarian. Brigid felt, deep in her heart, that the mother might have lived if she had waited.

And so now, while she waited for the paint to dry, she went back to the bedroom. She had been dreading this. She winced as if walking towards a knife as she started down the darkened hallway. The room was black. Towels and clothes and bed linens lay beneath her feet. She got down on her hands and knees to search for the candle and matches, her eyes avoiding the back wall. When she found them, kneeling, she lit the candle, and looked up. What she feared most had come true.

The painting of the trees had been slashed, the canvas torn back to look for evidence.

She sat back and began to sob.

The trees, his mothers, which Padmaj had clung to, which hundreds, thousands of people had clung to all their lives, had been destroyed. She thought of the wild mountains of New Mexico, carved into cattle ranches, split into pieces by fences, and then shaken from the inside by atom bombs. She thought of the abandoned stone houses all across Ireland, their roofs still missing after having been lit on fire and bashed in by landowners during the famine, so that the starving tenants who couldn't pay their rent would be unable to inhabit them any longer.

She cried then for India and Ireland and America; and for her sister, her mother, and her father, too; and for Michael, and Claire, and Miriam; and for Padmaj and Mattie. All of whom, she now knew, had loved her, in their own way, by giving her life or by playing a part so she could finally come to this point of healing. And then she cried for herself, for the girl she once was, and for the mother she was now becoming—for all she had lost and loved, and for the fragility of our feeling in the midst of such devastation.

It would be different, she vowed, for her daughter. This would be a moment she would remember—Brigid would pass it on to her in stories, she would pass on all the stories of what she had loved, the people and landscapes and living things that were being threatened with extinction at the same time that they were what we depend upon most for our survival.

***

She left the painting as it was. It had been a witness to all this, she decided, and she and Padmaj would honor it together by taking it down and having it repaired.

She rose slowly then, and began to fold the clothes and linens and towels, to make the bed, to rearrange the drawers in the bureau, to sweep and mop the floors. As she did so, she put each item back on the altar—the statues of Durga and Kali and Ganesh, the candles, the brass bowl, the peacock feather, the wooden carving of a coiled serpent, just beginning to rise—slowly, gently, she kissed each thing and placed it back where it belonged.

The last items to be returned to the altar were the eggs that Claire had given them at Easter, only one day before the bombings.

Padmaj's egg, painted like a lotus, was still intact, the tiny white petals almost invisible in the dim light. She thought of his name, its meaning, and wondered if Claire had known this about him, even then. She saw, in the hundred tiny lines painted on the egg, all the reasons that Padmaj and Claire would have loved each other in her absence.

They were the same reasons that Brigid loved both of them.

Their openness. To feeling. To pain. Their ability to drink it in. To hold it. To let it be. Neither backing away, nor probing too closely. They both had a kind of ability to accept—it was this that had drawn Brigid, with her wounded spirit, to them.

Brigid's egg had been injured, too. It was crushed on one side, the painted green shamrocks pushed inside, so that they rattled, like tiny bones. Brigid turned the egg over, let the pieces fall into her palm, and to her surprise, she found not only the shards of egg inside, but seeds.

Claire had inserted tiny shamrock seeds into the egg after emptying the insides and while it was still wet, so that they clung, when the egg was dry, to the interior walls. If the egg had not been crushed, Brigid would never have learned this.

Brigid put the egg onto the altar, and then she went outside to plant the tiny heart-shaped seeds, the colors of brown and ivory and beige and gold, into the black earth outside the house. As she did so, she whispered a prayer, the first one she had been able to utter since she was a small child—a blessing upon her baby, and upon Claire's baby, and upon Miriam—a blessing upon all the children of all colors and all nations, all the earth's children, no matter where they have been planted, no matter where they sprout, no matter where they will one day bloom.

***

Finally, late in the night, she went back to the living room and began to paint. She was tired and white paint dripped on her t-shirt and legs. Once, near the end, she swiped the brush across her protruding belly and stopped, realizing she liked the effect it made, so she took off her shirt and painted her belly white, giggling, playing with her baby girl who poked here and there at her mother through the skin, until Brigid held a large round glowing white ball in front of her body.

Then she went to the kitchen and called her mother, Rose, to invite her to come to the birth. Brigid wanted her to be a part of what was white and clean and new within her now.

After the phone call, she finished painting the wall quickly, and then lay down on her back on the hard wooden floor, the lights still on, her whole body sore, wrapped in the saffron blanket, her belly high in the middle of the new white room, and fell into a deep sleep, where she stayed the whole night long.

SIX

The day that Brigid left to clean the house, Padmaj and Claire stayed back at the apartment, alone. Mattie offered to go by herself to the movies, knowing they needed to talk.

"I have seen your trees," she said to him quietly, after Mattie left, as they sat across from each other, Padmaj on the couch, Claire on the leather chair, in the living room.

"How is that possible?" he asked.

"All my life," Claire said, looking out the window, "I felt something was missing. It was not exactly a feeling of emptiness, but a kind of constant sorrow, as if I'd lost something, but I couldn't even remember what it was.

"I tried to fill it up with things. When Michael started making money, I found myself buying things we didn't need, mostly things for the house, as a way of trying to make myself happy. And I turned to food, too—all kinds of exotic foods that I hoped would fulfill this ache I felt.

"And sex," she continued. "Sex..."

She stopped. She was going to say that Michael had been a wonderful lover, that their lovemaking was a kind of prayer, that it was Michael's love for her that had prepared her in the first place for what she had felt with him, yet she prayed that it was Michael's baby she was carrying.

But she said none of this.

She simply said, "And sex, too."

His lips turned upward into a slight smile.

And then she continued, "The day I walked into your restaurant, I was beginning to admit all this to myself for the first time. There was something, I don't know what it was, that affected me that day. I was never the same. And though we were both with other people, then, and I know you will be, still..."

She paused.

"I feel grateful to you in a profound way for what you helped to opened up in me."

She rose to move toward him, and she kissed his cheek, gently.

"So, thank you," she said, still standing.

"You are welcome," he said.

And then she sat down beside him.

***

For the rest of the night, Padmaj listened as Claire talked to him of hunger and trees, as she explained to him that the road her daughter had led her down was a road through history, but also, she understood now, one that looped back to the present.

"I thought, at first," she said, "that what I had been feeling was associated with some kind of knowledge that could be found in the past. I read history books, I visited museums."

She stopped, bit her lip.

"Go on," he said.

"But it was not there. It was not in the past."

She touched his cheek, the thin scar a slightly darker shade than his smooth skin.

"My first lesson had come from being a mother, from Miriam. I had no choice but to try to answer her cries for help, to try to discover the causes for her lack of hunger."

He nodded.

"But then, after Michael died, when I was alone in Connemara, I found I could not mourn because I had not seen his body."

She shuddered, and he touched her shoulder, briefly.

"I started thinking about death, about how, after our deaths, our bodies literally return to the land.

"We think death puts us in the past, but not really, it's not really in the past at all. History, I have learned, is something that is carried in the land, and lives on through us, in our bodies, in the way we hunger, in what we want or do not want, in how we touch or do not touch."

She took his hand and said, "One day I stood in the middle of a forest of yew trees at Kylemore Abbey, and I had the strangest sensation that I knew what you were also feeling, in India, and what Miriam was feeling, here in Dublin, and what Brigid and Michael were feeling, wherever they were. I knew that no matter where we are, we are on the same earth, and that when we love each other, we share the same body, and when others we love are hungry or in pain, then we are, too.

"We are, too," she repeated, searching his eyes. "Do you see?"

"I see," he said.

They sat quietly for a long time, not even speaking when Mattie came back from her movie and quietly went down the hall to her bedroom and shut the door.

They said no words but sat together holding hands in silence until dawn finally began to break beyond the mouth of the River Liffey.

"Now go," said Claire said to him, kindly, in the blue light. "It's time for you to go back to Brigid. Go to your home."

And he did.

His last vision of Claire as he left her was with the morning sun rising to her left as she sat once again beneath the southern window in her favorite chair, with her journal nestled beneath her large belly and her right hand in motion, writing.

***

In gold morning light, Padmaj drove out of Dublin to return to his house where found Brigid, wrapped in the saffron blanket on the living room floor, still sleeping.

She woke as he came toward her and, without speaking, wrapped the blanket around them both and led him down the hall to the bedroom.

Once there, she gestured toward the painting and then looked at him, blinked, and waited. "My trees are gone," he sobbed.

"Oh, Padmaj," she said. "I am so sorry. I am so sorry for everything. Can you ever forgive me?"

"No, Brigid," he said, looking at her fully for the first time since his return. "It is not for the painting that I am crying. It is..."

"What, Padmaj? Can you tell me?"

He led her to the bed and they sat upon it, facing each other, and he took her hands.

He breathed in deeply. "Many years ago, my mother told me to go, to travel, to learn as much as I could, to love as much as I could. I have done that."

"You have," she said.

"I knew even then that it was all possible because of the sacrifices my mother had made." His voice was low. "But this time, when I went home, my mother told me that, years ago, when I was in college, she had sold our land to miners."

His eyes searched hers, wild with grief, hoping she would understand.

"This was the money she had given to me in a white envelope when I left for Ireland fifteen years ago. This was the money I used to pay for the down payment on the restaurant. At the time, I did not ask where the money had come from. Perhaps, somehow, I knew. But I did not want to know."

Brigid's eyes were full of tears.

"It was not until this time, when I went home, that my mother finally told me. I could not believe what she was saying. I had to go back to the village to see it for myself. Oh, Brigid," he cried as she wrapped her arms around him.

"It is horrible. The trees have all been felled, the rivers are dry, all our homes are gone. The land is torn apart from the inside, and rubble lies in great heaps over the earth," he cried. She held him tightly against her breast while he wept.

For she was no longer afraid of such sorrow. She could lay grief against her body, and hold it now, because she was, finally, gaining the strength of a mother.

They made love again then, for the first time since her leaving, and they were once again, as they had been then, unalone.

After a long time, Padmaj said quietly, "I came back to find you, my Soul twin. I have found you again. And you are carrying my child—it is a sign of such hope to me. Perhaps we can find a way to teach our child about all that we have lost, and all that we have learned, and all that we have learned to love."

She nodded and said, "That is exactly what I want, too, my love."

"Brigid," he said, placing his smooth dark hands on her hopeful, freckled face. "*Brahma muhurta*, my sunrise, will you honor me by marrying me?"

"Padmaj," she smiled, her hazel eyes shimmering with specks of yellow and green. "Yes. Yes. I will marry you. Yes."

SEVEN

After seven weeks of pre-labor pains for Claire and Brigid both, which manifested themselves as sharp, quick, shooting lines of fire down the insides of Claire's thighs and a tightening and hardening around Brigid's waist that lasted for minutes at a time, they were both finally going to give birth.

It was the morning of New Year's Eve, and they were in Claire's apartment where they'd been living together now for their entire third trimester. Padmaj had moved back into his home after Brigid cleaned it because there was no more room at Claire's apartment and because Mattie said it was upsetting for a pregnant woman to move right before giving birth. The nesting instinct would go screwy, she said, and cause anxiety in both the baby and the mother. But the plan was that Brigid and the baby would move back to the house with Padmaj, after their wedding, which was planned for February 2nd, Brigid's Day. And, soon after, Claire had decided, she and Miriam and the baby would move back to Chicago. Miriam would start college there, and they could both be closer to her father in the time that he had still remaining. Most of all, Claire wanted to take what she had learned in the past year, and try to bring it back home.

When Claire and Brigid woke on the morning before the New Year, the sun was just rising over the Liffey outside the window, and the women looked into each other's eyes and knew it was time.

They called Mattie, in unison, like children calling for their mother in the morning. She came, wrapped in a white robe, and said, "Let's eat."

She led them to the kitchen where she made them each eggs and toast and milkshakes made with bone meal and honey. She insisted that they finish every last bit because they would need the energy later, when they wouldn't be able to eat.

Then she told them each to take hot showers—it would be a while, she said, before they'd be able to take a shower alone again. She presented each of them with small blue glass vials of liquid soap into which she'd mixed oils of lavender and vanilla for calming. Into Claire's, she'd also put a drop of sweet pea for friendship, and into Brigid's, a drop of rosemary for healing the wounds of the girl by moving into motherhood.

After their showers, they called Padmaj at the restaurant to tell him the news. He had been planning to close the restaurant that night anyway so he could come over to celebrate the New Year. Mattie told him the evening would be fine; there was nothing he could do until then anyway. Then Claire called her daughter and Brigid called her mother to tell them to come.

When Miriam and Rose arrived, all the women sat in the living room—mothers, daughters and grandmothers, together—playing cards and telling stories, some sad, some funny, to pass the time and to distract Miriam, who was more nervous even than the women in labor, especially when Claire's water broke all over the wooden floor and ran into the fireplace where it sputtered and shot up sparks, causing everyone but Miriam to squeal with delight.

Then Brigid's contractions came, hard and strong, late in the day, and Mattie made them all, except for Miriam, get up and go outside. The four women walked along the northern bank of the river, heading west, into the setting sun. When a contraction would start, Claire and Brigid would stop, lean into Mattie or Rose or each other and breathe until it receded, and then keep walking. This phase, right before the transition, was often when anxiety mounted for many women, and Mattie was especially concerned about Brigid, who had seen this many times before but had never experienced it for herself first-hand. The rhythm of the walking and the sunset gave them something to focus on aside from the tides of pain rising within their bodies. When they'd gone so far that it was completely dark, they turned around and headed home, with the current. Although they did not know it at the time, they would discover later that each of them, within herself, was repeating the word over and over as they walked back to the place where they would give birth: "Home. Home. Home. Home."

Once there they met an overanxious Padmaj, wringing his hands in front of the apartment building and pressing the intercom buzzer again and again.

"Oh my ladies!" he said when he saw them. "I thought something terrible had happened to you! Where have you been?"

Mattie smiled, congratulating herself on her wisdom for making him wait until evening to come.

"Calm down, sweetie," she said to him, giving him a bear hug. "Everything's fine. They're all right. Let's go on upstairs."

In the elevator, Claire squatted to relieve the pressure, and Mattie patted her hair gently as Claire held on to her legs.

Back in the apartment, Miriam was gone, and Mattie told Padmaj to wait in the living room, and asked Rose to draw Brigid a bath. Then Mattie made Claire lie down on the bed so she could check her cervix. Claire was already eight centimeters dilated, and was entering the in-between stage, which was often the hardest part of labor.

Claire yelled out, and Mattie called for Padmaj to come into the room as Claire started to cry, calling Michael's name and saying, "Why? Why? Why?"

Padmaj looked at Mattie who whispered to him, "Let her know she is not alone," and Padmaj took Claire's hand and stroked it and said, "I am here, my lady. I am here," his eyes dark and patient.

Soon there was a shriek from Brigid and Rose, and Mattie went to check on them and discovered that the bathwater had turned bright red.

"Come on out now," she said to Brigid, calmly. "It's okay. Come on out." She was speaking simultaneously to Brigid and to the blood. Mattie had seen bleeding like this in women before who had been wounded as children. She gave Brigid ten drops of Motherwort tincture and had her lie down on the bed next to Claire, where they immediately held each other's hands.

As they did, Claire's transition subsided and Brigid's began.

"Mum!" Brigid shouted. "I can't do it!"

"Yes, you can," said Rose. "Look at me. Yes, you can."

Just then Miriam came back in to the apartment with the three other members of her quartet. They stayed in the living room and quietly began to unpack their instruments. Unbeknownst to anyone in the birthing room, Miriam had composed a piece for the occasion, which they started to play.

It was a relatively short piece, about nine minutes long, but it had several distinct movements in it—at first, a hard, regular rhythm, almost like pounding, which quickened and then led to complicated sequence that ended in a long, slow sorrowful sound like keening, which gave way to a soft melody, a comforting lullaby that moved like steady breathing.

The four musicians performed the piece throughout the evening as Padmaj sat watching and listening to them, as they played over and over again, never stopping, dripping with sweat, and the four women in the other room breathed together and moaned and walked around and squatted and cried and laughed and sighed and gave birth—first Brigid, and then Claire—just after midnight on the first day of the New Year.

The candle-filled rooms of the apartment were lit then from the outside, as all nine adults joined together and the yellow lights up and down and all along the Liffey came on and the river glowed like a ribbon of celebration, as if the earth itself were also rejoicing at the safe arrival of the two children.

The first to arrive was a girl, Lotus, named after her father. With Padmaj's smooth dark skin and Brigid's sparkling hazel eyes, Lotus came screaming for contact with her parents' skin. She wanted from the start, as her name implied, to be a flower of connection, bringing together color and geography and history and faith. She would grow to become a beautiful woman, someone capable of turning destruction into creation, the mother of many generations.

And then came Hugh, a boy. He had thick black hair and thin dark lips like his father, Michael, and bright blue eyes like his mother, Claire. His name was chosen to honor the yew tree that reaches out across death, through legend and history, to be reborn again and again. As we are born again from the hearts of our ancestors, as we discover anew what they once dreamt for us, what they survived so that we might be possible, so that we might learn, finally, how to make peace with the past. As we learn how to lay the past to rest and give birth—not just to a new year, but to a new time—not just to a new nation, but to a new, living earth.

About the Author

Cassie Premo Steele is a Pushcart Prize nominated poet, a monthly columnist for Literary Mama, and the author of six books. She provides individual coaching, classes, and workshops through her Co-Creating practice, which teaches people to live balanced lives through creativity and connections with the natural world. Cassie Premo Steele lives with her husband and daughter along a creek in South Carolina, and would love for you to visit her at www.cassiepremosteele.com.

ALL THINGS THAT MATTER PRESS ™

FOR MORE INFORMATION ON TITLES AVAILABLE FROM
ALL THINGS THAT MATTER PRESS, GO TO
http://allthingsthatmatterpress.com
or contact us at
allthingsthatmatterpress@gmail.com

www.ingramcontent.com/pod-product-compliance
Lightning Source LLC
Chambersburg PA
CBHW051633260626
47170CB00004B/1161